Red Ink~ The SeQuel
Rites, Revenge, & Revelations

Butterfly Brooks
Thaddeus Kane

About the Authors

Butterfly Brooks is an author, historical research consultant, Love Warrior.
Thaddeus Kane is an author, musician, educator, playwright, Love Warrior.

Dedication

This work is dedicated to all of those that are still learning Love's lessons.

Acknowledgements

Eternal love and gratitude to all of those that love, support, and encourage creative fire. All of our mothers, fathers, children, family, and friends, especially Gwendolyn Elizabeth, Dora Louise, Verta Elizabeth, Marji Jihada and Brenda Faye~ We love you, forever, for always.

Supreme Love and Gratitude to our pen sisters, Gina, Phoenix, and Pamela. Your Love and encouragement empower us in our creative experience~ We Love you! Tera Kirksey, Helen D. Clark-Speedy, Rise Bullard, Sharon Armalin, Regina Williams are angels in the outfield~ We Love you! Xoxo

The Spider: I adore your wings, so fiery, so enchanting
The Butterfly: I admire your web, so captivating, so enthralling
The Spider: Can We be together? Forever, maybe?
The Butterfly: We are together. We have been, forever...for so many lifetimes. I am delighted to see You again.

CHAPTERS

"The world needs the soft, beautiful power of Butterflies."

Last time…Red Ink~ Bosses, Bullies, & Butterflies

✦Zing Post Tea Thyme Group✦

LaToya Tea Mitchell Post: Y'all read Bree's latest Sauce Mobb post? I know y'all have. I bet I know who she is talking about. ☐☐What do you think? This is a tangy one

Reactions: 1,246 Comments: 2,403 Shares: 889

(Load previous comments)
Shanika J.: Fuck her! She ain't that great a writer anyways.
Katerra Johnson: After all that talk about being original and bashing other people for ghostwriting smdh
Diminka Johns: Who is her? Tag me in the post. What did she say?
  Shanika J: @Diminka Johns I tagged you.
  Diminka Johns: Ok. Thanks!
Geneen Matthews: Yeah. But y'all just assuming it's Kendali. might not be her. could be anybody
Diana MacFadden: But you need to read the post. Sounds like she probably talking about Kendali.
Geneen Matthews: I read it. I still think y'all assuming a lot
Felicia Stewart: Wonder what this will mean for her career. Can't be good.
Geneen Matthews: Not good? maybe. But doesn't matter to me. I love her books. I will still keep reading.
Amber Michelle: I'm a fan. She used a ghostwriter. So what. Who cares. Keep the stories coming.
Heather Dunwoody: Yeah, but she talked so much trash about people who use ghostwriters. Like real bad. And now, she uses a ghostwriter. Wow. She ain't shit. I'm deleting all her stuff from my kindle. It's one thing to use a ghostwriter, but then to say you don't and then bash people who do? HYPOCRITE! AND I HATE HYPOCRITES☐
Paula Lelani: This is what I can't stand about this whole industry. This whole scene is so messy. Everybody has so much to say about Kendali, not even knowing it's her but what about Bree posting this bullshit. It's all too messy. And ridiculous. Just over it. All of it. I am going to start reading sci fi and

fantasy.☐
Jada Reynolds: Yeah. Throw the whole industry away.

And then…

Hiram ascended the stage as the audience clapped. Toni took a few steps aside and stood near the platform where the award was displayed. Hiram approached the podium dressed sharp and crisp, his walk, smooth and confident. With his eyes fixed on Kendali, he extended his right arm in her direction, presenting her to the crowd. "Kendali Grace," he began. "Tonight, we celebrate this beautiful and gifted icon and bestow upon her the honors, awards and accolades that she has earned. Rightfully earned. And anything that contradicts this is far from the truth." Dominion Publishing's CEO continued singing the praises of his top-selling author for another three minutes. Next, it was the moment of truth. "Kenni? Come up here! Kendali Grace everyone." The garden erupted with roaring applause as the literary star walked up the marble steps to receive her christening. She was about to be made a boss.

Hiram adjusted the mic stand for Kendali and then stepped aside. She took a breath and silence fell upon the garden as they anticipated her next words. A stranger's eyes homed in on her from a distance. "I don't know where to begin." Kendali smiled with honest, glowing appreciation. Butterflies danced and swirled around her. She felt royal and magical.

"I am honored even amongst the controversy," she said as she lifted the diamond and platinum plaque. "I earned this."

The butterflies fluttered around her. The attendees applauded. At that moment a sharp, piercing whisper was heard. It lasted for a split second. The butterflies' serene dance was disrupted into chaotic scatter. There was confusion. Yelling. Screaming. All watched in bewilderment as the beautiful Platinum Quill award recipient fell back onto the marble floor, her award shattering into shards of broken glass and broken dreams. Hiram rushed to her aid thinking that she'd fainted. As he got closer to his wounded lover, he saw the blood flowing from her chest.

"She's been shot!" Hiram yelled. "Dial 911! Now!!!" Some of the guests began a rapid exodus from the garden. Others looked around for the shooter while some took cover. Kendali's closest friends and colleagues rushed the stage to help their fallen star. "What the fuck?" Hiram shouted as he removed his jacket. He placed it under Kendali's head and his hand over her bleeding heart. "Somebody get me some fucking towels! Something! Shit!" His eyes welled with tears as he watched the blood mix with the glass on the floor. He looked into her eyes and rocked her. "Kenni. Hold on, baby girl. You gon' be alright. Just hold on." Georgette and others watched Hiram attempt to save Kendali's life, but Mrs. Rivers caught a hint of something else.

Kendali reached for Hiram. She tried to speak. "Hir...Hiii...Hiram..." She coughed, staining his white shirt with crimson.

"Where's the fucking ambulance?" Dre shouted as he rushed to the stage with a tablecloth. "Dali, baby! Dali!" he said kneeling by her side and clutching her hand. "Don't you die on me, girl!"

Hiram placed the tablecloth over her fatal wound as tears fell onto his cheeks. He pushed the cloth deeper into the bullet hole, knowing there was nothing else that could be done. Only he knew that his precious Kenni was crossing over to the heavenly side.

In ignorant hopefulness, Dre mumbled, "You gon' be okay."

An odd cool wind swept the stage as a bloody-handed Hiram and PQ attendees witnessed the last breath of life leave Kendali's body. The sirens wailed in the distance, but the aid and the rescue had come too late. Kendali Grace wrote her final chapter on the evening of receiving her greatest honor. She fell before the eyes of friends, lovers, fans, and foes without giving proper thanks. Not even a wave or a wink, or a warm kiss goodbye.

Chapter One
When Butterflies Cry

Sunday, 9:00 p.m.

Tragedy had stolen his Majestic Grace right before his very eyes. He heard his soul shattering a horrible din in his ears. Kendali lay on the floor, bleeding out. Hiram and Dre, her lovers, vying for the affection of a dead woman, was the quintessence of repulsion for Max as he watched them weep over her lifeless silhouette. Unfortunately, there was nothing he could do for her and no time to cry. He watched Hiram hold her heart with greater love in death than he did in life, scowling at the despicable beast named Rivers. Rescue teams were in route, so he focused his attention on the crowd, moving stealthily through the melee, thinking like a sharpshooter. Compelled by instinct, he pivoted to his left. There was movement in the botanical maze at the side door. Rushing to the manicured shrubbery, Max spotted a man in a black tuxedo running away. "Hey!" he yelled as he pursued the suspicious guest. The man glanced over his shoulder at Max and began running harder. The chase was on.

The G.W. Arboretum was situated inside two square miles of Hamer Hill Park, Seminole City's largest green space, a verdant oasis in the midst of the urban center. Max was impressed by the assailant's swiftness and mobility, easily managing the thickets of the inner-city forest. Before he knew it, the gunman had put seventy yards between them and continued to increase his speed. Max cursed his emotions, for they delayed his response to the situation giving the assassin a headstart. He pressed his way, rushing through trees, while the deer watched the human pursuit. He chased him for what seemed an eternity, arriving at the park's edge on a street bustling with traffic and everyday people. He scanned the darkness and scorned the night for aiding and abetting the escape of the culprit.

"Ayyy!" he screamed at the starry sky and arched his back in agony. A few people gawked at him, as he folded his body down to the ground, crying bloody murder. "I will avenge your murder, my Love. My Grace Amazing." He plodded heavy-footed and heavy-hearted back to the ballroom, breathing laboriously, and taking his time for he did not want to see his love again, decaying in a pool of her own blood, no mercy or grace for The Most Graceful One.

"Ahhh...whyyy? God, why?" Toya bawled in a baritone, like a wounded animal howling at the moon, waiting for death to come. Her estranged husband Jamal, an average height brawny built brother consoled her with a loving arm around her jerking shoulders. She sat at a table and he stood next to her, rubbing her back. They had been separated for a while but remained good friends. The entire area looked like a FEMA camp as medics treated minor cuts, bruises, and sprains that attendees suffered from the chaos. She and Jamal had no physical injury, but emotionally Toya needed an ICU. "I just can't believe it. I just can't." The entire Seminole City Police Department was on deck to handle the tragedy. They had taped off a perimeter around Kendali's body and designated an area for medical treatment and another area for interrogation. The chief of police, Everett Dempsey, quickly assigned his absolute best detective, Geronimo 'The Wolf' Blackfoot, to take the lead. Folks were dismissed from the arboretum, slowly but surely. Of course, most people left during the initial shooting, fleeing for their lives. Barely two hundred folks from a 600-person attendance remained by the time the police arrived. Detective Blackfoot questioned Toya.

"I didn't see anything. Just her body drop. I heard people say they saw a man running out the side door. Some said out the main ballroom door. Wearing a tux. Ha! That's everybody here. A Black man in a tux. Shit."

"Yes, that seems to be the consistent story. Don't worry, Ms. Mitchell. We will do our best. We have every man on this case."

"Oh, I am sure you will do your best because I will certainly do mine."

"We will handle this, Ms. Mitchell. You have to trust us."

Toya stood. She braced herself with her bare feet steady on the cold marble floor. Her shoes disappeared amidst the pandemonium as she had run to the stage and crouched next to Dre, mourning the last breath of Kendali Grace. "Yeah. And you have to trust. That's my sister's dead body layin' up there. And I will do everything within my power to find the killer. And I mean everything."

"Ms. Mitchell-"

Toya gave the detective her "shut your mouth" palm to his face. "Detective, please. I heard you. I don't have anything else to say." She turned to Jamal. "Just take me home." Her ardor awakened the wolf in him. No disrespect to her companion, but he sensed she was hungrier than the wolf, wanting a comfort that only an indigenous soul could provide.

"Yeah. Yeah. Okay." Toni finished up her conversation with the G. W. Carter Arboretum chief of operations and returned to Lesli, AJ, Brad, and Titus. "This whatcha call a Grade A nightmare. Primo. Supreme."

"Yeah." Lesli sighed and gripped Titus' forearm tighter. He wiped her face for the umpteenth time, her tears streaming quietly down her cheeks.

Brad was cradling AJ like a baby. Who would have thought she would be such a blubbering basket case.

"I was just starting to like her."

"Shhh." Brad soothed her patting her head softly. His wife Charlene had been appointed chief of the temporary medical team in the FEMA camp since she was a nurse. She circled back periodically to check on them and then returned to assist the emergency medical technicians.

"Everybody still okay here?" Charlene asked.

"Yeah. We alright," Brad said. She kissed her husband, stroked the back of AJ's head, and returned to her duties.

"Wifey doin' her thing, huh?" Toni said to Brad.

"Yeah. She is an expert in a crisis. I mean she's married to me; she gotta know how to keep a cool head." Everyone chuckled at Brad's comic relief attempt. The laughter lasted for the shortest second in history because their surroundings were undeniable. Kendali Grace had been gunned down and she was dead.

"I just don't know. I don't know if I want to do this anymore," Lesli confessed.

"Fly, you talking crazy," Titus chided, frustrated by Lesli's pessimistic statement

"No, T. For real, I think I am going to do something safer. Like fly fighter jets. I started to join the Air Force when I finished high school."

"Really?" Brad was surprised.

"Really."

"Well, I am glad you didn't," he retorted.

"Yeah, me too," AJ chimed in raising her head from Brad's chest, still holding him around his waist and laying her head on his bicep.

"I am serious. I am tired of this." Tears still flowed from her eyes and Titus dried them as she spoke. "I am over it. Being stalked. And threatened. Cursed. Just sick of it. Now, a whole woman is *dead*? Dead, y'all. She was shot right in front of us."

"Lesli, I get it," Toni began. "But we gotta push through, ma. I know you tired. Me too. I been at this thing for twenty years, plus. But her death cannot be in vain. This did not happen for you to give up. To give in. And just fold. No, ma. We all gotta take a few days. Think. Reflect. Cry. Mourn. Regroup. And come out swinging. This is a wakeup call. For us all. This is an alarm. We gotta journey forth stronger, better, and wiser. Period! We gotta make change. Right now." Everyone listened to Toni intently, nodding their approval. "So if you wanna fly fighter jets, by all means, go for it! I know you will be a helluva pilot. But do it, to do it. Not to run away from your passion. From what you have built. For what you are becoming. If you know this is your calling, you gotta stay the course. And if nothing else, Kendali was killed while doing what she loved. Be clear: I am not, in no way, justifying her murder. I am not minimizing the loss of life, none of that. But if you gon' be gunned down, if you gon' die, it betta be while in pursuit of your passions. That's just how I see it." The circle fell silent. For them, the surrounding buzz of the remaining PQ-ers was reduced to barely a hum.

"Well! I guess she told you!" AJ laughed for the first time in what felt like years. They had grown older since that bullet pierced the heart of their literary colleague. Even so, they enjoyed the lighthearted moment in spite of the tragedy, searching for something inside themselves, praying for peace and youth.

12

"I mean dammit. I couldn't stand her but I didn't want her dead." Bree looked around the ballroom, amazed by the scene.

"Yeah. We know." Shante had been walking around helping people regain composure, handing out water and assisting Charlene. She plopped down in a chair to rest. Monique sat silently next to Shante, staring at the yellow crime scene tape.

"Mo?" Shante nudged her friend pulling her out of a trance.

"Yeah, yeah. What is it, babe?"

"You alright?" Mo rolled her eyes. "I mean...You know what I mean." Shante huffed and crossed her arms.

"No, I am not alright." Mo's upsweep was now a down-do, her hair all over her head, straight crazy. After Kendali was killed, she wept, curled over, cursing at the floor. The power of her screeching cries burrowed through the earth's crust into the depths of hell, calling up demons to avenge Kendali's murder. Her husband Vaughn had to carry her out of the ballroom. He calmed her with a sedative, an old prescription that they carried with them for affairs like The Platinum Quill. A doctor prescribed Monique with the pills during one of Dominion's controversial madhouse streaks after Kendali published her fourth Vixen Notebook. "I saw her grow up in this industry. I watched her develop. I just cannot believe this."

"Yeah. Me either," Bree concurred. "I didn't even bang with her and I'm hurt, ma." Bree dabbed her tears. "I mean. I'm really hurt."

"This shit ain't even real." Mustafa squeezed Aminah's hand with all of his Black power might. She squeezed back. "I mean..." Mustafa shook his head vigorously in disbelief, rubbing away dried tears at the corner of his eyes.

"I know, King." Aminah brushed his face with her tender lips.

"Maaan. We gotta do better than this." Maceo cradled his Black Pearl, her afro locks entangled with his beard.

"I just can't believe it," Nikki murmured. "I just can't."

Maceo reflected, "I mean, I ran the streets enough." He massaged Nikki around her waist as he continued. "Seen too much. But this?! A woman...our sister...shot dead right in front of us? Nah, man. This is as cold as I have ever seen. I mean she writes books! Shiiid. Books, man."

"I know, bruh," Mustafa responded slapping Maceo on his back with brotherly love. "I know."

"Yeah. We gon' bounce," Maceo said to Mustafa, giving him a dapped-up hug. "I'ma see y'all soon. Already told you...I'm down for the Isis thing, my man."

"That's what's up." Mustafa embraced Nikki goodbye. They all took turns hugging each other, bidding adieu, still in shock by the most finite goodbye of Kendali Grace.

"Yeah. We are fairly certain that he was stalking Kendali and hacking me." Hiram flinched as the paramedic bandaged his graze wound. The bullet that killed Kendali exited her body clean, and brushed Hiram on his shoulder.

Detective Geronimo Blackfoot, also known as The Wolf, jotted notes on his phone while Hiram described Max as a primary suspect. Georgette and Khai sat nearby listening and consoling each other.

Coppertone skin, bushy eyebrows hovering over piercing pale brown eyes, a low cut afro, and full beard gave the six foot two investigator a looming, stealthy presence. His eyes changed color, like a wolf, with his moods, thoughts, and emotions. "Well, he was here attending the event *with* you all, wasn't he? Are you saying he hired someone to kill her? This Maxmillian Gray guy?"

"Are we sure he was *here* the whole time?" Hiram raised an eyebrow. Geronimo contemplated the question. Hiram continued his spiel. "I am telling you. This dude is smart. He ain't no lightweight. This a big brain muthafucka we talkin' 'bout."

"Uh-huh. A Mr. Know-It-All?"

"You got it. And he *does* know it all. Ain't no fakin' or frontin'." Hiram eased up from the makeshift emergency room gurney that the EMT teams set up in the ballroom.

Hiram slowly rotated his arm. "Go easy, bro," the young EMT cautioned.

"Yeah, okay," Hiram replied stretching his body upward, pushing his palms toward the ceiling. "I am telling you, man. For all we know, he could have had a remote-controlled robot clone do the killing."

"That smart, huh?"

"Yes. That smart."

"Well, it is clearly a professional job. One clean shot. Straight through the heart."

"Precisely."

"Again, Mr. Rivers. I am very sorry for your loss. We will find the killer."

"If you don't, I will."

"Leave it to the police, Mr. Rivers. We ask you to let us handle this."

"Man, look. You do what you do. And I'm gon' do what I do."

Geronimo grimaced at his retort as someone shouted, "That's him! It was him!" Other voices joined the outcry pointing at Max. He finally made it back to the arboretum. "Yeah! Yeah! He was running! Running away! He shot Kendali!" A panic laden buzz filled the room and the ceremonial butterflies fluttered through an open patio door, thankful to escape the tragedy; their sister, for she was a butterfly in her own right, was dead and they too needed to mourn like the humans.

Hiram fixated his eyes on Max as he looked around, confusion flooding his face. Hiram gave the lead detective an affirming nod. Khai rose from his chair, on guard. Geronimo spoke, "Mr. Gray. We just wanna talk to you." He motioned to several of the uniformed police who were manning the door. The officers responded by inching their way toward Max forming a semi-circle around him. Max realized the encroachment of officers upon him and gave chase. Hiram bolted past the police and was right on Max's heels within nanoseconds. Khai trekked closely behind his friend. Max followed the path previously trod by him and the alleged culprit he had chased into the deeper recesses of Hamer Hill Park. Max outran the despicable beast, Khai, and Seminole City's finest, disappearing into the streets at the park's edge.

The pursuers stood on the street corner catching their breath and looking up and down the thoroughfare for the very athletic Maxmillian Gray.

"I see no sign of this nigga," Khai lamented. "Not at all."

Hiram growled, pounding his fists against the night air. "Argh!" Max was ghost.

"We will issue an APB, Mr. Rivers," Detective Blackfoot reassured. "He can't elude us forever."

"That's what *you* think."

Lesli and Titus arrived home, at Lesli's place, worn, weary, and wondering.

"How did we get here, T?"

"I don't know, Fly. I know right now we need to wash this day away."

"Yes. We do."

They took a long hot shower, kissing, caressing and massaging each other, the gray marble walls and floors of the stall giving them calm from its muted coloring.

Titus sucked her breasts hungrily and perched his chin on her chest.

"Marry me, Fly."

"Yes, my love."

"You mean it?"

"Absolutely."

"I love you, Mrs. Dixon."

"And I love you, Mr. Dixon." He wrapped his body around hers, lingering in the elevation of their station. *She said absolutely.* His soul sang a song he made up in his head, inspired by the timeline of their loving experiences. He hummed in her ear and she melted inside the melody, her emotions taking over.

They finished their bathing ritual, spread their towels on the bed, stretched out next to each other and air-dried their bodies, listening to the silence that tragedy brings. Titus dozed off and Lesli Lyn typed on her tablet, posting to her Zing group, The Kaleidoscope:

☐Zing Post The Kaleidoscope☐
Lesli Lyn (post): Beloved Butterflies☐

I greet you in silky soft winged peace. I am sure you all have heard about the tragedy that has befallen us in the urban fiction industry. Kendali Grace, author of the bestselling *The Vixen Notebook* series, was shot and killed.

Many people do not know that the life span of a butterfly is short. They live on average for one month. Just one month. Isn't that amazing? One month is the average life span. Some species live close to a year, but that is rare. Hence, the butterfly is the symbol for transformation, for change. And the saying is true, everything must change. Change is a universal absolute.

In the past, I have been critical of Kendali and others like her. I explained my thoughts about their writing styles and content and my position remains unchanged. Overall, I have consistently rated her books three and four stars.

Even so, the thing that *has changed* is my overall perspective about her as a person, as a woman. I learned a lot about her tonight, in the whispers, tears, and hushed conversations amidst the aftermath of her murder. My eavesdropping and recollection of her interviews and biographic articles has forced me to draw a new conclusion: Kendali Grace is a butterfly after all, to me. She was constantly transforming and changing herself. She fluttered in an effervescent state of ongoing, unfurling evolution, from a wayward teen to a video vixen, to a college student, graduating with honors, to a self-published author, to a national best-selling writer, winning awards and accolades across the nation. I have learned that she was loving, and kind and sweet-spirited and sensitive. I regret not knowing, not seeing, not understanding these truths before her untimely demise, but I let go of the regrets. Instead, I am living in the moment and learning the lessons of the short life span of the butterfly that ultimately is not so short after all. The butterfly lives infinitely, eternally ever-changing, ever-evolving, fluttering throughout the galaxy spreading love with her wings.

Kendali Grace, may you flutter around heaven, peacefully. Float on, forevermore.

Reactions: 10,444 Comments: 8,888 Shares: 12,017
(Load previous comments)

Akilah Butterfly: I have nothing but tears and love. I love this, Butterfly!□

Rise Bullard: BB, yes. We will miss dear Kendali. I loved her books. She was so sweet. I saw her on Myesha Morgan and she was so graceful and beautiful. RIP, dear butterfly. Thanks, BB for the post.

Calvin Jones: Dang, ma. RIP

Niecy King: I guess she is a ghostwriter now□

Akilah Butterfly: That is so crass

Niecy King: What? Ijs

Akilah Butterfly: Saying what!? She is dead now, good grief!

Niecy King: I mean. All of yall was so crazy about Kendali. She was overrated. And a hypocrite

Rachel Crum: Yeah, I agree with Niecy. I mean it's horrible what happened but she wasn't all of that.

LaToya Tea Mitchell: I am intentionally ignoring all these comments about my friend because I am liable to catch a flight. Most of you all didn't even know her…AT ALL! So, back to the positive: GIRL! You always bring us full circle. I have no words. And thank you for posting this. I love you, Butterfly.□

Butterfly Brooks: I Love you, Tea♥ And yes, Tea. We really didn't know her.

Gina Hayes Fife: I am so mad about this! We ask God for strength. For guidance. RIH, angel.

Diamond Sherron: Yeah, me too. I am so upset. Cannot stop crying. And so angry. God is the best of knowers. May she be at peace. We love you, Kendali.□

Phoenix Ash: It's unbelievable. So, so sad. RIP□

Helen D Clark-Speedy: Let us pray they catch the killers and remember the best about her, her books, and her sweet spirit. RIP□

Chapter Two
HomeComings & HomeGoings

One Week Later
Monday 10:00 a.m.

One Lord. One Faith. One Baptism. The words were emblazoned on a gargantuan-sized mural of Black ancestors picking cotton in Seminole County's cotton fields. Gethsemane Baptist Church, pastored by Reverend Dr. Floyd Lassiter, served as the homegoing celebration tabernacle for Kendali. Reverend Lassiter and Hiram had an amicable relationship, for Hiram was a generous tither, even though he rarely attended church. The three-year old sanctuary easily accommodated 5,000 members and they needed every single seat for the memorial. Fans, friends, and family showed up for the homegoing, seated in designated sections pre-planned by Hiram, Georgette, and Kendali's family. She was her mother's only child, but her mother was one of five children, so there were plenty of aunts, uncles, and cousins in attendance. Belinda Grace, Kendali's mother, her sister, her brother, Hiram, Georgette, Toya, Dre, and two of Kendali's cousins occupied the first row of elegantly cushioned pews during the down-home traditional wake. Reverend Lassiter was from the Mississippi Delta, so he combined the more refined customs of the 'saddity' Baptist church with the bluesy, rural one-room dirt churches of his childhood, where wakes were conducted by a motherboard of moaners. The moaners with their tambourines and haunting, harmonious spirituals were ten elder women ranging in age from fifty years to ninety years, but one would never know by the power of their voices, the spryness of their gaits, and the smoothness of their dance. They had the entire church in a celebratory uproar as mourners entered the sanctuary and cried over Kendali's open casket, pausing to kiss the first row family on their cheeks and offer condolences to each other. The sagacious sirens slapped the jingly instruments and ran, walked, and skipped through the silver carpeted aisles wailing a glorious sound that Mahalia Jackson would envy.

Hiram was a basket case. He did not holler or shout, but he sobbed incessantly, his face sopping wet with tears. As funeral attendees offered their kind words of encouragement, he would cry even more, his shoulders jerking unashamedly. Georgette was shocked, along with many others, for Hiram's mourning was incongruous to his cool, cavalier demeanor upon which he founded his reputation. Moreover, for Georgette, embarrassment was her shroud. She was disgusted by his sniveling display of weakness. His utter lack of composure repulsed her in the worst way.

"Can you pull yourself together, babe?" she asked him intermittently throughout the wake ritual. "I mean, do you need to go outside?"

"I'm fine, Gee." He patted her thigh. "I'm alright," he insisted wiping his face for the fortieth time with engraved handkerchiefs that she bought. He refused to leave his station in the pew. Instead, he posted up, pouting between bouts of hushed blubbering.

"You sure you don't need a breather?"

"Nah, babe. I'm okay."

Georgette maintained her regal posture, the brim of her spaceship-sized black and white hat dipping down ever so slightly over her eye. She wore a long auburn weave under the milliner's special in honor of Kendali. It was an extraordinary sight to see the congregation dotted with auburn colored hair, especially the first few rows. Georgette insisted that all the women of Dominion wear auburn hair. "I don't care if you dye it, weave it, or wig it. You need to wear it! Auburn hair, ladies. In honor of our sister." Judging from the sea of auburn locks, it seemed everyone obeyed her order including Toya who sat stoic-faced next to a mute Dre, both equally stunned and drained of emotions.

One of the moaners rang a bell, signaling the choir to march into the sanctuary. They came in, two by two, in red and silver robes singing, *Mary, Don't You Weep*. Belinda Grace screamed in agony, stirring up rounds of weeping, wailing, and muffled crying from all over the auditorium including Monique, Lesli, Toni, Nikki, Maceo, and Mustafa. Even Myesha Morgan showed up with heavy heart and streaked mascara. The choir continued their journey to the choir loft, never missing a beat. The anguish of the people seemed to inspire them to sing harder. Reverend Lassiter and his ministerial council, dressed in gray robes with gold embroidery, followed the harmonizers and took their places in the pulpit.

The funeral director asked the family if they wanted to do a final viewing before he closed the casket. Dre and Toya declined; they had seen enough of her corpse. Hiram rose first and motioned for Georgette to accompany him. They walked to the white casket with gold, sculpted handles surrounded by hundreds of orchids, Kendali's favorite. She was gorgeous, perfectly coiled brown curls resting softly around her angelic face. A simple white V-neck dress with silver buttons and goddess sleeves, glitter stocking sheers, and four inch silver pumps were the perfect garb for entering the pearly gates. Hiram's upper torso quaked with heartbreak. Georgette braced him with a firm grip on the base of his spine, essentially propping him up. She buried her disgust in the bottom of her feet and used the force to keep them both upright and dignified. After Hiram placed a bag of Swedish fish in Kendali's hand, they returned to the pew.

Belinda made her way to the casket, flanked by her brother and sister, each of them cradling a forearm. Her mother was a slightly taller, browner version of Kendali, Amazon-built, strong, soft, curvaceous body, wide hips, modest breasts, and round face. Same hair, same eyes, same brown curls. She too looked like an angel, dressed in an all-white suit and pearl tone patent leather pumps with rhinestone heels. Clearly, Kendali had inherited Belinda's sense of style. Standing at the casket motionless, Belinda hummed *Amazing Grace*. A hush fell over the church. Even the balcony could hear the soft melodic tribute. She cried one last cry and her siblings escorted her back to her seat.

There were songs sung, scriptures read, and dances danced. Reverend Lassiter delivered his eulogy:

"... It's bad enough that we are losing our lives amid confrontation. It's even worse when we lose our lives in the midst of celebration. Death has no prejudice. It does not matter if you are sad or happy, rich or wealthy. Death is coming for us...coming for us all."

21

1:00 p.m.

There were strict instructions for the remainder of the day. Only the closest 200 funeral attendees went to the burial while the remaining friends and associates were directed to Gethsemane's Family Life Center for a repast. As they exited the church, fans were given small caches of lavender vanilla potpourri and bags of Swedish fish.

The procession to the cemetery seemed like the longest ride of Dre's life. He and Toya stuck close together, holding hands and sitting in silence. They rode with Kendali's cousins in one of the four limousines that Dominion ordered. Dre reflected on their estranged relationship, unable to process his regret. He detached himself from his emotions, at least for the ceremony.

"What are you thinking?" Toya probed.

"Just what I'm gonna do now, ya' know?"

"Yeah. I know." Toya twirled a lock of her kinky auburn weave and rested her head on Dre's shoulder. "I am going to spend the rest of my life searching for her killer with all of my power and all of my might."

"Yes. I am with you, but I am sure Mr. Dominion has it covered."

"He can do what he needs to do while I do what I'm gonna do."

Dre didn't respond. He kept his eye on the roads they were traveling, leaving Seminole City and entering Shoshone, home of Everlasting Eden Cemetery. He was making up his mind to move on. Maybe even move away. Whatever it would take to forget his precious Dali and purge his body of emotions, he was going to do it. He would only remember that they were separated, that he despised her whorish ways, her dishonesty, and her disloyalty. He would cling to the memory of her vixen persona, and all the things he hated about her. He resigned to forget their loving touches, passionate sexcapades, and parking lot picnics. He would forget that they were on the precipice of new possibilities on the fateful night she was killed. He would no longer remember how they toasted the night together and how he reassured her that she was the best and deserved all of her success. He would only remember that he was alone in his feelings, holding out hope for a new love affair and she would forever be Kendali Grace, certified free spirit, something he could never truly possess.

The Everlasting Eden Cemetery was fields of verdant green, soft rolling hills with small gardens and gazebos dispersed every hundred yards. A plantation house sat on a hill overlooking the memorial meadow where the groundskeepers and administrators conducted the business. Most of the tombstones were modest memorials, per the rules of the cemetery; no ostentatious, oversized headstones or mausoleums were allowed. The layout was uniformly lush, filled with flowers, surrounded by acres of oak trees as far as the eye could see. All the men had been given purple and white orchids to lay on Kendali's casket during the interment. Hiram, Khai, Maceo, Mustafa, Brad, Titus, Vaughn, Crispus, and several others took turns making their final tribute while several of the elder women hummed, *I'm Going Up Yonder.* The women mourners watched, cried, and prayed.

"My dearly beloved brothers and sistas, children of The Most High God," Reverend Lassiter began. The partly cloudy sky served as an apropos background for his final speech. "We are gathered here on this hallowed piece of earth where there lies a hole in the ground that cannot compare to the size of the hole in our hearts. Our sweet Kendali, who was slain in celebration of her accomplishments, a sister who fell during her rise, isn't coming back." Sniffles and muffled cries complimented the reverend's solemn words as his voice strengthened with each passionate syllable. "Her tragedy, like all tragedy, was senseless, detrimental, and a severe blow to what her intelligence, her love, her power, and her determination could've brought forth as a benefit to the community, to the world. A light isn't just dimmed today, my beloved brothers and sisters. A light is out, but it's a light that we must rekindle in our hearts, minds, and spirits. We must keep our daughter, sister, and friend's light alive. She walks with us in our thoughts and deeds. And so, her living is not in vain!

Let her memory motivate us to do better and be better. Let her memory motivate and inspire us to love each other more. Love each other greater. Love each other stronger. We must be the diligent and vigilant keepers of our brothers and sisters. Kendali Grace, we offer your body to the earth, for the Good Lord has already reclaimed your soul. You are in our hearts forever."

Folks dispersed slowly, having conversations, hugs, kisses, light laughter, so-good-to-see-you's, and it's-been-a-long-time's.

"Hiram?" Belinda beckoned Hiram's attention as he was conversing with his frat brother.

He looked at her, and then turned back to Khai. "Aight, man. I'ma see you in a few."

"Yeah, let me make sure everything is on point for us," Khai said, referring to his supper club, the venue for Kendali's repast.

"I know it is, bruh. I know it is." They hugged. Khai walked to his Alfa Romeo 4C and sped to the supper club to close out the homegoing of his favorite lover girl.

"Belinda." Hiram ushered her to a quiet area under a tree away from the dissipating crowd.

"So, what's happening with her estate? She never told me much, but she did say you handle everything."

"Belinda, you have nothing to worry about."

"What does that mean?"

"I made Kendali do a will. All her wishes are enumerated in black and white. And there is a generous policy just for you." Hiram hid his irritation with the cold, calculated questions of Kendali's mother, not so motherly. *What a low life*, he thought. *Asking about money and they hadn't even thrown dirt on her daughter yet.*

"A will? Hmmm." She wiped perspiration from her brow; the humidity of the midday sun peeking through the overcast, was besting her. "What's in the will? What does it say? I know you know."

"Can we talk about this later? We need to get to the repast and finish your daughter's send off."

24

"Oh, yeah. Sure. Sure." A hint of embarrassment laced her words, just a hint. A dash. A skosh. She was fiercely more concerned about her inheritance than her appearance of propriety.

"Good." Hiram motioned for Belinda to head toward her funerary chariot. "I'm gonna grab my wife. We will see you shortly."

"Okay." Belinda sauntered toward the limousine thinking, the cool chill running down her back was a warning that some bullshit was afoot.

4:00 p.m.

Khai Draper really outdid himself for Kendali's final shindig. On two opposite sides of the lighted bar at the club's center, were two vertical Kendali Grace photo banners hanging from the ceiling. She was dressed in all white, fresh faced with her signature auburn locks blowing around her cheeks. Beneath the banners, tables decorated with purple and gold orchid pattern tablecloths welcomed guests to partake in Kendali's favorites. There were big silver bowls of Swedish fish, MAC makeup and cosmetic tools, and bottles of lavender oil displayed on three tiers, making an ornate regal presentation. Various kinds of handmade vanilla candles were lined up like little aromatic soldiers saluting the memory of the celebrity author. Stacks upon stacks of her books were wrapped in sparkling silver gift paper, mimicking real bars of the precious metal. Silver, white and purple gift bags containing various combinations of Grace's goodies sat on the table and the floor, waiting to be scooped up by a loved one.

All the dining tables had silver, white, and purple orchid centerpieces, two feet tall. Silver glitter tablecloths and white cushy chairs made an inviting fellowship hall, in spite of the somber occasion. Khai had eight buffet stations set up to ensure no waiting for the hungry lamenters. Steak, lobster, salad, baked potatoes, a pasta station, a grill station, a Deucey's station with Deucey's catering staff on hand to serve because she loved Deucey's, and a dessert station guaranteed that every weeping palate was satisfied. Indigenous Soul played their traditional soul, funk, jazz fusion and folks' spirits were elevated, for a little while.

"This is so good." Bree smacked her lips as she swallowed KD's seafood pasta. She, Nikki, and Maceo sat at a table with some other people they did not know.

"What did you get?" Nikki inquired as she dipped lobster in butter sauce.

"The seafood pasta. It is sooo good." She hungrily ate another forkful.

"You never had KD's?" Maceo asked Bree. He bit into his Deucey's fish sandwich.

"I haven't. I don't know how I missed it."

"Me either," Maceo said. "Yo' ass go everywhere."

"Yeah. But I missed this one." She swigged her merlot. "And speaking of going everywhere, I think I'm leaving. Gonna take a long sabbatical."

"What?" Nikki stopped eating. "Bree-Wee. Whatchu mean? Going where?" Nikki's big doe eyes saddened, her lashes blinking slowly, fanning back tears.

"Where you *think* you goin'?" Maceo pressed sternly.

"Gonna go visit my father for a while." Bree kept eating, nonchalantly downplaying her announcement.

"What? All the way to Ghana?" Nikki screeched, calling the attention of the strangers at the table.

Maceo gave them an admonishing glare. They returned to their conversations. "Bree. I get it. And you should spend time with your father, but right now? Are you sure? And for how long?" Maceo quenched his mouth with water, stunned by Bree's new plans.

"Yeah, Mace. I'm sure, big bruh. I need a break. I have been considering it for a while. And now, with this...I just…"

"Awww, Bree-Wee." Nikki massaged Bree's thigh, still holding her tears.

Bree held her hand. "I need to go. It's gonna be good for me. For my children. My father has been begging me to come to the Motherland. Y'all know this."

"True. We know. How long do you think you will stay?" Maceo needed to know.

"I don't know, Mace."

"Are you going to keep writing? You owe me two books." He laughed.

"I know. I will probably ONLY write. It's the ONLY thing I will do. No phone. No social media. Just writing. Reading. Walking. And loving."

"We gon' miss you, baby sis. But I get it." Maceo stood and opened his arms for a hug. Bree leapt into his embrace. Maceo motioned for Nikki to encircle Bree on her back and Nikki obliged. They bear hugged a long time, soaking up some joy in the midst of the sadness. The newness affirmed for them that there is life after death, especially for Bree.

Hiram sulked in a quiet corner of the outdoor terrace of KD's, lounging on a sofa and chatting intermittently with the grill master between tequila shots and hot dog pick-ups from guests. Belinda found him, a bloodhound with her olfactory center suffocating on the scent of money.

"There you are." She had changed into a pair of flat white slippers. The sloshing sound of her feet angered Hiram.

"Yes, Belinda."

"You said later. Later is now."

"The probate will take place day after tomorrow. You will know everything then."

"Why don't you just tell me now?"

"Good gracious, woman! Ya' damn daughter ain't even in the ground yet and you asking' me about her money?" Hiram staggered to his feet, surprised at his level of drunkenness.

"You damn right. I heard about you, Hiram."

"Oh yeah?" Hiram responded with surly tongue. "And it's all true, gotdammit."

"Oh yeah?" Belinda leaned back dramatically feigning fear.

"Yeah. So you know not to come at me with no bullshit. Ya' betta come right and ready."

"Yeah. Okay, Hiram. We gon' see."

"No, you gon' see. I already told you she left you well off." He drank another shot of tequila. "I mean you can't quit your job. But you can tell them to kiss your ass. You can pay off your house and have plenty left over."

"Yeah, but what about her royalties?"

"They go to Dominion."

"What? To Dominion? What the hell?"

"It's all in the will."

"Oh, we gon' see. You will hear from my attorney! Low life thievin' muthafucka." She stormed back into the main venue.

"Yeah, yeah, yeah." Hiram wearily plopped back onto the sofa.

The grill master checked on his new Patrón loving friend. "You alright, my man?"

"Yeah, man. Just sick of hungry, greedy bitches." He slurred his words. "You wouldn't believe what I deal with in this business."

"Actually, I probably would," he replied, sprinkling seasonings on a lobster and tossing it on the grill.

"Ya' think?" Hiram slumped forward, holding his face in his hands, elbows on his thighs.

"No. I *know*."

Dre entered the terrace. "That's for me, bruh?" Dre asked pointing at the lobster sizzling on the hot grate.

"If you want it, my man," the grill master said cheerfully.

"I do."

"Alright, alright. Just another minute or two."

"Cool." Dre folded his python arms across his chest and gazed up at the twilight sky.

Hiram noticed him with inebriated eyes. "Oh, I guess you came out here for me too," he shouted.

"Man, ain't nobody thinkin' boutcha grimy ass."

"Wait. Grimy ass?" Hiram pushed himself off the sofa and stumbled toward Dre. He stood toe-to-toe in front of Kendali's day one beau, poked out his chest, and breathed angrily into his face. "Grimy?"

Dre didn't move. He raised his eyes to Hiram's pupils, the drunken publisher standing slightly taller and slimmer than Dre. Dre spoke with clenched jaw, "Yeah, grimy. And ya' need to back up before I buss ya' ass."

"Make me, nigga."

Dre pushed Hiram past the grill, smack dab into the wrought iron fence enclosing the terrace. In his liquor drenched stupor, Hiram was no match for the physically fit power of Dre Walker. He pinned him with his forearm across his neck and Hiram struggled underneath the weight of the mighty warrior. Dre realized he was drunk. "Man, you ain't even worth it. Your ass is high." Dre released the pathetic man, almost feeling sorry for him as he attempted to medicate his sadness with a prescription of Patrón. He stepped back and Hiram swung at him wildly.

"I ain't drunk." He swung again and Dre moved smoothly out the way. Hiram landed face down on the ground. Dre and the grill master picked him up and returned him to the sofa.

"Maaan. Let me get my lobster."

"Right on, brother." The grill master placed Dre's crustacean on a plate and gave it to him. Dre walked toward the main restaurant.

"Fuck you, Dre. You didn't love her."

Dre slapped the air, shooing Hiram's comment. "Go get sober."

"No. You didn't. You couldn't! Not like I did." Hiram lay on the couch and propped his head with a pillow.

Detective Blackfoot had been quietly observing the scuffle from the patio threshold. He approached Hiram.

"Mr. Rivers."

"What are you doing here?"

"It's Geronimo. I am working Kendali's case."

"Oh yeah. Okay. But what are you doing here? You are not the bereaved." His statements bubbled from his mouth.

"No. I am the concerned. I am the involved. I need to be here. To observe. There are many clues at the memorial service of the murdered. The culprit is probably right here. Right now. Moving amongst us."

"If you say so. I told you the culprit is a ghost. Maxmillian Gray."

"Yeah. I remember what you said. We went to his house. No answer. I will need more time for a search warrant."

"Yeah, yeah. I get it," Hiram said shifting his body to get more comfortable. "You move like Max. Like a ghost. Just poppin' up. Appearin' outta nowhere. I heard about you. I know they call you *The Wolf.* All y'all niggas crazy."

Geronimo ignored Hiram's comments. "Maybe so. We do know that the killer was a trained assassin. The bullet was high caliber, state of the art. It disintegrates after a clean shot. Went right through her, brushed you, and poof! There is little left for us to analyze."

"A magic bullet?"

"You could say that."

Geronimo rested his tall, beefy frame against the fence. "Who was that you were arguing with?"

"That nigga Dre. Dre Walker. He was her man."

"Right, right. Yeah. I recall. Yeah. I talked to him at the scene." Geronimo loosened his tie. "You two don't get along?"

"We do not need to get along. This is probably the most time I have spent around him. He was intimidated by my relationship with Kendali. That's all."

"Why?"

"I groomed Kendali. Made her into a bestselling author. Made her dreams come true. That's hard for any man to deal with, another man manifesting your woman's wishes."

"Yeah. I guess it is." Geronimo inhaled the stench of guilt from Hiram and exhaled the suspect possibilities. No matter how much he was grieving, Hiram Rivers was definitely a suspect. The guilty always cry the loudest and the longest.

10:00 p.m.

The past several days had been difficult for Mustafa. He was dealing with a lot in the wake of Kendali's death. There were questions, answers, and emotions that he had to sort out for his own sanity and clarity. Sitting at his desk at Isis' home office, he prepared to go live with his broadcast, Osiris Rising, a podcast he created as part of the Isis platform. He closed out his Zing Live to host a weekly talk show about all things multimedia. Isis headquarters, a newly remodeled bus depot, was approximately two blocks from Goddess Garments, his wife Aminah's boutique.

He had a message for all who would tune in to his voice. "Three more minutes," he said as he eyed the timer and poured more honey into his hot tea. He sighed while stroking his beard and scrolling through some pictures and video of Kendali on his computer. "Beautiful...sad," he mumbled. "Why oh why has the ink turned to blood?" It was time to go live. The red "On Air" sign illuminated outside his studio door. His producer pointed at him through the glass.

"Peace, love, and light, my beloved people. Let me remind everyone that I officially retired my Zing Lives. I will broadcast to you live, daily at 8 p.m. on Osiris Rising Radio on The Satellite Planet platform. I posted the link on my Zing profile. Osiris Rising Radio has a Zing page. Go like it. Our social media team will post daily. Come be with us where we are gettin' Back To Black. Isis has Resurrected Osiris.

Now, this is an extra show, the kind that I never want to do again. I speak to you today with love, as usual, but with an unusually heavy heart. I'm torn, Black fam. I'm angry. I'm tired. I'm confused. And I'm mourning. *We* are mourning the loss of our beloved sister and literary creative, Kendali Grace. I'm contemplating my own fate while reflecting on her cataclysm. Are you contemplating your fate tonight, brothers and sisters? And I know many of you feel indifferent about her murder and some of you are glad she is gone. I see the comments and the posts. And we are all entitled to our feelings. I get it."

Mustafa paused momentarily and adjusted himself in his chair. He took a long swallow of tea and continued his dialogue, his voice trembling ever so slightly. "But c'mon, Fam. This shit is crazy. Kendali's murder was senseless. I beg you, good people. We gotta do better. Love better. Communicate better. Seek to understand better. Resolve conflicts better. Poor communication skills. Misunderstanding. Disrespect. All of these diseases destroy us. *We gotta be better.*

It's either that or line up to get buried. We have to correct ourselves and each other in the spirit of love. The spirit of love will inspire us to be better. These ills cannot live in the same place where love thrives. Love does not destroy. Love creates. Creates beauty, harmony, peace, prosperity, and more love."

Mustafa stirred his tea, sadness surging through his veins. "You know, earlier today I was cleaning out a file cabinet. We are settling in here at Isis headquarters, preparing for the official launch and our building is an old dusty warehouse, fully renovated. Yet, some of its residents still remain, including the spiders. I encountered one of these arachnids as I was cleaning. And then the next day, I saw another one. And the day after that, another spider. And another. And another. Instead of killing the spiders, I studied them. I questioned the symbolism of the eight legged creature. What does this mean? Why am I seeing all these spiders?" He cleared his throat, choked up by a dam of his tears.

"So I asked Mr. Bing and Brother Wired and of course my wife Aminah, since she is spirit woman, about The Spider. The spider with its eight legs and its web spinning prowess, represents creativity, destiny, infinity, prosperity, patience, and the weaving of one's own fortune. I was reminded by the spider to be patient and focus on my creativity. What I'm building. You know? The web that I'm weaving is a destiny of which I am the sole architect. My web is my life. Your web is your life. And we must not only be patient in weaving our web, but be patient for what the web will capture. You see? We must be patient with self and others and honor the presence of the infinite possibilities. We must know that we are infinite beings weaving our destiny, creating our fortune in the spirit of love. If we are to love, if we are to live, we must be the spider. Be the spider, Black family!"

He paused and guzzled the rest of his tea. "So, in closing this brief broadcast, I send into the ethers love and blessings to Kendali Grace and all of the fallen. While they are no longer here in the physical, we know they live on infinitely just as the spider has taught. Write in power and peace, sister Kendali. Peace, love, understanding and power to my people. Get back to Black!" Mustafa, overcome with emotion, wept profusely and hoped her living, his own living, was not in vain.

Chapter Three
Chrysalis

One Week later, Tuesday 11:00 a.m.

❑Zing The Sauce Mobb❑

Bree McDee (farewell post): In the spirit of Sisterhood:
Most of your favorite authors, book promoters, and literary personalities have taken a long pause for the cause, a moment of silence for Kendali Grace, me included.

There are so many who feel that I and many other authors created a climate that got Kendali killed. I disagree with this, but everyone is entitled to their feelings and opinions. With that being said, I admit, I have not shown up in the most mature, loving, sisterly fashion. I fed a lot of unnecessary fire between me and Kendali, a legendary rivalry. This behavior, I regret. I've had some time to think about it, and while it may be too little, too late, I still have to share my current truth:

1.) I apologize to my sister, Kendali Grace, for the ugly words and the nasty posts. My anger had so little to do with you and more to do with your publisher. Either way, there are many more healthy ways to express anger.

2.) I hope to be a better woman now that she is gone, a huge lesson for me. Life really is short and we need not waste it being lesser, but seize its preciousness and be greater.

3.) I apologize to all those, my readers, my fans, my supporters, and especially my brother CEO of Gutta Butta, who I caused too much unnecessary strife when he has done nothing but show me love over and over in spite of myself.

On that note, The Sauce Mobb will be deleted, totally erased. As I reviewed the content, I realize there is too much negativity here. No need to save, there is little to salvage.

I am headed to the Motherland, for a much-needed sabbatical, to walk around, breathe deeply, write often, eat well, and love...myself a little more. I'm gonna go and grow the fuck up!

I thank you all for riding with me on this leg of my journey. I hope to see you on the next. RIH, my sister, Kendali Grace. Love, Love, Sisters!❤ ❤

Reaction: 2,345 Comments: 1,256 Shares: 4,567
(Load previous comments)
Pamela Hunter: Wow☐ I am speechless. Good for you, Bree!
Carrie Sanders: Bree McDee done grewed up☐Safe travels, boo!
Regina Williams: Bree, I wish you all the very best! You are learning and growing. Growth is good. Traveling mercies, sister❤
Marie Jones: I mean, I guess that's good. And I aint saying she should be dead, but Kendali had some shit with her. Ijs
Bebe Davis: Yeah, she did have some shit with her.
Amber Alise: Okay. I am gonna need y'all to roll off this post. This post is positive. #GirlBye
Helen D. Clark-Speedy: May God continue to bless you and your children and show you most favor. May the road rise up to meet you, baby girl.❤ Love you☐

    Bree McDee: @Helen D. Clark Speedy aww, thanks so much! I love you too!☐

    Ashanti Simmons: What?! You can't go! Noooooooooooooo☐ I get it though☐ I'm going to miss you☐ But I wish you the best! RIH, Kendali Grace☐

    Lesli Lyn (Butterfly Brooks): Good for you, Bree☐ ☐I wish you Love Peace and Positivity. All my Love to you!☐

    Bree McDee:@Lesli Lyn(Butterfly Brooks) Thanks so much BB☐

After reading Bree's responses, Lesli Lyn closed her Zing feed and continued typing. Brad entered her office and made himself comfortable in a chair facing her.

"You ready to compile your books?"

"My books?"

"Your women empowerment series."

"Brad, I am not thinking too straight. I'm just here. Not feeling very empowered."

"I know. I understand. I think you need to seize the moment, Lesli Lyn. This is a good time because everyone is reeling from Kendali's murder."

She stopped typing and turned to her boss. "I'm surprised at you, Brad."

"What?" He raised his hands and leaned forward, caramel skin and same color eyes glistening.

"Capitalize on the tragedy? That seems so 'Hiram Rivers'." She tapped her purple polished nails on her desk thoughtfully.

"Capitalize? No. Answer the call, yes."

"Answer the call?"

"Yes, Lesli. The people need guidance. They need healing. You are the healer. You are going to help everybody through this. Especially yourself. You have a duty. A duty to be who you are…to the people who need what you have."

"Hmmm. Bradford Meade." She sighed. "You got it all figured out, huh?"

"No. None of us do. But we *gon'* figure it out. And there's no time like the present." He leaned back and scanned the butterfly nuances throughout her office-the glass butterfly figurines on her desk, the butterfly photograph collage on one wall, the butterfly on canvas on another wall, butterfly napkins in a butterfly napkin holder, and her signature butterfly letter opener. "See all these butterflies?" He waved his arm in a semi-circle. "You got it. You are going to give the people your butterfly medicine. This is your calling, Lesli. Not an opportunity, love. A duty. Ya' dig?"

"Digging," she reluctantly agreed massaging her temples.

"I know," Brad said acknowledging her anxiety. "It's a great responsibility. That's why it is you who are called. You are a great big soul with those big, beautiful wings, so…get ready. Start getting your books together. I mean whatchu got the wings for?"

Her eyes rolled around in her head, a myriad of emotions powering her gesture. "Argh! Fine. I will start next week. I just can't right now."

"It's cool. I am going to get our PR people to get you started with a Myesha Morgan appearance. You need to show up as the voice of reason. The hand of healing."

"How soon?" she asked.

"Soon. So, prepare." He lifted himself slowly from his seat to leave.

Lesli returned to her Zing browsing and said nonchalantly, "Titus asked me to marry him again. I said yes, this time."

Brad stopped, dropped his shoulders, and shook his head. "It's about damn time."

"I knew you would say that."

"Damn right I'ma say that. Makin' that man wait. For nothing."

"Can't you just say congratulations?"

He jogged to her and gave her a big bear hug as she tapped her keyboard. "Congratulations, sis. I'm happy for y'all." He gave her a brotherly lip smack on her cheek and danced out of her office, singing, "...and I want the world to know...you're mine," from The Temptations' *Nobody But You*. Lesli laughed heartily for the first time in a long time. She felt good about Bradford's mandate for her next level move, but her soul was kicking and screaming, wishing she could give her wings back. In spite of her wishes, she kept fluttering:

☐Zing Post The Kaleidoscope☐
Butterfly Brooks (Lesli Lyn) (post):

I greet you in silky, soft-winged peace, Beloved Butterflies☐☐
Bad books. All I can say is they keep writin' 'em. One bad book after another. Part one. Part two. Part three. Part four. Part five. Heaven help us. What is most disgusting is the authors who are angry when the readers beg them to stop. I side with the readers: Cease Fire! We surrender already. We waved the white flag at book three! These same assaulting book writers are further incensed when readers recognize their goal with serial writing is simply to make money. We all know this is the truth in most instances.

Be not offended when a reader recognizes that you have attended the school of 'Series Make Profits'. This is an industry fundamental principle taught by all the book marketing and self-publishing gurus. All of them impart the first rule of thumb in the book business is to sell multiple books, preferably in a series. 'Bundle! Bundle! Bundle!' is the battle cry for all the book selling war strategists, training the minions to wield their pens as swords for a living and quit their day jobs.

So, beautiful people, stop trippin' when readers call you out. Instead, find a balance between passion and profit.

This is the L~ Double. I am silky soft and signing off. Float On. Especially Kendali Grace Butterfly.☐☐☐☐

Reactions: 868 Comments: 8,246 Shares: 2,356
(Load previous comments)

Felicia Dee: Omgeee! I am so glad you said it!!! Cease Fire! Say that, sis!

Pamela Hunter: There she go. Fluttering those wings☐ Folks ain't gonna like this post. B, you and Mustafa, smh. ☐☐☐#Truth2Power

Devina Dee: Say it again for the people in the back☐☐

Liz Ferro: Well…

Hanifah Akbar: Yeah. Making money and assaulting minds. Shame on them.

Kim Jackson: I mean they get they money how they get it. I ain't mad at them.

Rita Cunningham: Exactly! They tryna get their coinage just like the next person. whatever!

Lee David: The Butterfly has spoken💯 #AlwaysTruth

2:00 p.m.

Geronimo finagled a warrant to search Max's apartment. He had good relationships with several judges who afforded him ample leeway in these kinds of unsubstantiated cases. The police gathered little concrete evidence on Max. He was simply a man that people saw running from a chaotically emotional scene and whom Hiram revered for his intelligence, but vehemently disliked. Geronimo's previously unanswered visit to Max's seemingly abandoned house prompted Judge Finley to sign the warrant without hesitation.

Geronimo parked in front of the all brick, gable-roofed bungalow with its bright yellow shutters, sturdy carport, and pristine clean parking pad. An array of flowers and shrubs lining the lawn's edge and the large picture windows on the front of the house made the residence postcard picture perfect. The mail overflowed from the mailbox and the porch was riddled with debris. It had been almost two weeks since his first attempt to question Maxmillian Gray. Even though he was sure Maxmillian left town, he knocked on the door several times and rang the doorbell.

"Mr. Gray!" he shouted. "It's Detective Blackfoot. I just wanna ask you a few questions." He banged on the door again and then the window. "Maxmillian Gray!" There was no answer. Before picking the lock, he decided to inspect the other doors of the house. The side entrance was locked, but the rear French doors were slightly ajar. Geronimo stepped into the family area cautiously, wondering who had been in the house since his last visit. He detected the vibration of one of his kind, a kind with trained, intuitive skill. "Mr. Gray?" No response. The family area and kitchen were neat and tidy. The steel blue and white marble kitchen counters were clean. There was nothing in the sink and the trash can was practically empty. Geronimo surveyed the white wood cabinets containing standard non-perishables, cereal, canned goods, rice, pasta, and assorted cookies and crackers. The refrigerator and freezer were empty except for a jug of water and a few ice trays. The detective moved into the family room and studied the pictures on the mantel. All the photos were old; he guessed they were of Max as a little boy and then him growing up over the years. There was a collage of him as a bright-eyed smiling child with a cheerful married couple. The photos of him as a pre-teen and teenager depict a young boy with sad eyes and half smiles usually with a different couple-a woman that looked like the woman of the first happy couple and a man who was probably her husband. The young Max and his family were impeccably dressed and well-groomed on all the photos. There were several of him in his U.S. Air Force uniform and some of Max's graduations with the look-a-like woman and her husband.

Geronimo took his time searching the two tidy bedrooms. Clothes were neatly hung in the closets, shoes were lined up in shoe boxes, and suitcases sat unmoved. There was no sign of a man leaving town. He looked in the two bathrooms and the powder room. All was intact. But alas, there was the basement that measured the full length and width of the house. Detective Blackfoot turned on the light and carefully descended the stairwell. Upon landing on the chestnut-colored hardwood floors, he looked to his right and there was a living room set and television. To the left was something he had never witnessed before, a sanctuary of sorts with an altar and life size posters of Kendali plastered on the wall and hanging from the ceiling. "Damn," he mumbled. He pulled out his pocket flashlight and walked around the private church observing the burnt offerings of lavender oils, incense, dried orchids, bags of Swedish fish, vanilla candles, purple and gold embroidered fabrics, bowls sticky with honey, and dried orange peels. Various copies of Kendali's books were scattered about and upon closer inspection, Geronimo detected what he was certain were semen stains on the fabric and the floor. Several empty bottles of lavender vanilla lotion nearby confirmed his speculation. "What the hell," he murmured. He snapped pictures of 'The Kendali Temple' with his cell phone and jotted a few notes. He meticulously inventoried the rest of the basement, taking more photos and summarizing his observations in his note app. Several hand carved deer bone knives, new and antique, made Geronimo think of his own collection passed down from his grandfathers. "Ah-Wey-yah," he crooned. Blankets homespun from fine yarn comforted several hand-crafted corn husk dolls resting easy on a futon that served as the border of the dirt church, its sole deity, Kendali Grace. He thought of his sisters and cousins playing in the yard with similar dolls when they were children and in the midst of a maddening scene, he smiled. Just as he was finishing his investigation, he saw a safe tucked underneath the staircase. The door was closed but it wasn't locked. Geronimo opened the box to see nothing; it was empty. He took more pictures and made his way upstairs to the main floor. He snapped more photos of the kitchen, family area, and bedrooms. Extra special time was taken photographing the mantel with Max's life story. He exited through the back of the house, twisting the knob locks, and closing the doors tightly. He looked at the front of the house one last time and hopped in his police issued car. *This just got real interesting,* he thought.

5:00 p.m.

"Tell me what you need, detective," Belinda said, settling onto the sofa of her deceased daughter's condo.

"Tell me what you know." Geronimo sipped the lemonade tea that Belinda gave him upon his arrival.

"I don't know much." She brushed her soft brown curls away from her round face, an exact copy, older version of Kendali Grace. "I loved my daughter. She loved me. We weren't close, but we weren't distant. You see what I mean?"

"I do." Geronimo sat his tea on the table and pulled out his cell phone to take notes. He turned to face her, seated next to her on the sofa. "Tell me who would want to kill your daughter, Ms. Grace.

"I really don't know. She was in that hip-hop video world and she always told me, 'Mama, you wouldn't believe how grimy this business is. I've seen too much, Mama.'"

"Did she name any names?"

"Not that I remember. All I can tell you is that Dre was her boyfriend. Seemed to be a nice young man. She was good friends with Toya. Everybody calls her Tea. And Kendali was infatuated with Hiram's ass." Her final comment was laced with venom.

"Infatuated?"

"Yes. Hiram this, Hiram that. Hiram, Hiram. I understand he helped her a lot, but shit. He ain't gawd!"

"Hmmm. Okay."

"Do you know she left him everything?!"

"What do you mean?"

"All of Kendali's royalties go back to Dominion."

"All of her royalties?"

"All, detective. Yes. Everything."

"So, Hiram gets her royalties. This is notable," he replied tapping his cell phone display."

"Well, as he kept repeating at the probate, I don't get it. Dominion does. Yeah. Whatever nigga." Belinda sucked down her brown liquor, eating the crushed ice to cool her nerves. "And I can't do anything about it. I can't contest the will. She wrote it, signed it. He even had her make a video."

"Making a video will is common practice these days for large estates."

"Yeah. He is very shrewd. Not to be trusted. Hiram is a scoundrel."

"Tell me about the video."

"It is a video, time stamped and dated with Kendali very happily reading her will. Saying why she is making the provisions, on and on. The stipulations. All that."

"I see."

"Don't get me wrong. She left me this condo. It's paid for and a very generous policy. Very generous. I was surprised. She even left Dre the money in her savings account and a nice policy too." She gazed at the ceiling. "Yeah. She really was a sweet girl. But that Rivers guy, I don't trust him. At all."

"Duly noted, Ms. Grace."

"Is there anything else you need?"

"Just give us permission to access all of her personal effects. Her house. Her belongings."

"Definitely. Absolutely."

"We are gonna get to the bottom of this. Are you staying here for a while?"

"I think so, but you have my number. Find out who killed my baby, detective."

"I will, Ms. Grace. I will."

Chapter Four
The Guilty & The Gilded

One Week Later, Wednesday
12 Noon

Mustafa was the first to arrive at Nina's private banquet room. Sand-colored hardwood floors, snow white walls, soft track lighting, and gorgeously gleaming mirrors etched with still life portraits made Nina's one of Seminole City's most inviting bistros. He reviewed his task lists excitedly, proud and nervous about the next phase of Isis. The launch was nigh.

"My man!" Thaddeus Kane, BlackOut Media's number one author slapped Mustafa on his shoulder, greeting his publishing boss. Mustafa stood and hugged Thaddeus.

"Blessings, Brother Thad. Good to see you. How is everything goin'? We haven't talked in a minute."

"Yeah. Well, you went dark. I mean you Blacked OUT! Pun intended." Thaddeus stood at six foot five, café au lait skin, close cropped curly hair, medium thick build, toned belly pouch from eating well on royalty checks, keen facial features- thin lips, narrow, straight nose, slanted eyes, and a huge smile. And he hated when people asked him if he ever played ball. "Every tall Black man gotta be a ball player?" he would balk. He played guitar and graduated college with a biology degree, a minor in English. He ran track in high school briefly and that was it.

Mustafa laughed at his friend. "Yeah, I did. That sister's murder, man. That got me all kinda ways fucked up."

"Yeah. We all still reeling." Thaddeus removed his windbreaker and made himself a plate of Nina's famous hot wings and herbed cabbage. He sat across from Mustafa and ate while Mustafa tapped keys on his notebook. Maceo and Brad entered the area together.

"What's good, fam?" Maceo extended his arms toward Thaddeus who was facing the door. Thad and Mustafa rose simultaneously, and all the men exchanged hugs.

"Good to see the brethren," Brad said placing his tablet on the table. Maceo skipped removing his jacket and headed straight for the buffet. Brad followed after him. "You hungry, bruh?" Maceo's plate overflowing with wings and cabbage prompted his question.

"Maaan. I just left the gym."

"Nuff said," Brad replied with an understanding grin. "I been slacking myself. Been off about a week. I try to do three days a week at least," Brad shared as he picked up his silverware.

"I know it's easy to fall off. Life gets in the way." Maceo grabbed a bottle of tea and headed toward the table.

"It does," Brad agreed. He finished gathering his lunch and joined the rest of the media powerhouse.

The crew leisurely enjoyed their Nina's while they chatted, grieved, celebrated, and consecrated their mission.

"The sister's death will not be in vain," Mustafa mandated. "Isis will destroy and purge the old and bring about the new. Isis put Osiris back together and so she shall, y'all diggin' me?"

"You know we are," Brad confirmed.

"We are being put back together...for real," Thaddeus concurred. He wiped his mouth with a napkin and guzzled his water. "So, tell us the deal," he said to Mustafa. "Give us the updates."

"Beta testing is complete, and we are real close to launch."

"That's good news. That's what we wanna hear," Brad stated.

"So now, we are in the process of strengthening the cyber security of our platform."

"And physical security?" Thad reminded.

"Yeah, we definitely need to consider these things which is why I called this meeting." Mustafa turned to Maceo. "We need a tall order, my brother."

"Ah, shit." Maceo pushed back on his chair and moved his plate to the side. "I thought I was just going to bring my books, akh."

"Yeah. We definitely want those, but we need a li'l more from you."

Maceo glanced at Brad; Brad raised an eyebrow and smiled. He turned to face Mustafa again. "Go ahead."

"We understand Hiram is well-equipped on the security."

"Ah hell. Y'all want me to bring Hiram in?" Maceo rolled his neck, exercising his muscles and releasing the tension brought on by the current proposal.

"Just hear me out," Mustafa urged. Bradford and Thaddeus listened to the exchange as they savored their food. "Now you know I don't fuck wit' the nigga. He got ego issues. But for what it's worth, he is who he is. And who he is, is the man with the goods." Mustafa planted his elbows firmly on the table locking his pupils with Maceo's. "More than his books, we want his security team."

"And what makes you think he is gonna listen to me?"

"One, he is vulnerable right now. His cash cow and alleged lover is dead. Murdered. He is ripe for a personal revolution."

"Okay…" Maceo waited for more reasoning.

"Two, for whatever it's worth, he does respect you. Much more than anybody else in this group. And three, y'all got history."

"Hmph. Never even thought about it." Maceo pondered Mustafa's articulately delivered summation.

"You know what I posit is true."

"It may be, but Hiram is shady, Mustafa. Y'all sure you want to deal with him?"

"We not making him a partner, Maceo. We just want his resources. His people and their skill set. Dig?"

"I dig, but are y'all sure about this?" Maceo glanced at his phone; Nikki was calling. He swiped to send her personal decline text, *"My Black Pearl. I will reach out shortly. I love you."*

Brad explained, "We want Hiram on board. His publishing and his security. That's it. We will make sure he behaves. We have contracts and lawyers for his ass." The brethren laughed.

Maceo reluctantly agreed, "Ohhh…kay. If y'all sure, I will get him to give up the goods. The nigga does owe me a solid, or two, or ten."

"We know you will do your best Maceo. That's all we need," Brad reassured.

"I'm tellin' y'all. I don't think you even realize the force we have assembled. We are going to forge our own path, out of the gutter…no offense Maceo."

Mustafa nodded at him. "Out of the mediocrity and the idiocy. We are destroying all the bullshit and we are establishing a new era, a new way, a true way to create, empower, enlighten, impact, influence, and change us for the greater. Becoming the best that we are. All the way back to Black."

Thad put his fist in the center of the table. "Back To Black." He looked around the table at his comrades. Maceo put his fist atop Thad's. "Back To Black" Brad followed suit. "Back To Black" And Mustafa sealed the pact with his fist on top of Brad's. "Back To Black."

Wednesday, 2:00 p.m.

☐Zing Post Tea Thyme Group☐

Latoya "Tea" Mitchell (post):
Y'all know I haven't been on much lately. I am still grieving. Just trying to find my way after the murder of my friend, my sister.☐☐ I did tell y'all I am going to make it my life's work to find out who killed her. I don't have much. But I've got guts. And I ain't afraid of none of these muthafuckas that I think could be culpable. I ain't scared of none of y'all. Tasir at Palace Records. We all know he is a sick bastard. Wes Gilliam, Diamond Artists Management. A pure dee turd. All of those bigwig, wannabe, grand puba niggas at Big Mike Records, Fortune Records, Magic Disc Records. I can't think of all the names right now. But all these big kahunas at these labels were afraid of what Kendali was revealing in her books. Especially the last one. Now I do have some info about Maxmillian Gray. Y'all may have heard the police are looking for him as a 'person of interest'. Yeah, okay. Whatever. He used to be an author at Dominion. Word on the street, he was stalking Kendali. Figures. Fuckin geek nerd psycho. Thirsty as fuck. Y'all know she was so beautiful and so loving. A cheerful giver. Nurturer. Probably to get back at Hiram, Dominion CEO, because their relationship soured. He was mad that Hiram would not release his last book when he wanted. Max, if you killed my friend, be ready TO PAY YOU MURDEROUS FUCK! Y'all keep your ears and eyes open!!!!! Because I am! Here is this sicko's picture, description, and resume! Call Seminole City Police if you see him. Also, call the police station every day and make sure they

45

stay on these other rotten assholes…Kendali Grace, RIH sweet sister angel. I love you.□□❤□

(Load previous comments)
Reactions: 8,962   Comments: 2,456   Shares: 4,532

Akilah Butterfly: Wow. Rest in peace Kendali.❤♣And I will definitely keep my antennas up.□Still can't believe she was murdered. We pray for guidance, amen.
Helen D. Clark Speedy: God be with us all. I am glad you are helping the investigation. Rest in peace, Kendali. Amen.
Benny Books: Damn. She was such a beautiful woman. She will be missed.
Calvin Spriggs: If I see the nigga, I'm str8 splitting his skull💯 RIH, Kendali
Amber Alise: I miss her so much. Everything is different. Sad. Dominion will never be the same. We need to catch this killer. I can't believe it's Max. But we never know what a thirsty nigga will do. I am with you Toya. All the way. Until we catch this muthafucka. RIH Sweet Grace!
Latoya Tea Thyme: @Amber Alise Yes, babe! We will get this nigga! I love you
Amber Alise: LU2

Hiram was sprawled out on the floor of his office man cave, TV blaring the movie Pulp Fiction, paperwork spread around him as he lay on his belly in front of his laptop watching Latoya's Zing feed. Tears seemed to take permanent residence in the wells of his eyes since Kenni's murder. Reading Amber Alise's comment made one fall, leaving a bitter taste on his lips. Amber loved Kendali. They had a similar background. Amber had been a stripper; Kendali had been a video vixen, six in one hand, and half dozen in the other. He brought them both to Dominion around the same time and they became fast friends.

The public was not made formally aware that Max was a suspect; they called him a person of interest, wanted for questioning. There was an APB amongst law enforcement, but no police authority had updated the community on the case's progress with details. In true Hiram fashion, of course, he had launched his own investigation. He had Crispus searching for Max and retracing his initial surveillance of Kendali's stalker and Dominion hacker cases. He decided to feed Toya intel to post on social media, including the masses in the hunt for Maxmillian Gray. *Why would he do this? All of this to get to me? Why, Max? What did you want from me?* He rolled over on his back and released more tears.

"You didn't have to kill her," he sobbed out loud.

"Who didn't have to kill her?"

Hiram lifted his aching, agony ridden body from the floor. "Georgette? What are you doing here?"

"I live here."

"Yeah, but who's watching Dominion?"

"Dominion is taking care of herself."

"Yeah, but nobody can do it like the parents."

"Look, I just came home for a break. I will get back to taking care of your empire shortly. Tiyanna is there. And quiet as it's kept, she could run Dominion all by herself. Easily. And AJ, of course."

"That might be true, but-"

"Look Hiram. You need to focus on you. You are a wreck. When are you going to return to your duties? I am tired of running things. I hate it. You know I do."

"I don't know when I am going to return. I just need time."

"Time. Yeah, alright. Time." She walked closer to him, her navy blue dress, tied at the neck with a bright white bow, emanated executive femininity of the sexiest order. Hiram felt his dick throb for Georgette for the first time in many weeks. He had been jacking off to memories of Kendali, so unsatisfied with the final ejaculation. He had only been able to get an erection when dreaming of her, when longing for her. Khai tried to ease him with his powerhouse fellatio, commiserating with him a few times, but Hiram's grief mastered his feelings, emotions, and libido. After Khai's failed attempts, he would leave his house and drown himself in tequila at Nina's. Georgette bent over his body, clad in a white silk robe spangled with tiny black crowns, only a pair of fruit of the loom 'tighty whiteys' underneath. "Hiram Rivers." She leaned in closer to the floor and he moved closer to her face. "You cannot go on like this. You haven't shaved. No haircut. I guess you still washing your ass and brushing your teeth." She sniffed.

"Now you know I ain't lying around rancid."

47

"You haven't seen your children. You haven't been to the gym. You aren't working. You barely eatin'. You have got to pull yourself together." She noticed a few more grays in his goatee and the fledgling beard. "You gonna grow a beard now?"

"I don't know what I'm gonna do. I'm just here." He dropped his head. Crying had become his comfort.

Georgette palmed the top of his blooming afro. "At least get a shape up. Do something."

He looked at her face and swirled his eyes around her head and shoulders. *Kendali,* he thought. "Why are you still wearing that hair? I thought that was just for the funeral."

"Why?" she asked standing up straight. "You don't like it?"

"I like it, but I don't know if it's you."

"Well, *I KNOW THIS,*" she said, as she fanned the air, referring to the mess Hiram made of his office man cave. The stench of despair held him hostage in the room. She continued, "is not you!" She stepped back toward the door. "This is not the man I married. Not the man who made me and so many others bestselling authors. That built an empire with his own blood. His own sweat. And his own tears."

"I know. I just need time. Just give me some more time, Gee."

Wednesday, 4:00 p.m.

Georgette jumped in her hunter green Audi Q7 and started the engine. A deep desire to weep overcame her but the tears did not come. The agony of being unable to cry had been plaguing her for weeks. She loved Kendali, but she kept replaying the Bible verse in her head, *Let the dead bury the dead.* We must move on. Even so, she needed comfort in her journey. She decided to give into her comfort craving; resisting only proved more torturous.

She dialed his number and pulled out of the cul-de-sac.

"Yeah, yeah. This is Thad."

"You don't know it's me? You deleted my number?"

"Georgette?

"Yes."

"Of course I deleted your number. You a married woman."

"I don't know for how long. This kneegrow is goin' crazy. I might be a widow soon."

"Word?"

"Word. Either he will wither away, shoot himself, or I will put him out of his misery."

"Damn. What's goin' on?"

"He just there. That's it. Just there. Breathing. Crying. Looking crazy. I've taken over Dominion. Mo left us. Kendali murdered. It's just a lot."

"Yeah. That is a lot."

"He is too emotional. I know he was fuckin' that bitch, but he won't admit it."

"So the rumors were true?"

"I think so. They were real slick wit' it. I give them that."

"Everybody knew something was up. But it's good that he wasn't frontin' you off out here in these streets."

"True, but it doesn't matter. He lied and he is lying."

"Did you ask him about it?"

"No. Not yet. But a lie is a lie, whether spoken or unspoken. I don't even wanna hear his cool, cavalier response. I don't deserve that."

"You don't. You deserve me."

"Ha. Still so charming."

"Come hang out with me. Let's have dinner."

"You serious?"

"What did you call me for? Just to talk?"

"I thought so. We haven't talked for a while."

"Come on, girl. You need comfort. I got it for you." Georgette didn't respond, stunned by the possibilities of a dinner date with Thaddeus.

"You there?"

"I'm here."

"Where would you like to dine?

"Truly, a Deucey's fish sandwich has been my chief craving."

"Wow. Ain't that sumpthin? All the money. The fame. The power. Fine wines. Five star restaurants. Executive chefs. Private dining. And we still come back to fish, bread, and hot sauce!"

"You betta know it!"

They laughed exuberantly.

"Let's meet around seven."

"You got it."

"Georgette?"

"Yes, Thad?"

"I'm glad you called."

"Me too."

Chapter Five
The Unusual Suspects

One Week Later, Thursday, 11:00 a.m.

Georgette was correct about Hiram's state of dishevelment. As he dressed for the occasion, he realized he hadn't put on clothes for over a month. He didn't care. Kenni was dead, but for the interrogation with Detective Geronimo, he decided to throw on a pair of Levi's and a white t-shirt that he pulled from his man cave closet. No haircut, no shave, and little food was still the order of the day. Generally, Georgette would bring him some KD's and leave it on the counter. One dinner would last him about 3 days. He preferred tequila over anything else. He rarely looked in the mirror, for he despised the torturous reflection. The shadow of his former self disrupted his entire universe. Realizing that he loved Kendali had invaded the whole of his constitution and crushed his internal kingdom. Emotionally devastated, love and death punched him into a new place where he had no control, and they continued to beat him up, every day.

Hiram wrapped all his creature comforts that he had on the floor of his man cave in a big purple blanket and dragged the bundle into the walk-in closet. A lavender-vanilla room deodorizer freshened the atmosphere, complemented by a cracked window. He gazed upon the garden admiring the flowers as his spirit grew sadder thinking how much she loved orchids. Geronimo pulled into the cul-de-sac, the big silver grill of his Toyota F150 approaching with an ominous vibration. He hoped Detective Blackfoot had enlightening news. He already learned, thanks to Crispus, about Max's shrine to Kendali and his family ties were few. His parents died in a car crash and his aunt and uncle raised him as their own. They had no children. After Max's military discharge and completion of his college studies, the uncle took sick and died and his wife followed shortly after. Hiram knew in his gut, Max was gone forever, a ghost dwelling in the ethers with all other ghosts, past, present, and future. He put his tequila glass on a coaster and walked to the door. He welcomed Geronimo's six-foot plus bulky shouldered frame into the foyer with a wave of his arm.

"Detective."

"Mr. Rivers?"

"Yes. I'm in the study." Hiram directed him to his left. "Can I get you anything? To eat? To drink?" Hiram admired Geronimo's tall, broad stature, bearded face, and smooth, pensive demeanor. He was a mirror of himself and others that he loved and respected, like Khai and Maceo.

"No thanks. I'm fine."

Hiram rolled his desk chair in front of the brown leather sofa, reclined, and sipped his tequila. Geronimo settled onto the couch.

"That's a nice arm piece you got there," Hiram stated, eyeing Geronimo's wrist.

"My grandmother made it for me." Geronimo pulled his sleeve up, exposing the brushed silver bracelet carved with ancient tribal symbols. "She is the best. A true blacksmith."

"Your grandmother is still alive?"

"Yeah," he responded with a smile. "And kickin'."

"That is such a blessing. Does she sell those?"

"She used to. But not so much anymore. I can have her make you one."

"That would be nice, bruh. How much?"

"Oh. She would never charge for her pieces. Never. Even when she was selling them. It was up to the recipient to give what they felt was appropriate. Ninety-nine percent of the time, people get it. My grandmother has a kind of powerful, admonishing omnipresence."

"I am sure she does, making a stunning piece like that. She must."

Hiram placed his tumbler on the table.

"So, what do we have, detective?"

Geronimo tapped on his phone and scrolled to his notes; he had named the folder 'Grace Case'.

"Why do you have your investigators working this case, Mr. Rivers?"

"Because that's what I do. When something is important to me, I hold it close to me. I need to know everything about it. I need to protect it. Tend it. See to it."

"Control it?"

"Yeah."

Geronimo flinched at Hiram's honest agreement. "Okay."

"I readily accept that I seek control. I have to. I am building an empire."

"Yes. Alright." Detective Blackfoot relaxed his back against the sofa. "Well, we went to Max's apartment and he clearly had an issue with Kendali. Not so much you. He had-"

"I already know about the altar. The rituals."

"I know you know."

"Detective." Hiram eased forward locking eyes with Geronimo. "We just established my desire for control, so tell me something I don't know. Why are you here?"

"Like I said to you on the phone. I just want to check in with you. Ask you some questions. That's all."

"Then ask."

"What happened with Kendali's royalties?"

"You talked to Belinda?"

"She offered her perspective on things."

"I bet she did. Did she also tell you that she was not mother of the year? That Kendali had been fending for herself from age fourteen while Belinda did whatever she wanted to do? Have as many boyfriends as she wanted? Some who were savagely inappropriate with her girl child?"

"She did not."

"Yeah, I know she didn't. And fortunately, Kendali was a precocious kid. She had to be. She defended herself successfully against most of the wolves Belinda brought in their midst." Hiram gulped the last drop of his tequila, walked to the shelf behind his desk, and retrieved the bottle of Don Julio. "What do you want to know about Kendali's estate, her royalties?"

"Whatever you have to offer."

"There isn't much to tell. She left her royalties to Dominion. Left her mother and Dre sizable insurance policies. Belinda got her condo. But you already know this."

"What was your relationship with Kendali like? Beyond the books?"

"Listen, Geronimo," Hiram said sitting in his chair again. He put the bottle on the table next to his glass. "I know how this works. You have information and you want to see how I respond to these general questions and your new info. Just tell me what you have and I will answer you honestly. You wanna know, if I know, what you know."

"I know your background. So, I am clear on that. You have been down this road before. No stranger to police."

"Precisely. So, tell me what's up."

"Did you know that she had a relationship with Max Gray?"

Hiram was unable to hide his emotions after Kendali's murder. Before her death, he would have put on his poker face and gave a nonchalant response, *"Not surprising."* Post Kendali's death, he displayed his raging shock. "The fuck? You sure about that?"

"I'm sure. I take it you didn't know."

"I can't say that I did."

"Were you sleeping with her?"

"We had a relationship."

"A relationship?"

"We were lovers…and friends. Bonded by books…and love. It seems." He gulped the tequila, the news of Max and Kendali burning his brain.

"Does your wife know about the affair?" Georgette stood silently outside the door listening to their palaver.

"No. Nobody knows. They guess. Speculate. But no one knows. I guess you know now. And how do you know?" Hearing Hiram confirm her suspicion that she tucked away for the sake of a greater love left her feeling hopeless and hollow. Georgette gathered her sadness and went back to their bedroom to get ready for the office, filled with regret for eavesdropping.

Geronimo ignored his question. "Did you know she was sleeping with Khai? He is your frat brother? Good friend?"

"Sleeping with Khai? No way! Who told you that? Did Khai tell you that?" A wave of nervousness rushed down his spine. *Does he know about the gourmet sessions? We were always so careful.*

"I haven't spoken to Mr. Draper."

"No way she was sleeping with Khai."

54

"Oh she was. And she was carrying his child."

"Whaaat?!" Hiram growled. "Impossible! Who told you that? Lies!" Hiram leapt from his seat, drumming the air with angry hands. *How does this nigga know this?* He stopped mid drum. *Cell phone! See this is why you don't deal in all this emotion.* His thoughts were bubbling over in his brain. He admonished himself for losing emotive control and failing to use his poker face. "What else did you learn from her cell phone?"

"That's it. Just wondering if you knew that your number one author was sleeping with your frat brother and your arch nemesis Max."

"Max is not my nemesis. That would be Maceo Grant."

"I heard about you two."

"Who hasn't." Hiram checked his feelings and found a comfortable place staring out the window at the garden. *How could they? Khai? My brother?! How Kenni? I did love you!* And she wasn't present for a confrontation. The anger and anguish was testing him way past his limits.

"Is Maceo out to get you? Would he go this far to bring you down? Murder for hire?"

"Maybe. Who knows? We don't know what's in the hearts and minds of men. Or women." He grinded his teeth, thinking of Kendali. "He thinks I have been unbrotherly toward him. And his favorite author got in the middle of our rivalry."

"What do you mean?"

"She tried to extort me when we were investigating Max. He had been stalking Kendali. You know this. You know all of this, detective. She put herself in the middle and Maceo was displeased with my reaction to her actions."

"Displeased? Uh-huh. What was your reaction?"

"That is immaterial, detective." His eyes stopped at the orchids as he scanned the verdant oasis. He cursed them and asked God's forgiveness for his thought. *How could she?!*

"Yeah. Okay." Geronimo rubbed his silver amulet between his thumb and forefinger. "I think you are right about Max. He has evaporated."

"I told you."

"Anyone else you suspect?"

"Definitely look into those music industry people. That's a rotten lot. A nasty crew. They are upset about her books. Especially this last one. They don't want us to release it."

"I need to see a copy of the book."

"I can't give you a copy. It's confidential, top secret. Certain books, like Kendali's, are only revealed to a select group of people."

"I understand that, but this is a murder investigation, Mr. Rivers. I need to see that book."

"I can't."

"I *can* get a warrant. Your call."

Hiram gave Geronimo a ferociously irate glare. After fumbling through odds and ends in his drawer, he retrieved a flash drive and inserted the device into his computer.

"The Vixen Notebook, Part 10," he mumbled as his eyes darted about the screen, skimming the words and holding back tears. "I tell you what, detective." Geronimo widened his eyes. "I will give you a hard copy. Good enough?"

"Good enough," he agreed.

"It has been a tumultuous ride," Hiram expressed clicking the print icon. The printer hummed at rapid speed, ejecting the pages of Kendali's final tale of her vixen woes. They waited silently for the document to complete printing. Hiram assembled the manuscript, bound it with a paper clip, and handed it to Geronimo. "Detective. Just your eyes. No one else's."

"I can do that. I will keep it between me and me."

"I appreciate you, brother."

"Are you going to release the book?"

"I don't know." His soul was losing the battle against the dam of tears. Just as he was discovering the breadth and depth of his love for Kendali, here was a stranger revealing her betrayal. "Is there anything else, detective?"

"No. That's it. We will be in touch." Geronimo saw the tearful rivers rising in Hiram. There was no need to further disturb his tortured soul. "I can see myself out."

"Yeah. Thanks, bruh." He glanced at him and looked away quickly, returning to his survey of the cursed flowers and his ever present melancholy.

As Detective Blackfoot entered the foyer to leave, Georgette appeared from the kitchen. He turned around to see her standing statuesquely in a green and navy pantsuit, perfectly accentuating her oddly robust hips. *He likes them tall,* he thought.

"Mrs. Rivers." He bowed slightly.

"Detective."

"I was just finishing up with your husband." He reached inside his jacket and gave her his card. "If you think of anything you think I should know about Kendali's murder call me. I would like to talk to you."

"Okay." She accepted the card and started to walk toward Hiram's office. "I will do that."

"Yes. Please call me. I promise I will be brief."

"Thank you, detective."

"Yes, Mrs. Rivers. Good day, sister."

She watched Geronimo exit and contemplated her husband's confession. The investigator had Hiram against the wall of truth. When the rumors started about Kendali almost five years ago, she asked him. He answered, no, with clean, swift sincerity. She let it go. While she still had her suspicions, she didn't care. She loved what she and Hiram built, their business, their children, their home, their bond. As long as their empire remained intact, his fleeting flings meant nothing, yet today she felt so broken, so anguished by the revelation. Georgette slid into Hiram's office quietly.

"Babe. Should you talk to the police without an attorney?"

"I don't have anything to hide. I didn't kill Kendali." He was still melancholy at the window, cursing God's creation, especially Kendali Grace.

"Yeah, but you know how this works if they want to *make* you the killer."

"I know. They have nothing. I am telling y'all; it had to be Max. And he is gone. We won't see him again."

"But why would Max kill Kendali?"

"He was obsessed with her."

"Obsessed?"

"Gee, don't worry about this stuff. Go to work. Take care of our business." He plopped onto his couch. "Why you still wearing that hair?"

"Why are you brushing me off? Are you a suspect?"

"I'm always a suspect, aren't I?"

"Shit. I'm not in the mood for your cavalier conversation. Now, topped with despair. Fuck it. I'm leaving. I got work to do."

"Be safe." He waved at her as she sashayed away. Already mildly intoxicated, he merrily anticipated a deeper drunken stupor. *Deez bitches…*

Thursday, 12:30 p.m.

Georgette grabbed her Fendi workbag and exited their mini palace. She decided to take her Ferrari. When she needed to blow off steam, a top speed run in the sports car was the perfect release. Hiram's brush-off filled her with heat. She raced out of the cul-de-sac and came to a screeching halt at the main street of their community. Geronimo was parked at the corner. They made eye contact and he motioned for her attention. She swerved around next to his driver's side.

"Yes, Detective Blackfoot. I told you I will call you."

"Well, I told you I would be brief, Mrs. Rivers."

"I need to get to the office. I have a lot on my plate since I have assumed the role as CEO. And our CAO walked away from us."

"Your CAO?"

"Yeah. Mo. Monique Ellis. She was everything. She did so much for Dominion. So, we are dealing with a lot of loss. Lotta loss."

"I understand. Where is Ms. Ellis now? Why did she leave?"

"At Gutta Butta. With Maceo Grant. Why she left? Sick of my husband. Hiram is a stubborn, controlling CEO. We all put up with a lotta his shit." Confession of the affair with Kendali left Georgette careless, reckless, and ready to throw Hiram under the bus, over the moon, and anywhere else she could sling him.

"I see. How would you describe his relationship with Kendali?"

"He made her. Older brother, younger sister. Mentor, mentee. Teacher, student."

"That's it?"

58

"Basically. They were friends. Definitely. Confidantes, even." Georgette wiped her sunshades and covered her Tracy Ellis Ross eyes. Geronimo admired her bubbly-eyed countenance.

"Did you know about their affair, Mrs. Rivers?"

She was surprised that he asked her right there in that moment. "Affair? Well, yeah. But no. No, I didn't know."

"Yes or no Mrs. Rivers?"

"I mean there were always rumors. So, I knew about that. But an affair? Wow. Okay. No."

Geronimo etched a reminder in his brain of Georgette's ambiguous response. "Okay. That's all I need to know."

"Enjoy your weekend, Detective."

"Thanks. You do the same." His eyes meandered the neighborhood as he sat in his truck watching Georgette burn rubber down the street. Did she or did she not know? He never imagined the publishing industry was so scandalous. The plot was thickening.

As Georgette merged her race car onto the interstate, her mind, body, and spirit shook with bitterness. *What was Geronimo thinking? Maybe I over spoke?* She wished she could run away from home. With Thaddeus. They had several uplifting dinner dates over the past week. But alas, there was too much to do.

Thursday, 2:00 p.m.

Geronimo was amazed by the revelation of this case, the first ever where the boyfriend seemed the least likely suspect. Even so, he gave him a follow-up visit to feel his energy regarding Kendali and Hiram's affair. They arranged to meet while Dre was working, ironically, he had the lucrative contract that maintained the beauty of Hamer Hill Park including the G. W. Arboretum where his girlfriend was killed.

"Mr. Walker," Geronimo alerted approaching the hard-working entrepreneur. Dre was pruning a bush while his team worked diligently throughout the lush grounds.

"Detective," Dre acknowledged. "We can talk over here." Dre motioned him toward his work truck parked nearby. He grabbed two waters from his cooler and offered one to the investigator.

"I thank you, brother," Geronimo said, accepting the bottle. He opened the water and swallowed the liquid. "So-"

"Before you even start. There is no way I killed Kendali."

"That's what everyone says. But *everyone* is a suspect, especially you because it is always the boyfriend, the husband, the partner."

"I didn't kill her, man."

"I have heard that your relationship was tumultuous. She was less than faithful?"

"Less than faithful?" Dre drank half of his water. "Look, man. I understood Kendali. I knew she had issues. If you met her mother, you know why. Kendali basically raised herself and endured the evil of more than one of Belinda's fuck buddies."

"I see." Geronimo listened, watching the pulsations of Dre's arms, face, and neck.

"So, yeah. I know she was fuckin' that nigga Hiram. And who knows who else. I got fed up with the lies. I left."

"And you fought, true?"

"Of course we fought. I mean, damn. She was fuckin' around. And all I was trying to do was love her."

"Love her?"

"Yes, love her. But she was under Hiram's spell."

"Mmm, hmmm."

"He is a spell caster. A magician. He real nickel slick. Too cool for school type. He's rich. He's powerful. He's connected. All female attraction factors. I wouldn't be surprised if the bullet was really for him and Kendali was caught in the crossfire."

"Oh yeah?"

"Hell yeah!" Dre dropped his empty water bottle in the back of his truck. "The nigga got plenty of enemies. And I mean plenty! He is well-hated."

"I gather that."

"Yeah. Especially him and Maceo. And after what happened with Bree? Shiiid. I wouldn't blame Maceo for offing his ass."

"What happened with Bree?"

"He had her roughed up. That's what I heard."

"Why so?"

"Does it matter? Bree is Maceo's number one! For real! Like his sister." He wiped sweat from his brow, the heat of the day simmering on his face. "Now, of course, I got a lot of this from Kendali. Pillow talk. She kept a lot from me. But she shared a lot too. And for whatever it was worth, I know she loved me. And that's where I'm gonna leave it."

"Leave it?" Geronimo rubbed the fabric of his cabana shirt, the cotton absorbing perspiration beading on his skin underneath.

"Yeah, leave it. I felt like I was going to go all out to catch the killer. But I think the bullet might have been for that nigga. So, y'all can handle it. I am stacking my money. Probably leave the city. Start over somewhere else."

"Where to?"

"I haven't decided."

"Well, don't leave us just yet, Mr. Walker. Remember, everyone is a suspect."

"Yeah, I heard you."

"You enjoy your day. Stay cool. And stay put."

Geronimo gave him a salute and Dre nodded.

The detective sat in his truck for a moment observing Dre as he returned to his lawn care task. The young brother seemed honest, but one thing he learned early on in his career, seeming is just that-*seeming*. He further confirmed the possibility that the bullet could have been meant for Hiram. Even the best of sharp shooters have a one percent error rate, and Kendali may have been the one percent.

Thursday, 3:30 p.m.

61

The rivalry between Hiram and Maceo and the resignation of his right hand, Monique Ellis piqued Geronimo's interest. He found Maceo's information and decided to pay him a visit. He and his wife Nikki had recently merged their companies and rented office space close to his apartment on a quiet side street off Seminole Boulevard. Geronimo parked his truck and observed his surroundings. The design of the block allowed six businesses to house their ventures comfortably on Eutaw Street. All the offices were oversized spaces with two floors and big display windows. 'Black Butter Books' etched in the glass with black pearls dripping from a stack of books and a pearl handled knife spreading the 'butter' across the book cover made a striking logo. The staff were moving around in clear view, the Aztec-tiled floor sparkled beneath their feet. Their desks and work areas were minimalist art deco décor. An electronic display board hung on the back wall surrounded by several conference tables. Lush plants created an indoor arboretum in the corner, close to the display window on the right and to the left two rows of desks were separated by an aisle, lined with a black and white contemporary design rug. Geronimo waltzed into the publishing headquarters and a smiling young woman greeted him immediately.

"Detective Blackfoot! Welcome to Black Butter Books," she said walking toward him, hand extended. Her big, thick braids were piled atop her head in an ebony crown accentuated by big gold hoops and metallic gold lipstick.

Geronimo shook her hand. "I thank you."

"I am Renee. Mr. Grant is waiting for you in his office. I will escort you." She sauntered pass her own desk toward the back of the space. As they passed the electronic display board they turned to the right, and it seemed another world opened up. There was another area the same size as the entry area with the same desk setup, but these areas were enclosed with soundproof glass. There was a dining area with a complete kitchen and an even bigger conference area. "Would you like something to eat? To drink?"

"No. I'm okay. I thank you." He was impressed by the simple, inviting, layout. They arrived at Maceo's office tucked in the absolute rear of the building, completely closed off with a glass door and vertical blinds. His modest work space, smaller than Geronimo expected, was decorated the same way as the rest of the building and included a private bath. His door was wide open.

"Mr. Grant?"

He was talking on the phone. He waved his hand for them to enter. "Have a seat Mr. Blackfoot. He will be with you in a moment."

"Thank you. Thank you much." He sat and the young professional left.

Maceo continued his call. "Yeah, man. Always. It's gonna be big...yeah...soon...I will update you...you know that...alright, alright...yeah...peace, brother." He ended the call.

He stood and walked around his desk to the detective. "I apologize, my man." He shook the detective's hand.

"It's okay. We gotta get it done."

"Yes, we do," Mace replied seating himself in the chair next to Geronimo. "So, what we talkin' 'bout?"

"I just wanna ask a few questions."

"I don't think I can tell you much. I didn't know Kendali Grace. Just seeing her at professional events. Maybe here and there around town."

"Okay. I understand. Tell me about your rivalry with Hiram."

"Rivalry?" Maceo scoffed. "Rivalry is a strong word. He is not my rival. Hiram is an asshole. He knows it. Everyone knows it. I may know it better than anybody else."

"Why do you call him an asshole?"

"Ha! I am sure you have talked to him. You tell me, detective."

"I am more interested in why you see him as an asshole."

"Look. Hiram is shiesty. Shady. He has some good intentions, sometimes. But overall, asshole. He takes much and gives little. He walks unjustly."

"What do you mean unjustly?"

"I mean, I gave him the publishing game. He started his company. He took off. I asked him before the takeoff to merge with me and build something even bigger. He brushed me off. Ducked me out. Never followed up. Never reached out to me. But it's cool. As you can see, I haven't missed a beat, a book, or a meal."

"Yes, I see. Your setup is awesome."

"Patience. Perseverance. That's all you see."

63

"You now have Monique Ellis working for you, right?"

"Yeah. I told you. Hiram is an asshole. She got sick of him too."

"Why was she fed up?"

"Are you listening? Hiram is an asshole. I don't have any other way to say it."

"Mr. Grant, are you sure you have no vindictive feelings?"

"You fuckin' wit' me, right?" Maceo laughed loudly, stood up, and roared. "You trippin'." He returned to his desk. "You need to go look at all 'dem muthafuckas in that industry she crawled out of. Talkin' bout writin' books.

"Like who?"

"I don't know. You the detective. Go detect."

"I am detecting now. I know he had your author Bree McDee worked over. What was that about?"

Maceo hid his surprise, he hoped. "That's between Hiram and Bree. I told you he is an asshole. And he has shown his ass with everybody in this industry."

"I know you were angry about the Bree incident. Maybe angry enough to have Hiram killed. And that is understandable."

"But Hiram is still alive."

"Yes. He is. So far. But could the bullet have been for him? Mr. Rivers is quite notorious and you, Mr. Grant, know this firsthand."

"This conversation is over. Thank you for dropping by, Geronimo."

"You didn't answer my question, Mr. Grant," Geronimo said as he pushed up from the chair slowly.

"There is nothing to answer. You're asking me if I killed Kendali to get back at Hiram. And that is pure absurdity."

"Why is your number one author leaving the country?"

"I am sure you got that off Zing. And if you read it, you saw what she wrote. She said why. I need not speak for her. Bree is an incredibly direct, forthright, articulate young woman."

"I know everyone thinks that someone of great financial means had to execute this murder and Bree is not a likely candidate, but I did some digging. And it turns out that-"

"I know, I know. A lot of people don't know that Bree's father is a man of vast means."

"Yes. He has built quite a fortune for himself in Ghana. And we know that Bree hated Kendali, Dominion, Hiram…"

Maceo grimaced at the detective's insinuations. "I think I ended this conversation, detective Blackfoot."

"Okay, Mr. Grant. I thank you for your time." Geronimo reached out for a handshake and Maceo put his hands in his pockets.

"You are not welcome."

"I will find my way out."

Monique appeared in the doorway. She greeted Geronimo. "Hi. How are you?"

"Fine, thanks," he responded making his way to the exit.

She glided to the front of Maceo's desk. "You got a minute, Mace?"

"I got plenty minutes for you, Mo Go. What's up?" He pulled two bottles of water from his refrigerator. One bottle he placed in front of Monique, the other he opened and guzzled thirstily.

"I wanna hear about Isis. I'm so excited about it. I have been selling Isis ads all morning!"

"It's goin' good?"

"Beyond good! We have so many folks making their commitments to advertise on the platform. So all we need is for Mustafa's crew to arrange the bank transfers. I am waiting for them to send over the info. I have Chelsea drawing up the invoices." She danced with her shoulders and sipped her water.

Maceo raised his thirst quencher. "Mo Go! A toast!"

She stood up. "Absolutely!"

"May we keep churning, forever, for always. The Butta!" They touched bottles and drank.

Monique plopped joyfully back into her seat. "So, who was the dude?"

"Just some detective. Investigating Kendali's murder."

Monique's mouth dropped into a sad bend. She had been practicing erasing Kendali's memory. It was all too tragic, too mind blowing for her. "Why is he questioning you?"

"I have no idea. Asking me about me and Hiram's rivalry." Maceo smirked. "I told him, ain't no rivalry. Da nigga ain't shit. That's all." He saw the worry in her eyes. "But there is nothing for you to be concerned about. I told him, I don't know nothin' about what Hiram got goin' on at Dominion. And he need to go see what's up with that industry she was writin' about."

"Well, that is true. It was crazy over there after the Myesha Morgan Show. Every damn body was calling. It was a damn circus. I am sure it is even worse now."

"Yeah. And they losin' it without you."

"Hmmm. I'm glad I left."

"Not as glad as I am."

Monique giggled nervously wondering if she made the right decision. Maceo reassured her repeatedly that there was nothing to be concerned about, but her anxiety was not assuaged. She prayed intensely, beseeching her God to make everything alright.

Chapter Six
Whose Bullet Is It Anyway

Monday 10:00 a.m.

After spending a weekend studying his notes and browsing Zing, Geronimo concluded that a chat with Toya was in order. To his surprise, Zing was overloaded with revealing information. Kendali's page was still live along with plenty of dead people's Zing profiles. Many Zingers found this eerie, but he imagined the maintenance of the accounts as homage, a new age, techno ancestral alter.

Common Grounds had a delicious selection of teas and Geronimo was sipping their secret blend when Toya walked in.

"Hey, Detective Blackfoot." She looked amazing, gleaming cocoa skin, lean figure, all legs, pure mocha sunshine.

"Yes, Ms. Mitchell" He stood, bowed, and cradled her hand in genteel fashion.

"Please. Just call me Tea. Or Toya."

"Okay, Tea."

They relaxed in the booth; Toya set up her tablet and Geronimo scanned his notes. "I need to finish a few posts and answer a few emails, if you don't mind, detective."

"Of course not. And call me Geronimo."

"Okay." Her smile brightened her pretty face. "I need to order something."

"I will get it for you. Just finish your business. What would you like?"

"Turkey sausage and egg croissant. No cheese. Caramel latte."

"I gotcha."

"Thanks."

She ticked away on her machine, posting on Zing.

□Zing: Tea Thyme Group□

Latoya Tea Mitchell (post): I need y'all to keep your eyes peeled. Make sure you repost this rotten muthafucka Max Gray's picture, geek of the week fucka. Call and keep pressure on the local police. Call all those record companies and make them shake those trees loose. That fuckin' Tasir Samaan, crazy ass nigga. Arms don't move when he walk. Wes Gilliam and those fuckin' Eisenberg brothers at Big Mike Records. Those are the tops. But they got some more at Fortune Records and Magic Disc Records. You can always inbox me information or contact Detective Geronimo Blackfoot at the Seminole City Central District Office. Or call the tip line 500.800.TIPS. RIH Sweet Angel Sister.□□□ ❤

Reactions: 8,756   Comments: 5,692   Shares: 10,003

Calvin:💯

Mike Mike The Second: We on it! Baby girl will not die in vain.

Pamela Hunter: I still feel so sad. But I am going to do my part. Keeping my eyes peeled □□□

Letitia Stokes: look my cousins know these record company fucks. They have told me stories. I will see what they know

Ryan Carter: I know where Max lives. I rode by there. Looks abandoned.

Latoya Tea Mitchell: @Ryan Carter Yes I posted about this. The post is pinned at the top! I told everyone to leave his house alone! We don't want to corrupt possible evidence that could lead to an arrest. We just need to share information, possible suspects, tips...and we always use the words "alleged" and "allegedly" and "I suspect". Or we suspect. My inbox is always open for clarity and more info.

Ryan Carter: Okay. Gotcha sis□□

Tracy Jones: Yeah. My sister said she used to see all kinds of craziness when she was a video model. And she named a lot of names. I am going to tell her to call the tip line

Olivia Grant: I am still wondering about Bree. Didn't she go to Africa.□

Latoya Tea Mitchell: (@ Olivia Grant) Good people! I put at the top of the group and the cover photo Bree IS NOT A SUSPECT! Whoever killed Kendali was a heavy hitta. Very smart, well connected, with lots of resources. No offense to Bree McDee but she is a writer. JUST a writer. That's it! READ the pinned posts and the Kendali Grace photo album. These are the suspects.

Olivia Grant: Yeah. But I heard her daddy got plenty money, honey!□

Latoya Tea Mitchell: Wow☐

Geronimo placed Latoya's breakfast next to her tablet.

"Thanks, love."

"You are very welcome."

"So, tell me about you and Kendali," he prompted positioning himself in the booth to stare directly into her almond eyes and lust her black, liquid gold skin. Her full breasts spoke softly to him beneath her plain white t-shirt. To think she had been a photographer, working behind the scenes, never stepping in front of the camera was inconceivable to him; her beauty must have been captured somewhere during her hip hop photography days.

"You talk. Let me listen while I start on my breakfast." She needed to marinate on the news about Bree and her daddy's money.

"Okay." They sat in silence for a few minutes, the lightweight bustle of the Common Grounds' patrons and the R&B Pandora stream making a relaxing melody for their palaver. He cleared his throat. "I wish you would cease your cyber mob investigation gathering. I don't think it's helping. We are getting too many calls from all the crazies."

She dabbed her mouth with a napkin. "Y'all get that anyway. That's nothing new."

"Yeah, but there seems to be a whole lot more with this case and I think some of this madness is fed by your Zing group."

"You are getting a lot more because Kendali was a celebrity. You can't deny that we have given you good information too. Which, is why you want to talk to me now." She drank her latte and lingered in a long silence while Geronimo gathered his notes taken from Toya's Zing group. Her assessment was undeniably true. He had been monitoring her group for intel.

"I have no rebuttal." He smiled and she cast her own sunshiny grin in return.

"How do you know so much about Max?"

"I need not reveal my sources." Hiram had been giving her information, along with other people. She committed to protecting the identities of those who generously shared with her.

"That's true. I won't press you. At least not now." Geronimo thought of Hiram as Toya's wellspring of intelligence; no one in the civilian world, save the Dominion CEO, knew much about Max. He tired of the whole lot of them, all vying for control over the case, it seemed. "Did you know that Max was seeing your friend?"

"What?" she stammered. Toya batted her eyelashes rapidly and brushed an invisible dust from her tablet with an anxious stroke.

"Yes. Maxmillian Gray. They had a fling."

"I should have known," she mumbled.

"You should have known?"

"Yes. There was a period when she was talking about him. Just in general. Told me they had lunch or something. He was helping her with her writing. Hmph." Toya twirled time back in her mind, hearing the Max conversations with Kendali replay. She talked about his rare book collection, his smarts, and his gallant manners.

"So, you are not surprised?"

"Not really. So when are y'all gonna catch him?"

"We are working on it, sis."

"Well, work harder. My sister is gone. Forever." Teardrops trickled from her eyes. Geronimo eased a napkin into her hand that was resting on her tablet and laid his fingers on top of her other hand. She dried her eyes and they sat in the haunting aura of the dead author until Toya finished crying.

"Go ahead, detective."

"You sure?"

"Yes."

"Tell me about Tasir, Wes, Big Mike Records. You seem to know more about them than anyone else in Kendali's circle."

"She references them and others in her books, changing the names of course."

"Of course."

"Because I was a creative director for a lot of the industry's big budget projects. The heavy hittas. Only the labels' most precious artists and big money makers."

"I hear dat." Listening to her recount her professional prowess excited him. "They paid you the big bag, yeah?"

"Yeah and I saw a lotta shit. Too much shit. And Kendali saw even more."

"Why didn't y'all report this stuff?"

"See, and that is the part people outside the industry do not understand." She wiggled to the edge of her seat, closer to the comely wolf. "Many times you are seeing things happen, but you don't even realize what is really happening." She picked up a knife, opened a napkin, and spread it out, smoothing the folds, creating a makeshift whiteboard and pointer for a quick tutorial on the rotten gut of the music industry.

"Okay. You see a producer or an agent taking a young girl, or boy under their wing. You see the intense interactions and those actions look like a big brother, big sister or mother, father type of energy." She moved her knife around her whiteboard for dramatic effect. "But! You later learn, because you start to hear rumors, that the relationships are based on sex and sex secrets."

"I see."

"Good!" She tapped on her whiteboard as she finished her spiel. "So, this dude always has his protégé in tow under the guise that he is training him, teaching him, working deals for him. Fashioning him for a career. All the while, this nigga is stickin' his nasty rotten pedophile dick in this li'l boy's ass. But the average person does not know that. And everyone enters the industry as the average person, having no idea the evil that lurks beneath the surface."

"Right. I get it. Now what does this mean as far as Kendali's murder? Tasir? Wes? Big Mike Records? That's Stephen Eisenberg, right?"

"Yeah. And his brother Paul."

"Okay. I heard about them too."

"More scumbags." She looked around the coffee shop, shaking her head. "Kendali despised the industry after she started learning what was going on. That's why she left. Me too. Just could not take it anymore. Too much nastiness. And the child sex rings, you have no idea how deep that shit really is, and all the higher up's that are involved. They are all protected."

"Oh no. I have more than an idea. I been in law enforcement for many years. I have seen it all."

"Good. So you get it." She crumpled her whiteboard into the palm of her hand and dropped her pointer onto the plate with her half eaten sandwich. "Tasir is a sick fuckin' psycho. He is into EVERYTHING. And I mean EVERYTHING. A hole is a hole is a hole. Period. And he despised Kendali because she rejected all of his very expensive advances. He even sent her a fully decked out Lamborghini once, in her name. And she demanded that the delivery guy return it."

"A Lambo?"

"Yup! With all the customized extras. I mean this sand nigga got a lotta dough. Too much to count. But you already know that."

"I do."

"Yeah. Worst story I heard about him. He had some little girls out in the jungle sucking elephant dick."

"Yeah. Okay. He one of 'dem?"

"One of 'dem. You got it!" She shivered as she reflected hearing that story. "Yuck! I feel like I need a bath just talkin' about this muthafucka." A deep guttural sigh helped realign her thoughts. "I apologize for the language, detective. I am usually not so foul. But this is a foul subject."

"No apologies needed, sis. I understand."

"Yeah." She stirred her latte with a spoon. "So, he hated Kendali. Now, Wes. Wes is notorious for recruiting the boy bands and initiating them into *Club Hershey Highway*." She balled her fist as she spoke. "Runs clean through these boys' assholes. He is a reprehensible savage. He too hated Kendali because she was talking to some of his victims and convinced a few to run away."

"Did you say *Club Hershey Highway*?" Geronimo chortled at her description.

"Yeah, that's what I said."

"Okay."

Toya continued. "Kendali was deeply affected by the horror that she witnessed. She promised to write about it. A lotta folks came to her to talk because her reputation for being a warm, easygoing, easy to talk to, kinda chick was growing. Many did not want to press charges against the pervs, though she encouraged them to. Even more just did not want to leave the industry. But there were quite a few she persuaded to leave." She twirled the auburn curls of her weave around her middle and ring finger, her wedding band glistening in the sunlight, beaming through the big picture window where they sat.

"Wow. She seems like she was a really awesome woman."

"She was. I miss her so much." Toya's eyes watered. "She was working on establishing a non-profit to help more of these industry victims."

"Does anyone else know about her mission to help these people escape the abuse?"

"I don't think so. I think she only told me."

"I think you are right."

"We were so close." A huge tear sped down her cheek and splashed onto her chest. "How much do I owe you for my breakfast?"

"Stop, sista."

"No, no. Let me-"

"Tea, no way. It's on me." He winked. "If you really want to pay me back, let me take you to dinner." Latoya's eyes widened with surprise. "Strictly platonic. I see the wedding band, love."

"Well, we're separated actually."

"Why do you wear the ring?""

"I just slip it on from time to time. To deter the wolves." She licked her lips subconsciously, suddenly feeling aroused by the indigenous masculinity of her lunch companion. For the first time during their conversation, his tall, muscular frame, deep set eyes, beautifully groomed beard, and thoughtful smile resonated with her.

He laughed. "Wolves? Ohhh, you thought I was gonna be some kinda thirsty busta?" He laughed louder and she joined his tickled symphony.

"Yeah. Maybe."

"Really, Toya. No thirstiness. But I *am* a wolf."

"Oh, I know that *now*."

"I just love your energy. Your passion. And I may need to ask you more questions."

"Hmmm. Uh-huh. Okay."

"I have lots of women friends." He stroked his beard. "Just friends."

"Okay. Just friends." Toya rejoiced in Geronimo's approach. "Do you need anything else from me?"

"No. I don't. I see you are not going to stop your information cyber-gathering. So…"

"No, I am not."

"In your gut, Tea- who do you think killed Kendali?"

"Tasir. He has the most to lose. He has the capability. The resources. The hatred. The motivation. And he is a sick fuck. Word is he didn't like her writing the tell-all tales and especially after her revelation on The Myesha Morgan Show, he was livid, they say."

"He is at the top of the list with the other industry scum."

"Definitely. But I just learned…I don't know how true it is. That Bree's daddy is loaded. So, now I wonder…"

"Yes, I know this."

"You do?"

"Of course. I *am* a detective, love."

"Yeah, right. You are."

"That's why I humbly asked you to stop the cyber investigation. We are trained professionals, even though it may not seem like it to the public. We get our job done. Especially in Seminole City."

"Oh, I know about you. *The Wolf.* I heard. But I can't stop what I'm doing."

"I understand. Bree is certainly motivated. I know the history of her, Hiram, Dominion, the bad blood."

"Yeah." Toya drank the final drops of her latte, eyeing Geronimo's physique once again. "Damn, Bree."

"Yeah, damn is right. We cannot rule out anyone, but don't worry. I'm on the case…friend." He touched her hand gently. She smiled anxiously hearing her soul speak to her, *Kneegrow, back up before you have me out here in full freak mode. Shit! Fine mutha wodie…*

3:00 p.m.

□Text Message□

Hiram: What's up, bruh?
KD: Ain't nuthin. What's goin' on with you? We haven't got up in a minute. I'm still grieving too. It's going to be a while.

74

Hiram: Yeah. I miss her so much. I can't even express it. Where you at? What you doin'?
KD: My usual work from home for the rest of the week prep. Been letting managers manage a whole lot more lately.
Hiram: Aight. I'm gonna swing by
KD: Good. Be good to see you.
Hiram: 🔲🔲

KD jumped up from his office chair burning with excitement. He and Hiram had not seen each other in many weeks and communicated very little since Kendali's murder. A few notes attached to Hiram's meal boxes, arranged by Georgette was the extent of their exchange. He missed his friend and hoped they would get back to their brotherly love sooner than later. Whether either of them wanted to believe it or not, they needed each other now more than ever.

He took a quick shower, oiled his body down, and rubbed on some Dolce and Gabana. Smoothing out his close crop curls he admired the faint freckles on his cheeks that Hiram reassured him were enhancements to his beauty. He loved Hiram for removing childhood insecurities from his spirit. The doorbell rang and Khai's heart thumped. He raced downstairs and opened the door.

"Man, you must have been around the cor-" Whap! Whap! Khai dizzily stumbled backward landing on the foyer wall. His favorite painting *Warrior Prelude*, depicting men of a variety of tribes polishing their spears, fell to the floor. His vision blurred and his breath stopped in his neck, choking him. He forcibly heaved past the breathlessness and coughed up his astonishment. As soon as he regained an ounce of composure, Hiram was on him with another one-two punch combination. Khai conjured his strength and lunged forward, tackling Hiram onto the floor. He mounted him, weak with surprise and confusion.

"What the hell, nigga?" He panted his words. Hiram responded with a powerful leg press against the air and thunderous push of Khai's lower torso, jolting Khai from his mounted position hurling him backward. Khai tumbled onto the marble floor, still recovering from the initial blows. With anger fortifying his retaliation, he leapt into a fighter's stance. "You wanna fight? Fuck it. Let's fight for real."

He allowed Hiram to get on his feet and once Hiram squared up, Khai jabbed him full force in his chest, quickly followed by a left hook to the chin. Hiram fell back, coughed in agony, and slumped forward, resting his weight on his knees, catching his breath. His recent overindulgence of tequila, overall malnourishment, and inability to find a healthier way to grieve zapped his stamina. Khai relaxed his stance slightly as Hiram surrendered. "What the fuck is wrong witchu, man?" Khai moved toward the family room doorway and rested on the threshold wall.

"You were seeing her."

"What?" Khai stood up straight, breathing hard.

"I shared her with you. And you were fuckin' her behind my back?"

"Maaan…"

"Khai, don't fix ya' mouth to lie, bro. Don't do it. I know. I talked to the police. Geronimo told me." He shuffled heavy footed to the stairwell and collapsed onto the steps.

Head hung with sadness, Khai spoke carefully. "I have no lie for you."

"You supposed to be my brother, KD."

"I *am* your brother. And let's get honest; we both loved her. You just didn't know until after she was dead. I knew that I loved her all along."

"Oh, you knew all along?" Hiram raised his head laughing sardonically, the sarcasm shaking the ceiling. "Fuck you, man."

"Okay. Fuck me. But she needed more. And you could not give it. And we know she was freewheeling with her pussy. She loved to give it away. She couldn't help it."

"Yeah, but it was supposed to be us *three*. You don't have enough women that you run thru? You *had* to have her too?"

"Like you can talk? Are you serious?"

"Yeah, I'm serious.

"You have your share of pussy too *and* Georgette, the kids, the money, the empire. So what if I got a li'l' extra from her without you. So what?"

"So what? Fuck you, KD. You ain't shit."

"I ain't shit? For real, for real. I'm good. I loved her."

"What? Y'all were planning on making a family? And behind my back?"

"Why? I can't be a family man? You doin' it."

"When were you gonna tell me she was pregnant?"

Khai teared up at the thought of Kendali dying with his seed growing inside her. For a split second he envisioned a baby being the perfect blend of their good looks. His heart puttered a somber beat. "I don't know, man. She had just told me about it, right before she died. I don't know what she was planning. She wanted to abort. I told her no. And who knows if I was really the father. She seemed real certain, but I told her I was against an abortion."

"Wow. Fuckin' her straight raw, makin' babies. Plannin' a family. Behind my back." His head burdened the palms of his hands, weighty and weary. "Being a family man takes more than you know."

"Yeah, okay. You can be a family man, but I can't? Datz your problem, Hiram. In your mind, you are the only one that can do and be anything. Just you. Nobody else. That's why you are losing Georgette. That's how you lost Monique. That's probably why Kendali is dead. It's you. You. You!"

"Right. All about me, but I share everything I have with everyone around me."

"So you say. Share? Or control?"

"I can't believe you were fucking her behind my back."

"You were fuckin' her too."

"But I brought her *to you, for us.* You are a real low life, Khai."

"I'm the low life? Okay. I'll be that. But what does that make you?"

"Makes me ready to leave." He eased himself off the steps, staggering to his feet. He glared at Khai, who was still leaning against the wall. "Oh. Did you know she was fuckin' Max? Maxmillian Gray? The stalker?"

"No. But I am not surprised."

Hiram was irritated by Khai's indifferent reply. "Not surprised?'

"No, Hiram. I just told you. She loved to give away her pussy. The Premium Pussy Benevolent Society. She was the CEO and chairwoman of the board."

"But you didn't know?"

"No. But I suspected the night you told us about him being the stalker. She appeared uncomfortable talking about him. But those are the kinds of things you pick up on when you are not so self-absorbed. The kinds of things you pay attention to, when you love somebody." Khai fingered his face, planning his first-aid remedies in his head.

"Self-absorbed? Love somebody? Fuck you, KD."

"You didn't love her. You loved what she did for you. What you did for her. Having control over her. And her physical beauty, but you didn't love her."

"No, I loved her." He leaned against the bannister. "I loved her, but they think I had her killed because she willed all her royalties to Dominion and they think I knew about you and her."

"Did you know?"

"No. But deep down, I may have had my suspicions."

"Oh my God. Did you kill her, Hiram?" Khai moved off the wall and stepped toward his friend, standing at the foyer's center.

Raised eyebrow and evil teeth aimed at Khai's inquisitive countenance, he grumbled, "Fuck you, nigga."

"Did you?! Did you, Hiram?"

"Pshhh." The publisher meandered his way to the door, bleeding from his eye and mouth.

"Did you?!" Khai shouted.

"Did you?"

Khai bristled at his frat brother's insinuation as he exited, leaving the door wide open. He watched as Hiram skulked to his Range Rover, slid into the seat, and pulled away from the curb. He cried the whole trip home, mourning all the way down to the marrow of his bones.

☐ 4:00 p.m.

The chaos since Kendali's murder seemed unmanageable, yet Georgette put on her CEO stilettos and bossed all the way up. The calls were coming in at lightning speed, mostly from the same top two industry people, their bidders, and their henchmen, Tasir's Palace Records and Wes Gilliam's Diamond Management. Mrs. Rivers and the legal team designed a flow chart for the phone calls and emails, a grading system that selected the appropriate responder. For the most part, Schwiner was handling the task of answering the legal threats and Georgette was executing the person-to-person communication with Tasir Samaan's people, Wes Gilliam, Big Mike Records, Fortune Records, Magic Disc Records, and others of their ilk. Then there was a slew of lesser folk that the PR staff, led by AJ, were taking care of.

"Tiyanna, just make sure everyone is on point with the process. Send the email and cc me."

"Okay. I got it."

Georgette's mood lightened, comforted by her assistant's efficiency. Their hectic day was ending on a positive note. Tiyanna sat at her desk and texted her sister.

⬜Text Message⬜

Tiyanna: D, wyd?
Darla: Nothing. What's up?
Tiyanna: It's crazy around here. I will be glad when this is over
Darla: when will it be over?
Tiyanna: Dunno.
Darla: You need to leave.
Tiyanna: I will. I am planning. But look. Ole girl still wearing that auburn hair. It's kinda weird.
Darla: Well, you know she's a li'l strange. I keep tellin you, she married to Hiram's crazy ass. You don't know what she is going through.
Tiyanna: True, But that hair is creepy. She has it styled exactly the way Kendali used to wear hers.
Darla: well that whole idea was creepy. I told you that. All those redheads in the congregation at the funeral. Looking like a field of red hots or something, I don't know
Tiyanna: lol. Okay girl. You is crazy Bye
Darla: Bye

Georgette rolled her neck, stretched her arms and bent her body over touching her toes. Sadness had become her constant companion, watching her husband careen into a bottomless pit of inexplicable despair. She had too many emotions to sort. She opted to take a businesslike approach to her current life and Thaddeus was quickly becoming the only bright spot in her day. Her phone buzzed.

☐Text Message☐

Thad: Hey Beautiful you.
Georgette: Thad! I am so glad you reached out. How are you?
Thad: Good. Dinner?
Georgette: Of course!
Thad: Where we going? Not Deucey's?
Georgette: ☐Dang! Am I that bad?
Thad: yes. ☐But if you want Deucey's, What Lola wants Lola gets
Georgette: Yes she does But we can go somewhere else. I liked that spot you took me to over in West Village
Thad: The Spicy Feather?
Georgette: Yeah
Thad: I have somewhere else in mind. Let me pick you up
Georgette: Are you serious?
Thad: Yes
Georgette: You know that's not a good idea. let me just meet you
Thad: Fine. ☐ Nature's Wok 476 Powahtan Street
Georgette: Asian Fusion? all organic right?
Thad: you been there before?
Georgette: I haven't and it is on my to be et list
Thad: yeah, hmph to be et. I got a list too. Yeah ☐
Georgette: ☐☐
Thad: Text me when you on the way. See you soon
Georgette: Okay☐

She felt giddy after the text chat. Whirling around like Harlem or Hendrix did when they sat in *mommy's big work chair*, she laughed uproariously. Georgette knew exactly where this thing was going and she planned to take the journey with open heart, open mind, and a wide-open pussy, embracing much needed healing. *Bon appetit, my sweet!*

80

10:00 p.m.

Hiram gave the cashier at Renegade Spirits, a hundred-dollar bill. "Don't worry about the change.

"Oh, wow! Thanks, bruh!"

"It ain't a thing." Leaving the liquor store, he cradled a brown paper shopping bag, filled with bottles of Patrón clinking a comforting sound against his chest. He was definitely slumming; so desperate for the escapism of the alcohol he bought Patrón since they were out of his customary Don Julio. There were several cars in the parking lot, some sitting silently, others idling at various volumes, waiting for the next move. He jumped in his truck and headed to his mourning cave. Anguish strangled him since his fight with Khai. They rarely quarreled. He was baffled by his own anger; he and Khai never had an agreement about side sex with Kendali. Truly, he knew deep down in his soul that he was angry with himself, angry for taking Kendali for granted. Angry for not realizing the magnitude of her beauty, her love. Angry for being a self-centered sap, but most of all, angry because he failed to protect her. His bones ached, a mind boggling symptom of his grief. *How can I feel this kind of physical pain, Kenni? How?* He yearned incessantly for one last touch, one last kiss, one last squeeze, one last plunge into her juiciness, and one last vanilla lavender embrace, wrapped up in the aromatic warmth of her loving heart. The tears started. He wanted to pull over and sob and scream and holler. Instead he rang Georgette and continued making his way home.

"Hey. What's up?" Her tone was coolly polite.

"Oh, that's how you talk to me now?"

"What is it, Hiram?"

"That's how a wife talks to a husband?"

"What do you need?"

"Where you at?"

"Just finishing up my day. On the way home."

"You don't sound like you in the office." Silence stifled the airwaves. Irritated by her lack of response, he pulled over and parked in a very empty section of the White Springs Town Center near their house. "Where you at?"

"Leaving dinner."

"Dinner with who?"

"Hiram-" *POP! Pop! Pop!*

"Oh shit!" Hiram pressed the gas, speeding out of the lot.

Georgette started her car and jumped inside. "Babe! What is going on?! Were those gunshots I heard? Hiram! Where are you?"

"Awww, fuck!" He banged the steering wheel, looking in his rear view mirrors- left, then right. There was a car behind him, seemingly tailing him. Fortunately, the late hour blessed the streets with little traffic for him to maneuver. His eyes darted from the road in front of him to the peripheral of his left eye, then to his right. He curled his shoulders forward, hunkered down close to the wheel, still pacing his visual survey-road, left mirror, right mirror. Road, left, right. Road, left, right.

"Hiram?! My God! Where are you?" She peeled out of the restaurant parking lot swerving on two wheels.

"Gotdammit!" He mashed the gas harder, running a red light. The gunman's car stopped at the same red light and turned the corner. After the assailant disappeared, the boulevard returned to stillness. "Shit! Muthafuck!" Hiram decelerated his truck and scrubbed his burgeoning afro frantically.

Georgette raced through traffic and made a beeline for the interstate. "Hiram! Are you okay?"

"Yeah. I'm alright." He exhaled deeply, now cruising Seminole Boulevard, his heart thumping and his breath ragged.

"Were those gunshots?"

"Yeah."

"Oh my God!"

"Don't worry about it. I will take care of it. I already know it's some of them industry niggas. I'm so done with these music maniacs."

"Don't tell me not to worry. Somebody just tried to kill you! They do *not* want us to release this damn book."

"So it seems. The gunshots are just a scare tactic, Gee." He sucked wind from the base of his belly and blew it out gradually through his teeth. "But maybe I was the target all along."

"We talked about that, Hiram. It was a sharpshooter. Whoever it was, meant to kill Kendali."

"Yeah, maybe. But even a sharpshooter has an off day."

Chapter Seven
Mo, Maceo, & Muse

Next Day
Tuesday 8:00 a.m.

Maceo eased his Escalade into the drop off driveway of Eutaw Elementary Middle School.

"Alright, young soldiers! Disembark!" He shifted the gear to park. "Have a good day. A strong day. Learn something. And teach something."

"We know, Dad," Canaan replied as Maceo tousled his mohawk.

Cameron secured his backpack on his shoulders. "Yes, we will. Love you, Dad."

"I love y'all too."

Nikki hopped out and opened the rear door for her sons' exit. "Make it a great day, baby loves." She squeezed them both, one on each side of her. Canaan, the older, was just starting to tower over her, and Cameron stood at her eye level. They kissed her cheeks. "I love you, sugars."

"Love you too," they replied.

Nikki gave each of them a juicy lip smack on their faces and they trotted into the flux of children entering the school building. She slid into the passenger seat and buckled her seat belt.

"Off to the races, Pearl." Maceo kissed his wife's smooth brown lips while running his hand up her thigh.

"Yes, Mr. Grant. Let's ride."

Maceo reentered the main thoroughfare and the couple rode in silence for five minutes, listening to the news on the radio, and each of them mentally reviewing the day's agenda.

"So, are you ready to tell me about the police visit?"

"No, Nik. I told you. There is nothing to worry about."

"Maceo Grant." She turned to face him as they rode down Seminole Boulevard. "You are gonna tell me sumpthin'. This can't be like before."

"Like before?"

"Yes. Like before." She positioned herself facing forward, ordering her thoughts and choosing her words wisely. "Mace, before your arrest. You didn't want to tell me everything then. I begged you to walk away. I told you it was time. Time to leave. To leave the streets alone. You took too long."

"You doin' an 'I told you so', Nik?"

She mentally spanked her tongue for failing in the wise word selection. "Mace, you know better, honey. I don't do 'I told you so's."

"Yeah, well it's soundin' like you are right now. And you walked away, Nik. You were supposed to hold me down."

"And I didn't? I didn't make sure you had money on your books? I didn't make sure your sons talked to you every week?" She added hand motions, finger snaps, and neck rolls to her animated diatribe. "We didn't visit you every two weeks? I didn't help Violet start Gutta Butta for you? Every piece of paperwork filed by me? Administered by me? I didn't hold you *down*. I held you *UP*!"

"Yeah, Nik. But I told you I was gonna get out. And you walked away." He banged the center console. "And then got wit' Isaac?!"

"Mace, you have to forgive me for that. You have to. It won't happen again."

He swung his head left to right, navigating the traffic with ease in spite of his emotions. "You sure?" He stopped at a red light and paused for an answer while taking in her disgusted facial contortions. "You have no idea the sadness I felt thinking I would never have you again. The murdering loneliness. My spirit…my soul dying and decaying."

"Just tell me what's up." Tears pooled in her eyes, her anger giving way to her husband's sentimental confession.

Maceo pulled up to their newly established office, admiring the vibrant, dramatic logo. "Isn't that beautiful, Pearl?" He kissed her cheek, strawberry coconut fragrance inciting his desire and her single teardrop salting his lips. Imagining her luscious areolas in his mouth, he fingered her nipple through the purple and green flower printed dress she wore.

She moaned for a half second, grabbed his hand, placed it on her heart, and released a long breath of exasperation. "Honey, you gotta tell me."

85

He surrendered to the bright, shining whites of her eyes that victoriously conquered his ego in their battle and laid his head on her chest. "The detective questioned me about Kendali's murder. Insinuated that I hate Hiram enough to kill his number one author and I stole Monique from Dominion."

"What?" Nikki rearranged their posture so that they were eyeball to eyeball, holding hands. "Why didn't you just tell me, babe?"

"Because, Nik. I vowed that I wouldn't cause you any more pain or anguish related to me, police, and prison." He squeezed her fingers and brushed them with his lips tenderly. "I am not going back to prison. I am not losing you again. You. Our boys. I am not. I hate to think of you walking away from me again."

"Mace," she whispered, moving close to his face. She stroked her cheek with the softness of his beard and massaged his clean-shaven scalp anointed with the magic of myrrh that permeated the truck's interior. "Honey, that will never happen again. Trust. We are on our path now. Together forever. Wherever you go, I follow. Period. And you are not going back to prison. Over our dead bodies. They will not take you away from me again." She leaned back and popped her neck in pure brown sugar soul sista fashion. "Uh-huh. Fuuuck dat. That's all you worried about?" They gazed at each other still holding hands.

Maceo chuckled at his wife's reaction. "Nik, you know how this works. When they wanna pin something on a brutha, they make it up however they want."

She gathered the myriad of thoughts racing through her mind. "My dearest husband, I know you could never tell me if it is true-did you have Kendali killed?"

"Nikki Pearl?!" Their eyes locked tighter. He let her hands go.

"I am just clearing the air." She leaned back in the passenger seat. "I know you would not kill Kendali, but Hiram is another story. Word on the street is that the bullet was meant for him."

"Yeah, but the killer was a sharpshooter. A hired gun. He got his intended target."

"Yeah, but how can we be so sure? Anything is possible. "

He pressed her hand to the center of his chest. "Nikki, I did not have Kendali killed."

"I know that. But *did you* have *Hiram* killed? You hate him enough and he has certainly done enough dirt to be murdered." She propped his chin toward her, fingering the beard she adored so much. "Honey. I know you." Her sparkling baby browns burrowed into his soul. "You can forgive him for so much. For so many things. For all his trifling, evil ways. But you can never forgive him for Bree."

He plopped back and banged his head on the headrest. "We are gonna let this go, Pearl. Bottom line: I am not goin' back to jail. And they may be trying to build a case against me. Tryin' to send me back to prison. And I ain't goin'."

Nikki gathered her purse, workbag, and sweater knowing that whatever happened, Maceo could never tell her. "Yeah. You right about that! You *ain't* goin'. Ha! We gon' see 'bout dat. They ain't pullin' *this* pearl," she pointed her thumbs at her chest, "from *my* oyster." She pointed at her husband and he responded with laughter. Nikki opened her door and dropped her feet onto the concrete, pretty purple pumps making a summoning din. "C'mon, babe. We got work to do. It's our time."

Maceo jumped from the truck and retrieved his briefcase from the rear floor. He met his wife on the sidewalk and hugged her tightly. "Ahhh yes. My Pearl."

11:00 a.m.

"This looks real good, Mo."

"You like those numbers?" Monique asked her boss as they worked in the conference room.

"I do. Even more so, these clients. You have landed some big people for these Isis ads. The brethren will be pleased. We have done more than our part."

"Yesss! The account has been setup. We should begin seeing the money rolling in within the next week. We still on point for the launch in a few weeks?"

"Definitely. Everything is a go-go as far as I know."

87

"Excellent! This is so exciting." She wiggled her shoulders, dancing in her chair as she wiped dust from her laptop.

"It is."

Closing her computer, she zeroed in on Maceo's eyes. "So. Tell me about Geronimo. What's going on?"

"You been talkin' to Nikki?" he asked playfully with wrinkled brow.

"I haven't." She smiled. "What do I need to know?"

"Nothing. I told you it's nothing to worry about."

"Uh-huh." Monique's tone dripped with sarcasm.

Maceo sighed and conceded to her innuendo demand. "He thinks I stole you from Hiram. That our rivalry is so intense, that I would have Kendali killed to ruin him."

"Hmmm." Monique exercised her eyes, squinting and stretching them rapidly, then slowly. She glared at Maceo. "Did you have her killed?" she inquired nonchalantly.

"Mo!" Maceo boomed, as he pushed back from the table.

"I'm just sayin'. I'm just sayin'." She bounced her hands across the air holding them up in a praising manner.

"Woman. What? You actually-"

"I mean shit. Hiram did you dirty. I would certainly understand. Maybe the rumors are true-the bullet was for him. He was the intended target. And no, I actually don't think you would kill Kendali, but Hiram...hmmm... I just threw it out there."

"Well throw it somewhere else. Be clear. They are probably going to question you."

"I figured as much. Shit, I thought about killin' the nigga. I hope they don't ask me 'bout that! Ha ha ha!"

"Mo, girl. You crazy." Maceo grinned.

"Shit. I'm serious. I love Hiram. But damn. He be hard to love." She laughed uneasily.

"That's real talk." Maceo picked up his tablet and started for the door. "Alright. Let's make our next move."

"Let's." They returned to their respective offices, Maceo feeling stressed, yet comforted after Nikki reassured him with her warrior woman force and Monique wondering if she went from the frying pan into the fire.

▢Text Message▢

Monique: Hey Love
Shante: My sister! wyd
Monique: Girl. work! Hands full at Gutta Butta. I mean Black Butta
Shante: That's right. the merger. How's it goin'?
Monique: It's goin' Doin' some new things big things on the horizon. lotta surprises. But you know I can't talk about it yet.
Shante: girl stop. EVERYBODY is talking about Isis!
Monique: Y'all make me sick But y'all still don't know everything
Shante: We know enough. It's gonna be world changing. Unprecedented! I am excited. Can't wait
Monique: Me either. How about dinner tonight? Vaughn is traveling. So…
Shante: So I get sloppy seconds▢
Monique: ▢
Shante: I'll take em. You the best sloppy seconds!▢
Monique: Teavolve?
Shante: I really want KD's. Cheesecake explosion.
Monique: Hmmm. I don't want to be anywhere Hiram could be
Shante: Oh, sis. Please. A whole murder. Y'all need to skip all that dumb stuff. water under the bridge.
Monique: Alright. KD's 6pm
Shante: Cool. Love you.❤
Monique: LU2❤

2:00 p.m.

"Mr. Meade, we want to talk with your board. Have a formal meeting. We want you to consider our offer. Most seriously."

"And I am telling you, Chuck. We are not interested. I have no more to say."

"I think you should reconsider. It will be for your benefit."

"Our benefit? Right okay. I need to prep for my next appointment."

"Certainly," the freckled face red hair white guy said. He rose, buttoned his suit jacket, picked up his briefcase, and extended his hand.

Brad stood and shoved his hands in his pockets. Chuck walked toward the door and Brad followed. "I will walk you out." They strode in silence to the elevator. Brad instructed the security staff to escort Chuck to his car.

"That isn't necessary," Chuck interrupted.

"Oh no. It is." Brad saluted the two officers and they returned the expression. He watched as they boarded the elevator with the Muse representative. Once the doors closed, Brad strolled back to his domain. His chair rolled as he plopped down to call Mustafa.

"Yo, yo!"

"My man, what's goin on bruh?" Brad greeted his partner-friend.

"Everything, bruh. Team No Sleep."

"I know, man." Brad laughed.

"Whatchu got for me?" Mustafa said shuffling papers on his desk, sitting in his office at Isis.

"Look. We know Thad was on point with his whitey speech. Whitey just left here. Lightweight threatening posture."

"Uh-huh. Fuck 'em. I told you I am sure they followin' me. Listening to our conversations. Watching our movements. That's alright. We got something for they asses. Brother Nati and our elders are on guard. And the youngbloods are in place. They ain't the only ones that know how to keep tabs on people. Only The Almighty is ALL MIGHTY!'"

"I know that's real."

"Yeah, so. Man your battle station, my brother. You know what's up and whatchu gotta do.

"Riiight. The pen *is* the mighty sword."

"You got it. Now wield that sucka, my brutha!"

"I'm on it."

"My brutha."

90

"Alright, Mustafa. We will catch up soon."

"Definitely. One Love."

"One."

He disconnected the call and texted Lesli.

"I'm right here," she sang as her phone buzzed in her pocket.

"Your timing is always impeccable."

"I *am* a butterfly. You know. The antennas." She flopped her head side to side, batting her eyelashes and twirling random afro curls around both forefingers then patting her afro puffs. "What do you need of my wings?"

"I need you to write a piece."

"Okay. Does it have anything to do with the white dude I saw?"

"Your antennas workin' overtime, huh?"

"No. The usual hours, 24, 7." She winked.

"I need a manifesto. Your words. Coming from me. It needs to be a mighty blow. Pen as a sword and serving as a circle of protection." He moved to his computer and started typing. "I am sending you this email with my thoughts. It needs to talk about Jim Crow. How it has never ended. Mention the books that discuss this truth about Jim Crow still existing today. Talk about our fallen brothers and sisters from all walks of life. Black Wall Street. The attack on Black economy. All of that. Talk about if I should die, go after Muse."

"Whoa. Wait. Die?"

"Yes. Die, Lesli Lyn. Die. This shit is serious. No games are being played."

"Shit."

"Yeah. Deep shit. Big shit. We are talking about taking a huge chunk out of Muse's profit while dominating an untapped market they are too egocentric and white centered to even think about. Our conscious community and our Black studies community. Isis is bigger than we can even fathom. We are simply moving in the spirit."

"Wooo! Okay. I hear you."

"Keep it short. Powerful. All points bullseye. You know. Do what you do."

"I gotcha. I will get on it right now." She sashayed to the doorway.

"Hold on. What did you wanna talk about?"

She turned around. "Seems so minor now, B."

"No. Never that with my favorite butterfly. What's goin' on?"

"The Myesha Morgan Show will be scheduled in a few days. Waiting for the confirmation call. I have two books just about ready for editing. And the covers are being finalized. I just wanted to get your input about the show."

"Just be you."

"Should I talk about Isis?"

"You can. Do whatcha feel. I trust your antennas." He imitated her twirling her curls and patting her afro puffs. She licked her tongue and left. He laughed heartily, the roar of his amusement following her down the hallway. The laughter soothed his soul, for he was mildly shaken by the espionage encircling their mission. He decided he would increase security and put his *own* Isis on point. He didn't want to burn Muse to the ground because they miscalculated his capability and capacity.

He rang his wife.

"Hey, babe."

"Charlene Sunbeam! I gotta hip you to some things."

7:00 p.m.

As they finished their meal with KD's cheesecake explosion, Monique self-disclosed to her friend.

"I am a little concerned about my new position, sis."

"I knew it was something. Spill it." Shante dunked her spoon into her Pina Colada cheesecake mountain, coconut cascading down its sides onto the plate.

"I don't know, Shante. Deep inside, I am feeling like I want to walk away from this whole business."

"Gurrrl...you talkin' crazy. You love books and you love the book business."

"Yeah, but now Maceo is telling me some shit about the police suspecting him for Kendali's murder."

"Whaaat? Really?"

"Yes. And it has me very uneasy. I mean I don't feel like he did it, but he despises Hiram and he has sharp, innate killer instincts. Remember he went to jail for murder. He paid to get released."

"Paid?"

"Yeah. He had a helluva legal team. And it cost him damn near half his fortune. Millions."

"Damn."

"Yeah. I need to go to law school."

Shante agreed, "I know right." She scooped a pineapple into her mouth. "I will support your decision. But you know you will be miserable without the book business. And what about your own house, MoJo Publications?"

"What about it?"

"You are going to start it? Maceo said he will support you, right?"

"Yeah, but I don't even know if I wanna be bothered."

"Mo. Listen. We are all reeling from Kendali's murder."

"Yeah many of us are, but a lot of us ain't. A lot of people couldn't stand her. Glad she's dead."

"This is true and understandably so. I mean Kendali wasn't a terrible person, but she *was* a video vixen.

"Yes, she was. And so misunderstood." Monique massaged her fingers, thinking about her time with Kendali, having watched her evolve. "At her core, she really was a sweet girl. She really was. Just trying to find her way. But hey. What I know. Karma spins her wheel..."

"Yes. She is a some next level wheel spinner." Shante leaned back in the booth. "Now, on Maceo. Ultimately we don't know who did it. I ain't goin' to the guillotine on it, but I don't see Maceo as a killer."

"Yeah. Not of Kendali. But did he hire someone to wack Hiram."

"Did you say wack? Ha ha ha! Girl, stop watchin' *The Sopranos*. Ha ha ha!"

"Shante! I'm serious."

"Okay, okay," Shante responded lessening her laughter. "You are fretting over all this madness because it is 'frettable'. Truly, who knows how far people will go. We never know these things. We have experienced a horrendous, horrific tragedy. So you just need to give it time, babe. Just give it time. All will be revealed."

"Time. Yes, sis. Time."

Chapter Eight
Does Music Calm The Savage Beast

Wednesday
10:00 a. m.

The average joe would not believe that Wes Gilliam was the monster that Toya described. His face was almost hairless, except for a faint mustache that gave him a pinch of masculinity. Otherwise, translucent skin dotted with freckles, thin eyebrows, and gray eyes made him appear younger than his fifty years. Medium height and medium build topped with a close fade haircut of wispy strands made him even more non-threatening and unassuming. Surely, Detective Blackfoot knew better. It was always these types who turned into monsters behind closed doors, wantonly ravaging others with their sick twisted desires and ravenous appetites for the inconceivable.

"I apologize for the delay. Can I get you anything, detective?" The executive greeted him in the reception area where he had waited for over twenty minutes.

Geronimo stood and shook his hand.

"Your assistant has been a dutiful hostess," he replied pointing at his water bottle.

"Good. Good." The two men walked down a long corridor to Wes' office passing worker bees along the way. Other than various awards and plaques hanging on the walls, the ambience of the place was surprisingly sterile for someone in the music industry-gray carpet, white walls, and black furniture. They settled at a rectangular conference table and sat next to each other. "What do you need from me?" Wes asked.

"Just a few questions about Kendali." Geronimo scrolled his cell phone notes.

"Okay." He tapped his foot in an agitated tempo.

"Why don't you want Dominion to publish her book?"

"I wouldn't say that." Wes waited for a conversational prompt. Geronimo did not deliver. He pushed back in his chair and expounded. "Look, I know Dominion is in the business of selling books and Kendali's series does just that-sell books. I am a businessman myself, so, I have no qualm with that. But this final installment may go too far and really, I am just helping Hiram out."

"Helping Hiram?"

"Yeah. She ruffled feathers with these books for the past several years. And now this one is supposed to be the death blow. They are going to be slapped with all kinds of lawsuits. I am merely helping them to avoid the blitzkrieg."

"The blitzkrieg. Hmmm. Okay. Lawsuits you say. You and who else?"

"Name a label. Anyone you want."

"But not you and your company?"

"Well, I don't make those kinds of decisions about who to sue. This is a corporation. We have a board. I didn't decide to make the phone calls and issue the cease-and-desist letters."

"You didn't? I understand differently. I hear you are The Man."

"No. I'm really not."

"What do you do here, Mr. Gilliam?"

"We manage artists. So we do a lot of different things."

"Such as?"

"Everything. Negotiate record deals. Arrange studio time. Hire producers. Set up tours. Arrange promotion. Styling. Booking. Everything. We make sure everything is everything for the artists. They call it branding now."

"Okay. Are you referenced in Ms. Grace's books? May her soul be healed in the spirit world."

"Honestly, I don't know. I haven't read her books."

"You have never read any of the nine published books? Not one page?"

"No."

"So, you are unaware that she may have referenced you and some of your history? Your character? Your experiences?"

"Am I being questioned in general or are you implying I have culpability in Kendali's murder?"

"Just asking questions."

"Just asking questions to help you? Or asking because I am a suspect?"

"No. Not a suspect. A person of interest."

"Okay. This conversation is done. I don't need to say anything else. You can leave your card and I will have my lawyer call you."

"Who is your lawyer?"

"Just leave your card."

"No need. I have what I need."

Geronimo's response unsettled Wes. "Ohhh-kay." He moved toward the door. "My assistant will see you out." His eye twitched and his teeth grinded, an automated reaction. "Kimmie!" he called for her.

"That's cool. Good day."

Wes ignored Geronimo and walked to the door.

The Wolf dropped his briefcase on the table and assembled his belongings inside the bag as the perturbed mogul returned to his dailies. The assistant stood at the threshold watching Wes walk to his office. She studied Geronimo's movements, then looked down the hallway at her boss again. She switched back and forth between the two men anxiously. When she was satisfied that Mr. Gilliam had totally disappeared, she tiptoed to Geronimo.

"Detective Blackfoot, I will escort you to the lobby," she said loudly. She then mouthed the rest of her communication. "Everything you hear about Wes is true, but I don't think he had Kendali killed." The detective paused and looked at her with pensive eyes, bouncing his briefcase against his calf. "Not his style." She turned to the conference room door, checking for eavesdroppers and nosey onlookers possibly passing by. "So, you have everything, Mr. Blackfoot?" she asked in an animated tone.

"I do. Thank you."

"Just follow me outside."

They took the elevator to the lobby, making one stop at her desk so she could get her purse and tell her subordinates she was going to pick up some snacks. They walked in silence onto the main street and went to the bistro on the corner. Once at the bistro patio, Geronimo asked, "So what are you trying to tell me, love?"

"Look, I don't really like the guy. At all. Wes is another kinda, next level asshole. I have worked with him a long time. He has done a lotta dirt, but a hit? Not his thing. He ain't even made like that. Now if she had been stabbed up in a fight, I would put Wes at the top of the list. But an orchestrated hit, look at Tasir Samaan."

"Oh yeah?"

"Yeah. Means, Motive. He hated Kendali, they say. And hated her books even more. And he's a twisted bastard. Into some sick shit, they say."

"So, I've heard."

"Yeah. And it's true."

"I appreciate you, love. Anything else come to mind," he began reaching into the side pocket of his briefcase. He pulled out his business card and gave it to her. "Give me a call."

"A briefcase. Hmmm. That seems unusual. A detective carrying a briefcase."

"I equip for the occasion."

She chuckled flirtatiously. "Yeah, I *will* call you. Now does it have to be about the case?"

"No, it doesn't. I have plenty of women friends."

"I bet you do. Have a good day, detective."

"You too, love."

12 Noon

"Hiram." Maceo nodded angling his shiny cue ball head to the entrance of Nina's.

"Aw, c'mon, man. Hug a nigga." Hiram opened his arms. "Hug ya' brother, man."

Maceo reluctantly embraced his nemesis and to his surprise, the warmth of their exchange felt good. Rivalries were burdening, exhausting, and frustrating. In the moment, he hoped that they were going to cease fire and establish a new relationship, founded in the brotherly love that initially brought them together. Maceo held the door while Hiram entered the restaurant. The hostess greeted them cheerfully and escorted them to their usual meeting room, always reserved for Seminole City's publishing heavy hittas, Hiram, Maceo, Mustafa, Brad, Monique, Georgette, and Nikki Pearl.

"I will send your server over right away, brethren. Or are we setting up a buffet?"

"No," Maceo answered. "No buffet today, sista."

"Okay. One server comin' up!"

"Thanks, baby girl," Hiram said.

The two men made themselves comfortable, actually looking at the menu for a change.

"I think I am going to try something new from Nina's kitchen."

"I think I will too, bruh," Hiram concurred. "We get stuck, too complacent sometimes. Doing much by rote. By habit."

"That's true. Need to shake things up. Move things around sometimes. Change our moves and our minds." Maceo flipped the page of his menu.

"Especially our minds," Hiram added, placing his menu on the table. His motion prompted Maceo to look at him. Now, eye to eye, face to face, mano a mano, Hiram apologized. "I have always loved and respected you. I never meant to hurt you, Mace. I was wrong. And I'm sorry. I hope you can forgive me."

Maceo gazed in disbelief as mistiness took over his eyes and his heart beat an awestruck rhythm. He held out his hand and Hiram cupped it in fraternal love. "Thank you, man. All is forgiven." Their handshake emanated the fire of a loving friendship, long overdue for a rekindling.

Hiram perused the menu again. "I think I am going to get the grilled salmon. I have never had here."

"Good choice. I get it with the grilled vegetables."

"Sounds good," Hiram replied, still reviewing Nina's selections. "And whatever you are going to ask me to do, I'm going to do. Short of killing my mother."

Maceo laughed. "You sure you want to say that before I ask?"

"Oh, I'm sure. I owe you, bruh. So, I know what I'm saying. It's already done."

"I appreciate that."

Their server came to the table, gave them a water pitcher, two tall glasses of ice, and a tray of lemons. He took their order and trotted off to fulfill their request.

"Alright, tell me what I'm doin'."

"I know you heard the rumors about Isis."

"Of course."

"Well, everything's a go, but we need security, cyber and otherwise. We hear you have the best."

"I do. That's it? You want a cybersecurity team and a physical security team?"

"That's it."

"Awww, man. That ain't nothing but a thing. I will link you all with my main man Cee and you can take it from there."

"You think he will do it? I know some people shy away from the Black thing."

"Not Crispus. He is on it already. He will be down. And his cybersecurity guy is Toussaint, so…"

"I got it. They were born ready."

"And you know this!"

"I do. I do." Maceo filled their glasses with water. "Now, Mustafa wants you to bring Dominion's books to Isis. Exclusively. There is a whole crew of us that have agreed. I have dedicated some of my staff to sales and advertising."

"That's what's up. How is it going?"

"Real good. Better than we expected. Ya' girl Mo is a helluva woman. I almost hate I snatched her from you." Hiram chuckled. "Almost hate, that is. In light of Kendali-"

Hiram held up his hand pausing Maceo's speech. "I know. I know, bruh." Swallowing his emotions, he switched to the Monique accolades. "Yes. Mo is the love of my life, second to Georgette."

"Yeah, man. I'm already in love with her. She is such a hard worker. Pure boss."

"She is. She has had plenty of practice bossing me around."

They laughed. Maceo commented, "As it should be."

The server brought a platter of seafood appetizers, and two beers. "Your entrees are coming up soon."

"Thank you." The two said a quiet blessing and dove into the platter of shrimp, fish, and crab vittles. "I know you don't want to talk about it, but who do you think killed Kendali? The detective dude questioned me. Seemed like he wants to finger me in this."

"Finger you?"

"Yeah. Like I'm tryin' to take you down. I stole Mo then had your number one seller killed to destroy you."

"Uh-huh. Did you?"

"You fuckin' wit' me, right?"

"Yeah, I am. But that may be my fault. I will take care of it."

"Your fault?"

"Yeah. He caught me at a vulnerable moment." Hiram dipped his shrimp in remoulade sauce. "All my moments are vulnerable. Since her murder. I just can't seem to get right."

"Time, my brother. Time will get you right. It is the only thing that will."

Hiram stared at a canvas hanging on the wall behind Maceo, depicting a robust woman singing and dancing in the rain, reminding him of Her Graceful Juiciness. He longed for the solitude of his man cave and imagined swimming in a tequila bath with her, splashing about, making love until his pain ceased. It was an evasive wish, an unanswered prayer. "He asked me about us. I said we were rivals. I will talk to him. Let him know what's up."

"Yeah, bruh. Cause I ain't goin' back. I told Pearl, by any means necessary. X cap to da back, suited and booted, I'm fightin' 'til somebody's death, not necessarily mine. Dig?"

"Oh, you know I understand. Geronimo is an alright dude. He has probably already figured it ain't you. I told him to find Max's ass. If he could. Dat big head nigga is ghost. Too damn smart."

"You keep the heavies around you."

"I got to. I ain't all that bright." They laughed. "But for real, I was sure Max was the shooter up until a few days ago. Somebody fired off at me. Right in traffic as I was leaving the liquor store."

"Word?!"

"Yeah. So, now I'm thinking about them industry fucks. Especially that damn Tasir asshole."

"I heard about him. Tasir Samaan?"

"Yeah. Sick fuck. I was thinking Max, but I am certain Max is gone for good. He wouldn't come back to shoot at me. But he could still be the killer. But, now, I am thinking harder about Tasir. Kendali exposed his evil deeds in this last book."

"That's right. Her final book. Y'all gonna release it?"

"I don't know, man. I'm leavin' it up to my wife."

"It would be a turbo boost for Isis. Her final book as the first release."

"It would. Yeah, that would be huge. You think Mustafa would agree? You know he is an uppity kneegrow."

Maceo burst into hearty laughter. "He is that, but he backs it up."

"Yeah. He got a big brain too."

"I will tell Mustafa to call you. I asked for this meeting to open the door. That's it."

"Cool. Just let him know that Georgette will be the one he talks to. I'm just not there yet."

"I gotcha. I understand, bruh. Take ya time. Time is always on our side."

"Yeah. I hope so."

2:00 p.m.

"This is Detective Blackfoot."

"Follow the merry go round, detective."

"Pardon me? Who is this?"

"Are you not taking anonymous tips?" The caller was using a voice alteration app, sounding like a cartoon character.

"I am. What do you mean, merry go round?"

"You are investigating the murder of that author, right? Grace Kendali?"

"Yeah, Kendali Grace. What merry go round?"

"You will see. You *are* going to question Tasir Samaan, right?"

"I cannot say. What do you know?"

"Just follow the merry go rounds. All of them. You will see. When you question him. Just remember when you get there." The caller paused. "Don't forget, detective. Write it down if you need to."

"Okay." The informant hung up.

Geronimo swerved around in his chair to face his computer. "Merry go rounds," he mumbled. He tapped his keyboard, updating his Grace Case file, then turned on his cell phone. He jotted his thoughts about the caller and the merry go round in his notebook app. Chief Dempsey, who had been on the case from day one, approached.

"Wolf! Tell me your instincts have us close to solving the case." He sat in the chair next to the detective's desk.

"Your timing is incredible. Would you believe that I just received an anonymous tip?"

"A good lead? Or a crazy?"

"Both."

"Both?"

"Yeah. The tipster is definitely crazy and his message was cryptic, but I have a feeling that it's a good lead."

"Alright."

"I just have to figure out what the hell he's talking about. And I won't know until I pay Tasir Samaan a visit."

"The psycho music guy?"

"Yeah. I'm headed there now." Geronimo assembled his investigative gear, preparing for departure.

"Okay. Good. Keep me posted. Directly to me on this."

"I know. I got it, chief." The two men stood, gave salute, and went their separate ways.

6:00 p.m.

"Welcome to The Oasis, detective." The butler stepped aside allowing Geronimo entry. "Lord Samaan is...in dispose. He will be with you shortly."

Lord? "Okay." *Lord?* Geronimo thought. *Yeah, all the rumors are true,* he noted in his brain. *Bat shit crazy.*

"Please wait here in the salon," the butler directed after closing the gargantuan sized wooden door and walking to the threshold of a room housing a grand piano.

Geronimo followed the servant, surveying the mansion. The peach-colored exterior reminded him of his grandmother's house that she adorned with turquoise accents, the shutters, the patio furniture and such. The interior reeked insanity and savagery, from the ominously dark vibration of the family portrait in the entry foyer, to the long creepy hallway, to the strange coldness of the salon. Even though it was decorated in vibrant colors, there was an underlying sinister aura. "Take a seat on the flower printed sofa. Do not sit on the green chaise."

"Okay."

"May I offer you a beverage? A tray of garden-fresh vittles perhaps?"

"No. I'm fine. I thank you."

The servant bowed. "Lord Samaan will join you momentarily."

Geronimo sat and waited until he was sure that the butler was gone. He walked gingerly down the hallway, peeping into the rooms along the way. *Merry go round.* The words played in his head cartoonishly like the voice that revealed the information. There were four doors total, excluding the salon. Door one was a library, ornately decorated, loaded with vintage books. Door two was a sitting room with chairs and sofas and nothing more, no decorations, no accentuating lamps or tables. But alas, door number three stopped Geronimo in his tracks. The mural over the fireplace depicted a merry go round. A plethora of merry go round ornaments and whatnots were in display, everywhere. The mantel, the tables, and three enormous glass display cases housed countless merry go rounds of all shapes, sizes, colors, and materials. Merry go rounds of gold, silver, brass, diamonds, pearls sparkled, inviting onlookers to its magnificence. Geronimo scanned the room with his wolf instincts, memorizing every single atom of the space.

"I see you have found my dedication to my favorite childhood past time, detective."

"Yes. It is remarkable." Geronimo turned and faced the alleged psycho.

Tasir grimaced at Geronimo's unperturbed disposition, smooth and cool, unmoved by him creeping upon him. "Would you like to take our meeting in this room? Although there is nowhere to sit." He brushed a tendril of his long black wavy hair away from his face and rested the same hand under his chin in contemplation.

"You da boss. Your house. Your call."

Tasir brush the ruffled sleeves of his white blouse that hung loosely over his stirrup pants, tucked inside his ballerina style man slippers.

"I am the boss?" He curled his lip with craziness. "I am!" he shouted.

Geronimo took one step back from Tasir, calmly and coolly. "Yes."

Tasir was miffed by the detective's ease. "Suddenly, I am inspired to play." He stretched his arm pointing toward the entry foyer. "To the salon!" he bellowed and marched skipped to the salon, his shoes making a sloshing sound on the mosaic tiled floor. Geronimo walked behind the skipping mogul, entered the piano room, and sat on the flower printed sofa.

Tasir settled at the piano and plunked the keys. Geronimo listened, admiring his musical skill and the sunset spangling the sky, giving auburn love to the flower garden beyond the patio. He played for ten minutes and then made a dramatic stop. "Tell me what you want, detective."

"Talk to me about Kendali."

"Dear God! Is she all anyone talks about these days?!"

"Well, she was murdered. Probably by a trained assassin, which is odd and strange, especially here. In Seminole City."

"True enough. Which is why I have a house here. Such urban serenity." He plucked the keys looking at Geronimo. "You are a big guy."

"You and Kendali, what was your relationship?" Geronimo asked ignoring the nutty flirtations.

Tasir switched to playing his ten-minute rhythm softly, the background music to his own voice, the star of a one night only concert playing in his head. "I sent flowers, you know?"

"I do."

He kept playing. "There is nothing to tell. She was just a video girl."

"And she refused your advances?"

"I did not advance her. I sent her gifts and she declined."

"Very expensive gifts."

"Therein lies the theory of relativity, detective. For a man of means, a Lamborghini is a bouquet of flowers. A box of chocolates."

"You were angry about her book. She depicted you in an unpleasant light.'

104

"Me? Unpleasant? Ha!" He banged the keys loudly for a few chords, his hair swirling wildly around his head as he jerked to the angry song. Then, he returned to the soft stroking of his instrument. "She didn't depict me at all."

"She isn't referring to you in her book? And your staff people haven't called Dominion offices threatening cease and desist orders for just about every volume of her *Vixen Notebook*, especially this last one?"

"I don't involve myself in such menial tasks. That's what those legal beagles are for. *Dogs!* I am an artist. A maestro." The music drummed louder under his fingertips. Geronimo sat completely still the entire time, only his mouth and eyes moving and his hands resting comfortably on his thighs. The maniac mogul banged the grand piano for another forty-five seconds and then he ceased his one-man symphony. "People say that. They say it is me. But it could be anyone. This business is overrun with sickos, detective." He smacked his lips on the last word he spoke, *detective*.

"What is your sexual orientation, Mr. Samaan?"

Tasir tossed his head back clutching his invisible pearls, feigning surprise. "I don't talk about sex, detective."

Geronimo brushed his pants and rose from the sofa. "I thank you for your time. I can see myself out."

Tasir was shocked by Geronimo's abrupt ending of their conversation. *How dare he interrupt this interrogation*, he thought. He jumped from his seat and rushed to the hallway. He called after Geronimo, "But I am the boss, detective. You said so!"

The investigator kept walking, throwing his hand in the air, never looking back. "Good night, Mr. Samaan."

Tasir stomped back to his piano and strummed a frustrated tune, stretching his neck, his face aimed at the ceiling. The butler peeped in. "Is everything okay, Lord?" Tasir did not hear, his bitter composition too loud. "Lord! Lord!" He shuffled to the side of the piano, waving his arms. "Lord!" Tasir stopped and pulled his hair back to the nape of his neck. "Is everything okay? Where is your guest?"

"He left." Tasir wrung his hands and closed the piano. "I want to get on the merry go round."

The butler hung his head. "Very well, my lord."

Chapter Nine
Osiris Redeems Isis

Thursday
10:00 a.m.

Hiram dialed Crispus. "I need you, bro."

"I am working the case. But we already know what's up. Max is in the wind."

"I know, man. I don't even think it's him anymore."

"I told you I didn't think so from the rip. I mean he definitely has the coo-coo profile and all that, but hire an assassin to kill her, or kill her period. I don't think so."

"Yeah. I agree with you more now, especially since I've been shot at," Hiram relayed.

"Whoa! What? When?"

"A few days ago. I'm alright but it certainly has me looking at these music industry savages. One time for Biggie. One time for Pac." After pouring two shots of tequila in his glass, he continued his libations. "Two times for Roger Troutman. Four, five times for Sam Cooke and Otis Redding."

Crispus heard the splashing alcohol. "Bruh, you ain't gon' drink all that?"

"Every drop."

"Maaan, when you gonna come outta this? You gotta-"

"I know. I got time. I won't be here forever."

"Alright then."

"I didn't call about none of this. Two things. One. Mustafa Akeem. He has assembled the brethren and they are launching the first and only completely Black owned and operated multimedia publishing, production, and retail platform."

"Isis?"

"So you heard the rumors?"

"You know it."

"Well, they asked me to sign on. An exclusive publishing deal for Dominion...and...they need security. Two times. Cyber and physical."

"I'm already on it. I'm glad to be a part."

"They sent Maceo at me."

"That apparently went well."

"It did. I apologized to him. For everything. I think we are on our way to better days."

"Now that! My man, is good news!"

"Yeah. I'm glad about it. Real glad."

"Alright." Crispus pumped his fist in the air. "And the other thing?"

"I need you to follow Gee."

"Georgette? What's going' on?"

"Just follow her and give me a report. I don't want to discuss it."

"Alright. Will do. Text me. And email me everything I need for Isis.

"You got it. Thanks, Cee"

"Yeah, bruh. You know I'm your man. And stop drinking, Hiram."

"I will." Hiram hung up and gulped his Don Julio, giving great gratitude to the tequila gods.

He reclined in his work chair and messaged Toya.

☐Zing Message☐

Hiram: Hey, baby girl. How are you?

Toya: Makin it. What's up? You read Butterfly Brooks' blog?

Hiram: Yeah. She real short and to the point these days.

Toya: Yeah. Has anyone seen the book? Are you gonna release it?

Hiram: We have the book under lock and key. No one has seen it. Release-not sure. I am thinking yes. But I don't know. We are wading through the legal b.s. Not the first time we dealt with this on The Vixen Notebook

Toya: Right. I remember. Seems like every installment, somebody had something to say.

Hiram: And I got the legal bills to prove it

Toya: Yeah. What else is happening?

Hiram: New intel. Point the people more toward the industry assholes. Not so sure it was Max. Not positive it was not him, but definitely a lot less sure that he's the culprit.

Toya: Really?

Hiram: Yeah. Somebody shot at me. Car chase. That ain't Max's M-O.

Toya: Shot at? You alright?

Hiram: I'm cool. You can lightweight mention it in your next post while pointing the people toward the music industry assholes, especially Tasir.

Toya: I gotchu We will find her killer

Hiram: Yes, we will.

Toya jumped right on her tablet and started keying her post.

◻Zing Tea Thyme group◻

Latoya Tea Mitchell (post): Haaay Tea Thymers. In the spirit of Kendali my sister. RIH Sweet Angel. Thanks to all your hard work and my sources, we can look more closely at the music industry evil doers. Maxmillian Gray could be the culprit but in light of recent events, folks in the publishing industry being stalked and shot at, yes bullets fired, and then chased down in unidentifiable vehicles, we are concluding that the probability of Max being the murderer of my sister has decreased dramatically. Tasir Samaan, Wes Gilliam their probability has been increased. And those damn Eisenberg brothers! Y'all stay diligent! Inbox me. Call the tip line. Let's keep gathering the information! Knowledge is power! RIH Sweet Angel Of Grace!

Reactions: 2,890   Comments: 9,863   Shares: 4,857
(Load previous comments)

Ben Amin: Me and my crew with that hootie hoo. str8 up like that. hmu if you need us, sis #thesehands

Latoya Tea Mitchell: @Ben Amin: I hear that brother

Halimah G: Wow. Not Max huh? Well I'm glad. I love his books. I hated thinking he was a killer. Yay for Max!

Natalie Bates: Yessssss! Such a relief. He is actually one of my favorite authors. I hate that he stopped writing. I guess we will never hear from him again.

Tera Kirksey: Yeah. I guess not. But I wanna know more about the industry low lifes! They really would have her killed? I can't believe it. Over a book?
Phoenix Ash: The pen, my dear sister, is a mighty sword. It wields immeasurable power!□
G. Fife: @Phoenix Ash So true, sis!
Tera Kirksey: I know about those music industry types. My cousin was signed to a label. They shelved her album. Wes Gilliam approached her about managing her. She said he seemed slimy. Had a circle of very young boys around him. All the time. smh
Mica Jennings: wow. buncha sickos. RIH Kendali.❤

11:00 a.m.

"I guess she can see you. You are here very close to show time." The effeminate assistant was impeccably dressed in a houndstooth checkered suit with purple tie, purple socks and flamboyantly adorned with a purple feather boa. "I mean since it's about Kendali. She's real broke up about it, you know?" He twisted his body toward Geronimo, taking in his physique, and curled his lips with approval.

"I know. It is a shocking tragedy. And I appreciate the consideration. I know Ms. Morgan's time is beyond valuable."

He batted his eyelashes. "Let me check with her. I am sure she will see you. Wait here."

"Okay. Thanks." Geronimo reorganized items in his briefcase while he waited in the lobby of the studio's dressing room suites located on the second floor of the building. The non-descript decor surprised him since Myesha was known for glitz and glamour. Everything was black and white, simple office furniture with hints of red. A few dramatic art pieces hung on the walls and that was all. The assistant returned quickly.

"Follow me, detective."

Geronimo walked behind the young cream-colored man as he switched down to the end of the hallway where Myesha lounged in all her television glory. She was reclined on a red leather styling chair, dressed in gray sweats with an aesthetician applying a clay mask to her face.

"Have a seat, detective," she invited warmly. Her assistant fluffed red and white floral print pillows on a black silk sofa situated across from Myesha. Geronimo sat and her sassy helper took a seat next to her. He commented, "A police officer with a briefcase? Hmmm. That's different."

Myesha lifted her body from the recliner to study her guest. "Hmph. That's no briefcase. That's a handmade amulet. Probably designed by an elder and blessed by a shamanic circle of healers."

"I am impressed, Ms. Morgan."

"Don't be. I know how you native boys get down. I have certainly had my share." She grinned at Geronimo, a series of seductive thoughts racing through her mind, surely showing in her facial expressions.

Geronimo noticed her flirtations and continued talking. "My grandfather made it and my grandmothers prayed over it. Prayers of protection."

"I know." She offered another sly grin, simultaneously scissoring her thighs.

He ignored her again and spoke to the occasion. "I will not take up your precious time. We can get right to the point."

She lay back on the chair, exhaling a sigh of defeat while the aesthetician positioned her for optimal service. "What do you want to know?"

"What you know."

"I know EVERYTHING!" she bellowed.

"Tell me what you think I need to know. Who killed Kendali?"

"Have you read her books?"

"I haven't."

"You need to. All the answers are there. The industry killed her. They are all culpable."

"We can't charge the industry, Ms. Morgan."

"I don't see why not." She breathed in exasperation. "That's the problem. You need to go after all of them. You know she was on my show right before she died?"

"I do know."

"She revealed the ugliest side of the business in her final book, but she has been leading up to this finale the whole time. That's why you have to read her books."

"Okay. Duly noted. What can you tell me about Hiram Rivers?"

"What? That we had a tryst a while back?"

"A while back?"

"Yeah. Hiram and I go way back. We used to travel in the same circles. We have a mutual respect and understanding. We know a lot about each other." She paused momentarily thinking about Geronimo's questions. "He definitely knows a lot about me. Probably too much. I was a naughty girl, detective."

"A naughty girl. Okay."

"Yeah. I guess the affair has come out, I'm sure."

"Hiram and Kendali? Yeah."

"Well, I have always known. Everyone else speculated, but I *knew*."

"How did you know?"

"Because that's what I do. My business is knowing. Knowledge and information. Once you know one thing, you become a magnet for intel."

"I can see that."

"As for Kendali's murderers-all the big record label execs, movers, shakers. Those are your culprits. People have no clue how much power these assholes wield."

"How much?"

"Too damn much." She sat up in her seat, the clay hardening on her cheeks. "Read the books. She tells it. Tasir, Wes, everybody at Big Mike Records, and some others. The Eisenberg brothers. They are all in there. And these niggas don't have skeletons; they got whole cemeteries in their closets. Ha!" She sneered with an agitated jaw, as she shared her suspect suggestions with the detective. "If I had to put money on anyone, I would actually go with Wes Gilliam. He is as slimy as it gets. And you never see him comin'. Fuckin' low life."

"Hmmm. Cool. I gotcha. I appreciate you, Ms. Morgan."

"Read the books, Geronimo. Call me for clarity, if you need."

He rose from the sofa and eased his bag onto his shoulder. "I will. I am on it."

"And don't be a stranger. You are welcome here any time."

"Thank you, sista. Have a good show."

"Thanks a bunch, detective."

12:00 Noon

Observing the audience from the wings calmed her anxiety. A Butterfly with butterflies, go figure. Women in vibrant colored dresses, with painted faces and the few men with full beards dotting the sea of femininity made her smile. The studio's yellow and red geometric shape art deco style backdrop Lesli Lyn was rarely nervous before interviews, presentations, or book discussions, but since Kendali's murder her sensitivities heightened. Her emotional responses intensified. She was more prone to crying and she emotionally analyzed everything around her. She didn't feel ready for her new transformation, but Brad insisted that she had shed her cocoon again, and her wings were primed and pruned for fresh flight. A silent prayer eased her thoughts. She asked God to remove the unready sensation from her spirit while the two shots of ginseng and wheatgrass that Titus made for her earlier to smoothed her out.

"Fly, all is well, babe." He kissed her neck and hugged her under her voluptuous rack. She pressed her weight against his strong torso, brushing his hand with her fingertips and he squeezed her tighter. "I'm going to sit with the people. You always be you, God takes care of the rest."

"I love you, T."

He spun her around softly and kissed her. "And I love you, Mrs. Dixon." She watched him walk away and repositioned herself amongst the buzzing production staff.

"Okay, Ms. Brooks. Lemme double check your mic." The cheerful production assistant tested Lesli's microphone and unraveled the wires making them more inconspicuous. "Okay. You are all set."

"Great!" She relaxed more, Titus' breath still lingering on her neck and his cologne hovering around her head, an aromatic halo.

"I thank you. Thank you." Myesha bowed to her audience as they clapped adieu to her guest. "Now, our next guest has been with us before. She used to be signed to Dominion Publishing. Wrote some outstanding books while there. Definitely some of my faves. She is so many things and really needs no introduction. And I am sure you all follow her world-famous blog and Zing group, The Kaleidoscope." A quiet, intermittent cheer rippled through the crowd, acknowledging Myesha's point. "She is now morphing again bringing us more of her greatness with her gorgeous wings. Let's give a grand welcome to the incomparable, one of a kind, one and only- Butterflyyyyyy Brooooooooks!!!"

Lesli strode onto the stage surprised by the boisterous reception of the crowd. Inundated with threats, snide emails, and drive-by attacks over the past year assured her that people had no love for her. Hence, her resistance to Bradford's push for her new projects was born of her experience with an angry audience. The splashing sound of the car speeding past her and the stains on her green Adidas flashed in her mind; the drive-by at Teavolve left a scar. She relished the healing reception of Myesha's audience, smiling and waving. Her purple capris, accented with silver grommets down the legs and her turquoise, front tie, collared oxford blouse, unbuttoned just enough for a peek of her purple lace camisole, dazzled the people. She tiptoed to the lounge area, violet butterflies fluttering on her sandal heels. The hostess greeted her with a sincere bear hug and loving peck on her cheek. She stepped back and waved her arms presenting Lesli again and they showered her with more rambunctious applause. Lesli bowed, her zig zag parted afro puffs saluting the gleeful onlookers. The two women nestled in the sofas and started their interview.

"Gurrrrrrrrl, you know I love us. We always show up and show out. You look maaah-vahhhluzzzz!"

"Thank you-thank you. And of course you always speak volumes of Black beauty."

"You are such a poet. Let's talk about that. Gosh! I have so much I wanna talk about. Talk about the new Butterfly. What's going on? How are things with The Kaleidoscope?"

"The Kaleidoscope is good. Meade Comm is my second love."

"Second?"

"Yes. My-"

"Oh, wait. Jewelry cam, Tony. C'mon. I see it. That's a helluva rock." Tony zoomed in on Lesli's finger. Myesha lifted her hand toward the camera to display the butterfly shaped ring. "And shaped like a butterfly?"

"Yes. He knows me well."

"Girl, I love it. Y'all set a date?"

"Not yet. But it will be soon."

"Congratulations, doll face."

"Thanks so much, Myesha."

"Now, Tony. One more. Without being too invasive. Because she is giving us a lotta *Cleve-land*." Myesha puckered her lips and pointed at Lesli's her signature diamond encrusted butterfly pendant, sparkling betwixt her breasts. "You are the envy of all us little flat chested girls." Lesli laughed. "Okay, y'all see that? Gorgeous! A gift from the soon-to-be-husband?"

"Not this one," she responded, rubbing the butterfly pendant like a good luck charm. "My daddy gave me this one."

"That's right. Your dad is the man to know here in our city."

"That's what they say."

"And what they say is true, honey. Lesli is being modest, y'all. Her father Delroy Faulkner is a serious powerbroker. And not just here. But all up and down the coast."

"My dad has done well. He has been good to our family. A lot of families. A lot of people."

"Yesss." The audience applauded. "So look. Tell us about your latest project."

"By Any Wings Necessary. A Black Woman's Guide To Evolution. It is a series of empowerment books. One for body. One for mind. One for spirit. One for soul. "

"Oooo. I am loving it already."

"Bradford Meade, our CEO insisted that it was time for me to share these compilations with the world. The books are essentially my journals, detailing my journey. My journey to me."

"Wow. Any juicy stuff in there? I know it is." The audience laughed.

"It's all juicy." Lesli glanced around the studio, spotting Titus at the top of the amphitheater. They winked at each other. "And in the way you mean, yes. It is honest and bold and loving and sincere."

"So you give explicit details about your life?"

"I do. I do."

"Because we do know you get a lotta flack about your book reviews and your opinions on the state of the Black publishing industry."

"I do. I have."

"Talk about it. Didn't somebody try to run you over?" The audience released a collective, harmonic gasp.

"Yes. They did."

"Did you ever find out who did it?"

"No. I didn't. We never filed a police report. None of that. We handled the situation privately."

"Bodyguard?"

"Well, yeah. Essentially." She zoomed her eyes on Titus' loving smile.

"Like our beloved Kendali."

"Yes, like Kendali. May she rest in heaven."

"Yes. Yes." Myesha's tone shifted. "I'm speaking of the late Kendali Grace. Best-selling author of *The Vixen Notebook* series. You all know she was slain recently. Snuffed out at the PQ gala. Which you, Butterfly, are a major player in that event, right?"

"I wouldn't say major. Significant, yes."

"Okay. Significant. Which brings me to why you have been on folks sugar honey iced tea lists. You were highly critical of Kendali's books and a lot of authors at Dominion, which was once your home." Myesha crossed her legs and rested her upper body on the back of the sofa.

"Yes. Dominion got me started in the fiction business. I am grateful to The Rivers. Highly critical? If you say so."

"I would. And so would plenty of other folks."

"True enough. But I think I have been very diplomatic, politically correct in my manner of reviewing books."

"You think?"

"Yes. My reviews are given in the spirit of betterment for authors, publishers, and me. As a writer. I am always improving. Seeking critique and constructive criticism to evolve as an author. I am a butterfly, so transformation is part of my makeup. This is an evolutionary journey for me." The audience clapped and whooped at Lesli's response.

"Okay. I hear ya'. I hear ya'. Let me read something you wrote about *The Vixen Notebook*." Myesha picked up her cue cards from the coffee table and her reading glasses which she slid onto her face. "Quote. While Ms. Grace has certainly improved her writing style and I am sure she had tons of help, she fails to develop her characters enough for us to care about them. Or maybe she doesn't want us to care. Does she know how to create character depth? I don't know. I do know she will greatly benefit from continuing those writing courses. She owes it to her readers. These one-dimensional characters must die. Learn to layer, Kendali." Myesha placed her glasses on the table and dropped the cue cards next to her on the sofa. "Now, c'mon BB. Much shade, yes?"

"Shade? No shade. There is absolutely no shade in my critique. Those are my sincere thoughts; from the only space I operate from and that is the space of love." The audience hollered their approval of Lesli's rebuttal. "Now read last line of the review, Myesha."

"Okay." She picked up a printout of the book review and positioned the paper a good distance from her eyes. "Girl, I'm old," she remarked. Lesli and the guests chuckled at Myesha's antics. She read, "Ultimately, I am delighted to see her evolution. I wish her continued success as she tells her story. Salud! Three and a half stars!"

"Now, Myesha, that is a positive closeout."

"True but..."

"No but's. I always offer balanced critique. A mother raising a child, a teacher teaching a student. A friend helping a friend. If we really love each other, we have to be honest. We have to tell the truth, even if it stings."

"Oh...you a butterfly that stings?"

"So, I have been told."

"Gurrrrl...Well, we love your books. And we love your blog. Tell us again about your Butterfly Connects."

"It's a women's evolution series of books based on the four stages of a butterfly's birth. We are doing a four-city tour to start. Then four more. Then four more. Per the seasons."

"Oooh. I like. What inspired this undertaking? It's gonna be huge."

"It is. Actually my publisher. He insisted. He feels I have a strong voice in the literary arts and demands that I use it in a big way."

"I am inclined to agree with him. You do. All of my staffers here are subscribed to The Kaleidoscope and are members of your Zing group."

"Really?"

"Yes, girl. You are a superstar!"

"Wow. I am so humbled. I thank you all. I am ever grateful."

"And we are grateful for you. Aren't we, lovelies?" The audience cheered. "We want you back on the show when your books drop. Release date yet?"

"No, not yet. But soooo soon!"

"Now, your boss and a cadre of bosses got a big thing brewing. We are starting to see the ads. Isis, right?"

"Oh my goddess! Yes! It is going to be huge!"

"That's what we hear All forms of media?"

"Girl, yes. And all of my books will be on Isis only."

"No more Muse?"

"No more. Isis only."

"Wow! Do y'all think this will work well? So many people are loyal to Muse."

"True. But so many are loyal to us. To all the brands, the publishers, the authors that are brought together with Isis Power in numbers. This is our key."

"Definitely power in numbers. I will certainly subscribe. I can't wait!"

"Me either, sis. It's gonna be extraordinary."

"Y'all give it up for Butterfly Brooks." The show goers stood on their feet and stomped and clapped and gave up the love. Myesha continued, "Check out her blog, The Kaleidoscope. Subscribe and buy her books on her website and at Isis.com, exclusively! Make sure you get ready to get Isis." The two women embraced as the audience kept up their roar of appreciation. Myesha whispered in Lesli's ear, "Trust your spirit. You are more ready than you realize."

Lesli murmured, "Thanks so much, sis."

2:00 p.m.

"I gotta kick this off with a real quick read, brethren." Hiram inventoried his comrades sitting around the glossy cherry wood conference table located on the top floor of Isis Communications headquarters. "May I, Brother Akeem?"

"By all means, my man."

Hiram tapped his tablet and read:

Battle Of The Gods

Ole jimmy crow seemed to be a god, but just like The Wiz played by the late great Richard Pryor, he back there, in the back, in an ole funky robe, sleeping on a cot. It is all an illusion.

But we are real.

The jim crow rears his rotten beak once again, family. He flaps his wicked savage wings all around us, stifling the air with the stench of oppression, war, domination, jealousy, gluttony, and wanton pursuit of blood. A blood sucker. A blood eater.

The rumors are true. Isis is real, a multimedia production and publishing platform, all Black, all strong. You will begin to see the billboards, the commercials, the cyberspace ads, the trade show booths, the celebrations, the interviews. All of it. The brethren and sisteren have come together and designed the ultimate all Black media experience.

Oh, but woe. Here comes Mr. Charlie with his offers, which, by now we must know are never offers. They never have been, not since the 24 dollar 'purchase' of Manhattan Island. They don't make offers. They throw pennies after punishment, toss pittance after waging war and raining hell down upon their target. The people at muse are waging war against us, Black family. We need you to know this and to stand strong with us. Even if you do not sign up with Isis, we ask you for your prayers of protection in the spirit of The Creator. Protect Isis.

Protect Osiris. We are family. We are powerful. We are magic. Ole jim crow is over; he is dead, a thousand deaths he dies everyday defeated everyday by us and our repeated refusal of muse's offers. They come for us and we wield sword and shield on behalf of you and us, as a united Black family. And we are winning. Our destiny is to win and destroy jim and his minions finally and forever.

He is destroyed by the power of love and resurrection. The Love force between Osiris and Isis as she births him anew. Together, they are the all-encompassing fierce goddess and god of all, manifesting our truth, and our purpose.

Black kingdom, Black empire, Black family, we know you got our backs and we damn sure got yours!

Aka~weah~yah!

Bradford smiled. Mustafa, Maceo and Thad pumped fists. Crispus spoke, "Good move, bruh."

"You think so?" Bradford wanted reassurance.

"In general, it is a good practice to look the devil in the eye and call him by name. For the most part, he will retreat and return to hell."

"Amen, Brother Crispus," Mustafa affirmed.

"Amen," Hiram concurred, reclining in his chair pushing his tablet away from him.

"I'm glad you read that to kick off our meeting," Mustafa said.

"Of course. It's got Butterfly Brooks written all over it." Hiram grinned.

"You betta know it! We only rock with the best." Bradford pounded the table rhythmically. "They *are* Isis. For real."

"Yes. Just like Mo." Maceo raised a finger. "And Nikki Pearl. They are our resurrectors, our feminine fire and protection. The force."

"Word." Mustafa added, "Like Aminah."

"And Georgette. She has risen to the grand occasion at Dominion. For me. For us. Because it has been a madhouse."

"We know." Mustafa thumped his chest two times, his fingers forming a peace sign that he waved toward Hiram. Hiram nodded, accepting the love. "Rest in power, Kendali."

119

"Rest in peace, sis," Thaddeus acknowledged. "Rest peacefully sister." The other men uttered their respects.

"Now, my brethren. This is a short meeting. I brought us together to simply say, everything is a go. We are ready for launch!"

"Yeah, yeah!" They all clapped and cheered and banged on the table, drumming their excitement.

"We will have a formal launch celebration in a few weeks. You have already seen the commercials and ads popping up." The kings of Isis shook their heads affirmatively. "You will see more. And more. We have an awesome staff, that has swelled to about 100 employees and contractors. So we are well founded with only the absolute best and brightest. All Black, by the way."

"My brother," Crispus voiced.

"Yes. So. Look around the table. Get a good look at each other because you, my brothers, are the newly formed Board Of Directors of Isis Communications."

"Word?" Maceo questioned.

"Doesn't it make sense? Who else should it be?"

"I guess so," Maceo agreed. A toothy grin formed on his mouth. Mustafa walked to the neighboring kitchen area and returned to the roundtable with bottles of champagne.

"A toast, family." He went back to the kitchen and retrieved three more bottles and several corkscrews. He distributed the bottles and the openers.

"No glasses?" Hiram asked.

"No glasses. Straight from the bottle...to the dome!" The roundtable laughed.

Maceo said, "I hear that! That's what's up."

Mustafa popped his bottle first and let the cold carbonated elixir spill onto the table. "For the brothers and sisters who ain't here." The other men followed suit, releasing the corks from their flasks drenching the table with liquor. "Kendali Grace!" He bowed his head. "Now call out the names of your fallen loved ones. Your transitioned loved ones." The men called the names of grandmothers, grandfathers, mamas, papas, aunts, uncles, cousins, and friends. "Ashe, ashe, ashe ashe-o! And to us, to all of our Isis Queens, to us, The Osiris

Kings and all the Osirian forces of the universe, may we reign righteously, divinely forevermore!"

The men called out, "Ashe! Salud! Black power! Right On! Sho' ya' right!" They drank merrily; the deal was sealed.

After everyone left, Mustafa keyed his first official Osiris Rising Zing post:

☐Zing Osiris Rising Radio☐

Osiris Rising: The rumors are true, Black Family! Isis has resurrected Osiris and she is taking her rightful place on her throne. The brethren and sisteren have answered the call and we rise each and every day to the occasion. Isis Communications is all black, all strong. The first and only completely Black owned and operated multimedia publishing and production corporation.

You have been seeing our beautiful ads and commercials and hearing the buzz on stations all over Planet Radio satellites. I am confirming it is all true. We are here and here to stay.

We got books! We will have a variety of publishing houses, book companies and indie authors selling their masterpieces on Isis.

We have film, TV, music, and radio.

Isis is original and classic TV streaming lectures at its finest. The best of episodic serials, classic movies, documentaries, and educational programming.

Education...Black studies and Black history and science textbooks...online courses...extensive online library with subscription...an authors, designers, and musicians and filmmakers institute...no more jive test readers who do not have command of Isis' English...

We offer publishing services for those who want to do it on their own cuz that's alright with us

No bully Zing groups...Isis has a built in social platform where you can build your audience interact with your audience and grow your readership within the Isis universe. No more flying blind about who is buying and not buying your books. Isis is the queen overseeing her queendom with love nurturing understanding and wisdom.

There are strict guidelines for participation, family. No bullshit allowed. It must be all love. We have real live humans in our customer care center no more zing bots bits ding dongs Real people who share the same vision. Our official launch gala is coming up soon. There are a limited number of tickets. So download the app, subscribe, and get your tickets. Right now the app shows gala tickets and a mockup preview. So, go get a taste of the throne. We all the way Back 2 Black! I Love y'all!

6:00 p.m.

☐Text Message☐

Thad: Hey baby love
Georgette: Thad!
Thad: How was your day?
Georgette: Still here. Haven't eaten. Just a smoothie. And granola bar
Thad: Dinner?
Georgette: DEFINITELY!
Thad: I'm cooking for us
Georgette: Huh?☐
Thad: Yeah. Slide thru
Georgette: Hmmm.
Thad: I will send you a Lyft. leave your car at Dominion
Georgette: Okay☐
Thad: Girl stop. Just get over here
Georgette: ☐
Thad: ☐

She danced around her office pirouetting gleefully. All was quiet, just her recital and one maintenance man humming her accompaniment as he cleaned offices. She grabbed an overnight handbag from her closet. Its contents were all the things a girl needed for a rendezvous, toiletries, makeup, robe, underwear, head scarf, and a slip-on maxi dress, easily styled up or down.

▓ Text Message ▓

Thad: Your Lyft has arrived
Georgette: Thanks, see you soon. ☐

Thaddeus set the mood with soft jazz playing on his big screen TV and candles lit throughout the sunken living room. The kitchen situated next to the living area pumped delightful aromatics around the four-bedroom, two-story contemporary style house. He had been cooking and anticipating a tête á tête with Georgette all day, even while giving dap to her husband at the Isis meeting. He felt no remorse.

The doorbell rang. He skipped from the kitchen into the wide foyer, singing along with John Legend, excited and carefree. He opened the door.

"Georgette."

"Thaddeus."

He welcomed her into the house with a long, sincere hug. Unbeknownst to the star- crossed lovers, Crispus was on the case. He had tailed her from Dominion to Thaddeus' residence, found a comfortable, inconspicuous bird's eye view of the house, and watched, waiting for their bedtime story to unfold. "Wow, Georgette," he muttered as he observed the affectionate embrace.

"I've missed you." He gazed into her glowing eyes; a kiss naturally followed.

She savored the minty freshness of his tongue, speaking into his mouth. "I missed you too." His arms tightened around her body while she caressed his back. Her whispering, "It smells so good in here, love," made him tingle; an erection raised the material of his gleaming white sweats.

"Hmmm, yes." He led her by the hand to the kitchen, through a wide foyer, past the stairwell to the right and a billiard room on the left replete with two tables and a variety of old school arcade games. The buffet he prepared had copious amounts of everything a health-conscious Georgette would not eat, especially on a weeknight. He had been spoiling her with Deucey's and all kinds of fattening foods.

"I keep tellin' you I don't eat like this."

"Yeah, but you keep gobblin' it down." He laughed. She playfully nudged him in his side.

Her mouth watered at the chafing dishes filled with fried chicken, mashed potatoes, candied yams, collard greens, waffles, eggs, bacon, and banana pudding.

"You made all of this?"

"Everything except the pudding. I got that from Deucey's." He kissed her cheek.

"Let me wash up."

He took her bag. "Right over there." He pointed to the powder room down the hallway.

When she returned from the bathroom, Thaddeus was preparing her plate.

"For you, beautiful."

They sat in the kitchen, the peanut butter colored wood of the floor, ceiling, and cabinets radiated a copper glow from the full moon shining through the patio doors. Earthy and deliciously romantic. Thaddeus said a simple blessing and Georgette scooped mashed potatoes into her mouth. She couldn't wait to taste. "You really made these?" she asked, swallowing another heaping forkful.

"Yes, sweetness. I am from a family of women. Me. My mom. 3 sisters."

"Wow. That's right. I remember."

"I took good notes."

"You did. I can't believe your wife left you. I would have stayed just for the potatoes."

"She had her reasons. I, too much a dreamer."

"She regrettin' that shit now I know."

"Maybe a li'l bit." He poured her a glass of wine.

"How are your children?"

"Everyone is well. How 'bout yours?"

"Missing me...and their father. Missing home."

"How long are you gonna keep them at your mother's?"

"I don't know. Maybe all year. I don't want them in this semi warzone me and Hiram got goin' on."

"I understand, but it seems so unfair."

"It is. But nothing is fair in love and war."

"You switched that up."

"Yeah. They got that adage wrong."

They continued talking, sharing memories of their fleeting, unconsummated romance, catching up on family, work, books, and projects.

"Let's have our pudding on the sofa," Thaddeus suggested.

"Okay."

They cleared the table together, the clanking dishes were the only sound serenading the silence of their minds, thinking of the infinite possibilities building between them. Thaddeus loaded the dishwasher while Georgette wrapped the leftovers. She ladled healthy servings of banana pudding into two bowls.

"I will finish up and meet you on the sofa."

"Okay," she replied, eyes twinkling and vagina pulsating. After arranging their desserts on the coffee table with a water pitcher and two goblets, she located a soul music channel on the television and set the volume to low.

"Why didn't you just tell alexa?" Thaddeus playfully asked plopping onto the sofa next to her and stretching his arms across its top edge.

"I don't like those things. Too invasive." Nervousness bubbled under her skin as she rested her head on Thaddeus' arm. He made circles on her shoulder with his fingertips. "Thank you so much for dinner. You feedin' me too much." She snuggled closer to him, libidinous anxiety burning up and down her spine.

"You think so?"

"Yes. I know I have gained weight."

"Yeah. You a li'l thicker." He patted her head with his own crown and they smiled simultaneously, watching the LCD slideshow of waterfalls and city skylines.

"I love these pictures."

"And I love you." The depth and sincerity of his baritone rippled in her ear like purple water from a sexual fantasy of two lovers bathing in a paranormal pond. He clutched her waistline and lifted her onto his lap with commanding ease. Her hips spread across his thighs exciting him and he buried his face in her small bosom inhaling the exotic fragrance of her perfume and the vanilla scented hairspray wafting from her auburn weave. He heaved his hot breath on her flesh, the v-neckline of her dress giving him just enough skin to ignite. She liquefied under his passion as he squeezed the ample flesh of her buttocks. He tenderly bit her nipples through the printed fabric. The gentle bite compelled her to arch her back and Thaddeus responded by moving his hands up her graceful torso. He pulled her toward him, and the kissing started. Their tongue play was perfect, in and out, up and down in smooth loving rhythms. She untied her dress, and he rolled the material down to her elbows. She raised her arms out of the dress and wrapped them around her lover. "Ah, Georgette," he hummed in her ear. Her dormant joy was finally erupting into a welcome river of lava, ready to commence the fiery baptism of Thaddeus Kane. They loved each other one thousand and one ways, on the sofa, the floor, and eventually in his bedroom until the wee hours, an overdue healing for her and a much obliged service for him.

2:00 a.m.

"Dammit!" Georgette jolted from a comatose slumber. She checked her phone on the night table and sprung to her feet "It's two a.m."

"And?" Thaddeus said.

"*And?* I'm in your bed. I gotta go."

"No, you don't."

"Yeah. I do. He is already suspicious."

"Did he say something to you?"

"Yes and no. Don't worry about it." She did an inventory of the room. "Your bedroom is really nice. You're such an artist."

"I try."

"Now where are my clothes?"

"Downstairs."

"Seriously?"

"Yeah. You don't remember?"

"I mean I do and I don't."

Thad sat up in the bed. "Damn. That ain't good."

She laughed. "Oh no. I remember all of this." She waved her arms around her body and twirled like a snake. "And all of that!" She plopped next to him rubbing his mild erection.

He chuckled. "Okay. I was about to say, damn. I might need to go see about myself."

"Ohhh, no, my brother. You deliver." She pecked his neck. "Diligently." She kissed his face. "And I thank you."

He kissed her mouth. "You are welcome."

"Okay. I'm gone. Get me a Lyft, please."

"Why don't you just let me take you?"

"No. No way. Just order the Lyft, love."

Thaddeus ordered the Lyft and they went downstairs so she could dress.

"You gon' be alright?"

"Yeah. I am sure he is passed out drunk. As usual. He doesn't even know I am not there."

"Look at my phone." She handed him her cell. "No calls. No texts."

"He might be waitin' you out." He gave the phone back to her.

"Baby, you don't know Hiram Rivers. He is cool and cavalier about a lot, but this ain't one of the lot."

"Okay. If you say so." The Lyft alert dinged on his phone. "Your ride is here. Call me when you get in."

"Okay."

"Call, Gee. Don't text."

"I hear you. I will call." They shared a long goodbye kiss. "Yeah. Maybe I should have married you."

"You know this."

Georgette exited Thaddeus' and jumped in her Lyft. Crispus followed her back to Dominion headquarters and then to the house. He sat and watched the Rivers' residence for about twenty minutes making sure everything was calm. He sent Hiram a text, "Let's meet up soon." Hiram did not respond. "Translation: negro hungover on that Don Julio", Crispus mumbled. He tossed his cell on the passenger seat. "Damn, Georgette." He drove home.

4:00 a.m.

Geronimo poured himself a shot of moonshine, grabbed a gallon of water from his fridge, and pulled out his pipe from the kitchen drawer. He tucked *The*

Vixen Notebook under his arm and made himself comfortable on his couch. He opened the flexi binder and started reading again:

The Vixen Notebook Part 10:
Age Is More Than A Number
I wanted to tell, but they begged me to hold their secrets...
xoxo,
Kendali Grace

Prelude

Hey, Loves. I am giving you my final story and Stacy Capricorn is putting down her pen on these chronicles.

After my father died of a heroin overdose, my mama zoned out for three years. They never married, just loved each other deeply. He worked a good blue collar gig at a chemical plant and she worked as an office manager at the same plant. He had been a careful, conscientious, highly functioning addict, so the overdose devastated her. When she snapped back to reality, I was a blossoming thirteen -year old and she was an insatiable sex addict. All she wanted to do was screw. Too many of her boyfriends trained me to fight and fend off sexual advances. I gave into a few, some because I simply tired of fighting, others because I liked the gifts and attention. There you have it- my baptism as a vixen.

He bought a few of the books on Muse.com and skimmed the pages. Apparently, the same prelude was in every book. An image of Belinda Grace appeared in his mind. So sad, he thought. His notebook pages filled quickly as he correlated the characters to their real life counterparts.

Geronimo had spent all day and all night communing with chief video vixen, Stacy Capricorn, highlighting passages and texting Myesha for clarity. The stories were mind blowing smut, so unreal that you knew it was real. The obscenity of it all repulsed Geronimo. These people only understood debauchery, wanton sex, money, and more sex and more money. They knew nothing of love. Fortunately there were silver linings in the sewer of her experience. One was her relationship with Naomi Proudfoot, which was definitely Toya in real life and another was her boyfriend Tommy which was probably Dre, making his first appearance in book seven. After his studies of the lightweight pornographic tales of the series, Detective Blackfoot concluded that Tasir and Wes were strong suspects. She all but said, if I end up dead, Tasir did it.

Chapter Ten
Taste The Breath Of The Wolf

Friday, 12 Noon

On Fridays, Black Butter hosted lunch for the staff. Usually, Mo would have one of the administrative coordinators order the food for delivery, but today, Maceo wanted to show love to Deucey. He went to the restaurant, talked to Deucey for about an hour, and ordered almost every item on the menu. Driving down Seminole Boulevard, excited about his fish sandwich, he sat anxiously at a red light, bobbing his head to DJ Raphael's latest Chill-Hop Mix #27. Isaac Cole pulled up next to him, in a black corvette, top down.

"Everything alright?" Isaac asked.

Maceo waved deuces at him.

Isaac grinned, mischievously tapping his fingers on his steering wheel. "I mean is everything really alright, cuz your wife is still textin' me." Maceo pushed up to his wheel and mean mugged the scorned taunter, his son and student of the street hustle. He wanted to shoot him, but of course he knew better. Isaac waved his phone at Maceo so he could see Nikki's picture flashing on the display. "See? There she is, calling me. I gotta see what she needs."

"Fuck you, Ike."

"Ha ha ha!" Isaac laughed as he sped away.

Maceo's ears burned with rage. *There is no way Pearl is still dealin' with this nigga!* He peeled down the street, tires screeching, music blasting, driving wildly through the traffic. He swerved into the Black Butter parking lot and leapt from his Escalade, barely putting the truck in park. He left the keys in the ignition and stormed into the building. "Renee, get the lunch from my truck. Set it up for everyone."

"Of course, Mr. Grant." Renee cautiously moved from her desk to the door, avoiding contact with Maceo, the veins of his smooth bald head bulging, pumping blood angrily into his reddening eyes.

Maceo raced upstairs to Nikki's office where he found her talking on the phone and typing on her computer. "Get off the fuckin' phone, Pearl. Right now!"

"Mr. Anderson, I have a client coming in. Let me ring you back later this afternoon. Okay, that's great! Bye for now."

"Nicole Pearl Pennington Grant. I ain't never seriously considered killing you until this moment. This very moment. Please tell me, you are not fuckin' around with Ike. Please, Pearl."

She shuddered at his demands. This was the first time seeing him so enraged. Generally, Maceo was cool crazy. When angry, he managed to express his emotions in a mellow manner. "Mace, you cannot be-"

"Gotdammit, Pearl! Just fuckin tell me the fuckin' truth because I swear to God...Pearl..."

"What are you talkin' about?"

"Nikki, I know you just talked to him. What the fuck you communicatin' with this nigga for?!"

"Huh?" *How the hell does he know this?*

"Isaac pulled up next to me at a red light, wavin' his phone. Your picture on the screen. You callin' him!"

"Maceo, calm down. You jumpin' the gun."

"Don't tell me to calm down! And please, don't mention gun. Don't encourage any ideas, Pearl. Just tell me you fuckin' him. I will burn this whole building down...and everything...and everybody in it!"

"Are you fuckin' for real? Hell no! Not since we got back together. I haven't even seen him."

"But you talkin' to him?"

"Well, yeah."

"The fuck?"

"Only about him coming to get his things. And the legal stuff. Making sure he has all of his books and that Black Pearl...Black Butter is not obligated in anyway. The same process I am doing for everyone who is not renewing contracts."

"Pearl. Pearl. Ahhh." He bounced around, a silly dance. "Whyyy? You want me to go back to prison? Shiiit..."

"I just wish you would calm down."

"Calm down. I am calm. If I wasn't calm, I would have killed that nigga at the red light. Fuck! Why, Pearl?"

"Maceo, we were not together. And you certainly have had your share of ass."

"I have always been straight with you, Nikki. I never cheated on you."

"Yeah, but you had your share in the beginning and while you were locked up. Now don't lie."

"I have always been loyal to you, Pearl. But Isaac? Shit. He was my student. My brother. You need to dead this. Wrap it up immediately, Nikki. I'm trusting you to do that. And no more phone calls. Delegate that shit."

"Mace…"

"Pearl. I'll burn it down, babe. To the ground."

"Argh."

He walked to his office and slammed the door.

2:00 p.m.

Big Bro!

How are you and sis? I miss y'all so much! How are the boys? I hate that I didn't bring baby boy's big wheel. He asks about it every two days. Even so, the kids love it here and so do I. You will have a book from me soon! Give Nikki my love. I Love y'all!!!

Oh, and congrats on Isis. Yes, we know what you are up to over here!

Maceo typed his reply:

Sis!

We miss you too! Yes! Isis is HUGE! I'm glad to hear you are in good spirits. Give my love to the children and of course your father. And send me my books! Godspeed!

I love you.

Humble Peace,

Mace

He welcomed the tranquility that Bree's communication brought, quelling his anger about Nikki and Isaac's shenanigans. "She betta get her mind right," he grumbled.

Tap Tap! Mo knocked on his door.

"C'mon, Mo."

"Can we talk for a few?"

"Yeah. Come. Sit."

"Ummm. I think we should go outside. Or somewhere else."

"Ah, hell. One of those talks?" Maceo tapped his temple. "Yeah. Okay. Anybody here?"

"No. Just us. They are all at the workshop I signed them up for. About contract bidding with the schools."

"You had to send *everybody*?" Maceo questioned her decision with wondering eyes.

"I got this. I'm vetting. They don't even know it's all part of the interview for the new position I am creating."

"Oh yeah? When am I going to hear about this?"

"Just be a CEO. Me and Nikki got this one. You gonna be good with it. Trust!"

"I know. I know." He swiveled his chair to face his credenza and opened his cigar drawer. "Smokes?" he mused, waving the Cuban imports at Monique.

"And drinks?"

"You got it!"

She took the cigars from his hand, swooped an ashtray from his roundtable, and sashayed onto the rear patio of their building. Maceo grabbed a bottle of cognac and two tumblers. He stopped at the kitchen and filled Mo's with ice. She liked ice with everything. Milk on ice. Coffee on ice. Ice on ice, crunching it from her cup throughout the day.

"It is so beautiful out here." Mo received her icy tumbler from her boss, which he filled halfway, then gave her a cigar.

"It is." Maceo sat in the cushy patio chair across from his left hand, his wife being his right. Their feminine covering empowered him, secured him. "We need to work out here. I think I'm gonna start bringing my laptop out here on days like this."

"Yes. I agree." They lit up and puffed. Maceo sipped and smoked while Monique talked. "You know y'all can't come in here fightin' like that. Not a good look. Not good for morale. Some of the staff heard y'all. Do you realize this?"

"I know, Mo. That's usually not my demeanor. But maaan...Nikki Pearl, Nikki Pearl..."

"What is goin' on?"

"She been communicatin' wit' dat nigga Isaac."

"Ssss, eeewww," Monique hissed, dramatizing a painful reaction. "Dammit, Nik."

"Yeah."

"She cheatin'?"

"Nah. Talkin' to him about his books. She still tying up loose ends with Black Pearl."

"Yes. This is necessary."

"Yeah, but I told her she needs to delegate that. She need not talk to him. Let somebody else do that."

"True enough. Even so, you cannot argue in here. Period."

"You right. Say less. I am clear."

"You ever cheated on her?"

"Hell no. That shit is for suckers. Loyalty is everything to me. Now, me and Pearl had our ups and downs. Separations here and there in the beginning. We agreed to see other people. Date. Just keep that shit tight. We would see each other too, but we were free to do our thang. But she fucked around with Isaac while I was in exile. It's been hard for me to get past it. I mean, I raised this nigga. In the streets, he was my son."

"I know. But you gonna have to get past it. Y'all love each other. Move on with the love."

"I know, Mo. But dammit. Ike?"

"Maceo. Charge it to crazy and let it go. She was in a crazy place. Y'all were in a crazy place. Have you ever thought about how distraught she was and what that does to the mind?"

"Well, yeah. I have."

"No, Maceo. I mean, putting yourself in that place. Two children. The absolute love of your life locked up for life. The loneliness. The sleepless nights.

The questions. The fear. All the hauntings. And all the while still making sure you were good. C'mon, Maceo."

"I hear you. Really I do."

"Let it go. Charge it to crazy. And be glad she didn't wind up on drugs or in a strait jacket."

Maceo nodded pensively. "Okay, Monique Ellis. I appreciate your insights, sis. I am gonna let it go. I won't kill her." He chuckled.

Monique frowned at his joke. "Eh hem. On that note, one final time, did you have Kendali killed?"

"Mo! I ain't that nigga. If I wanted to hurt Hiram, I would kill him. Myself. One bullet to the brain. The end. Goodnight. Forever."

"Geronimo is coming to talk to me. I wanna be sure. I wanna be convicted in what I say.

"I know they have me on the list, persons of interest and all that bullshit. But that ain't me. Just tell him the truth."

"You right. Just the truth." She puffed her cigar and flicked ashes in the ashtray.

And they smoked and sipped away the remains of the day.

5:00 p.m.

"I will not take up much of your time. I know you are a busy woman."

"It's okay," Monique assured, closing her office door as Geronimo settled in a chair facing her desk.

"Is your boss here?"

"On a conference call. Do you need him?" She fingered her silky straight locks behind her ears and made herself comfortable in her seat.

"I don't." Geronimo eyed her family photos on the wall behind her. "How long have you been married?"

"Long time. Nineteen years. Been together twenty-one."

"Congratulations to you. That is awesome. I love to see Black love lasting."

"I do too. It's been quite a ride."

"I know it." He tapped his phone and the display lit up. "Talk to me about your bosses. Who is the better boss?"

"Wow. You dig right in. The better boss?"

"Yeah. Talk about them."

"Detective, ask me a question and I will answer."

"Okay. Why did you leave Dominion?"

"It was time to move on."

"That's a nice stock answer."

"It's true. I did all I could do there."

"I have been told you are the only other woman alive that knows Hiram Rivers at least as well as his wife. Maybe even more."

"Maybe."

"Tell me what you know."

"You tell me what you want to know."

"You think he had Kendali killed?"

"What? His cash cow? No way!"

"What makes you so sure?" He set his phone on the edge of her desk.

"Hiram is too greedy for that."

"Greedy?"

"Yes. You tellin' me he is a suspect?"

"Everyone is a suspect."

"Not me."

"Well no. Not you."

"But I thought you all were narrowing this down to the music industry nuts?"

"They are definitely in the running."

"Hmmm."

"Did you know about Hiram's affair with Kendali?"

"Is that why he's a suspect?"

"Surely."

"I guessed they were seeing each other. We all thought so."

"Who is we?"

"Just everyone. In general. Everywhere. Whoever. Some folks thought yes, they were gettin' down. Others thought they weren't."

"But you, you thought yes?"

"Yeah. They were so close. Too close. But kill her? For what?"

"She was involved with other men."

"Uh-huh. Hmmm. Now, hmmm."

"Are you changing your mind?"

"Not exactly. No, I'm not. But that is interesting. You mean other men outside of Dre?"

"Yes. Other than Dre."

"Well, she *was* a video vixen."

"True."

"But Hiram killing her, or having her killed? I can't see it."

"You know she willed all of her royalties to Dominion."

"Whaaat?! No. I didn't know that. Hmmm. Wow. All of them?"

"Every cent. To the chagrin of Belinda Grace."

"I bet. Wow."

"You changin' your mind now?"

"Who knows, detective. I mean ultimately, I don't think so. But Hiram, I mean. I love Hiram. He was very good to me. Very, very good. He will always be special to me. But yes. Hiram is a supreme asshole. And I mean supreme. But he has some truly beautiful qualities too."

"Yeah, okay. And what about your current boss?"

"Maceo? No way."

"He was in prison for murder. And he and Hiram are archrivals. You do know this?"

"Of course I do, but Maceo is from the streets. And he operates by an old school code. Involving other people in his beef with Hiram, that ain't his thing. At all."

"You seem so sure. How long have you known him?"

"Long enough. We have worked in the same circles for the past year or so. But I really know him through Hiram. Maceo is the more positive reflection of Hiram. You see?"

"I do see. So you came to work for Maceo on your own? He didn't steal you from Dominion?"

"No. He didn't even know I had left when I did. We had no conversations prior to my departure. He found out through the grapevine like everybody else."

"Have you considered that the bullet may have *not* been meant for Kendali?"

"Not for Kendali?"

"Yes. Maybe the bullet was for Hiram."

"But a trained assassin is what I heard. Isn't that right?"

"Well, yes."

"Meant for Hiram. Wow. Hmmm." She scratched her head. "You tellin' me much more than I can tell you, detective."

"You've told me plenty, Mrs. Ellis. I am thankful for this palaver." Rising from his chair, he gathered his mobile device and his briefcase. "Be well."

"Good luck, detective." She escorted him to the door. He paused at the threshold, turned, and bowed. She offered a half smile. "This is so devastating for so many of us. I loved Kendali. We need you to find the killer."

"I know. We will bring the murderer to justice. Know this."

Monique watched Detective Blackfoot leave the office wondering what the truth was; it seemed a many 'unsplendored' thing.

7:00 p.m.

As he studied his cluttered peg board diagramming the Kendali murder case, his phone buzzed. He picked up the device and smiled when he saw Toya's name pop up in the notification bar. They had been texting periodically over the past several weeks, Toya constantly declining his dinner invitations.

☐Text Message☐
Toya: Hey, handsome
Geronimo: You owe me dinner
Toya: Just right to your point No greeting?
Geronimo: Greetings! You owe me dinner
Toya: ☐
Geronimo: What's it going to be?
Toya:☐

Geronimo: I understand. I'm not pressuring you. I know you're separated from your husband. Those emotional ties...that bind. I am clear. Most honestly, I just want to get to know you. Your inner woman. You are such a powerful being. I want to be around you.

Toya quivered, reading his words. She was intensely attracted to him but still married and attached to her husband Jamal. She contemplated the experience of Geronimo, swooning as the countless possibilities flipped through her mind. What did she have to lose? They *were* separated, no loyalties needed to be honored. And she was bored with the aftermath of the split, the leftover emotions and the dried-up feelings.

Toya: Okay. Nina's. One hour

Geronimo: Yes. I will see you there.

His soul did somersaults. *Finally*, he thought.

Nina's was unusually quiet for a Friday night and Geronimo was glad. He and Toya would be able to talk and get to know each other. He found a comfortable spot at the bar and stretched his long thick legs to the side of the bar stool. A couple dressed in all black were sitting in a far corner whispering and giggling. Two other patrons nursed their drinks at either end of the bar enjoying the live band. The lead singer of the group belted out jazzy blues lyrics reminiscent of Nina Simone laced with Layla Hathaway's vocal inflections.

"What can I getchu, my man?" the bartender asked.

"Bärenjäger. On the rocks."

"My brother." The bartender admired his choice of spirit.

Geronimo absorbed the ambiance thankful for the day's end but still troubled by Kendali's case. He spent more time in the past week reading her Vixen Notebook which intrigued him. The descriptions of the starring savages, Raul, who was allegedly based on Tasir, and Phil, allegedly based on Wes Gilliam, proved haunting. The appetites of the music industry ranks made him wonder about many of the greats he loved. He imagined himself sorting through his vinyl record collection the way he sorted through clues to a case, creating a list of sexual deviant suspects and pedophile profiles and tossing the evil doers wax compilations onto a pyre.

"Hey, detective." She crept up on him, a welcome interruption from his record burning ceremony.

"Toya, the light of Gabriel." He stood and embraced her, marveling at the thin flowy flower printed sundress that hid her curvaceousness. Sandaled feet, purple polished toes, and the lavender vanilla perfume gave him reason to squeeze a little tighter.

"Yes. It's me." She chuckled at the nickname he had christened her in a conversation. He had begged her one final time to end her cyberspace manhunt and she naturally refused. He told her she was the light of Gabriel, the force of his trumpet's sound, sending out her call to the world. They lingered in the hug, caressing each other with tenderness.

"I am glad to see you." He looked in her eyes. "Is the bar okay? You want a table?"

"No. This is fine."

He motioned for her to sit next to him and they ordered drinks and a variety of appetizers. They chatted as the bartender kept the cocktails and vittles flowing.

"I love that you jog too. We must go together some time."

"We must. I used to jog in Hamer Hill Park. But not since Kendali was killed."

"I can dig that. Knowing the culprit escaped through the park. The arboretum is there." He ate a jalapeno shrimp popper. "Yeah. Too much."

"Way too much. I jog around Mother's Garden now." Toya savored a spicy meatball and gulped water afterward.

"That's a beautiful park. Tucked away."

"Exactly. Away from everything. I do yoga in one of the gazebos from time to time too."

"I do yoga too."

"For real?"

"Yes. Good for centering the chi. In my line of work, this is key."

"So that's how you stay so damn cool."

"Uh-huh. And my grandmother named me Kawoladesgv Waya." His lips curled into a smile showing off his beard, glistening with patchouli oil.

"Kawo? Help me…Kawo-"

"Kawoladesgv Waya. It means 'breath of the wolf'."

"Breath of the wolf," she repeated.

"Yes. The wolf is an animal of precision, instinct, stealth. An animal of great spiritual force. But it is his breath, my grandmother taught, that is the source of his true power."

"Wow. Hmmm." She absorbed the wisdom, mesmerized by his regal omnipresence.

"Yes. My grandmother. She is the light."

"Yes. She is." Toya bit into an avocado egg roll and dabbed her mouth with a napkin. "I don't know many men who do yoga. When I was going to classes, there might be one per session. Maybe. But that's it."

"We out here. As a matter of fact I belong to a group, Yang Yoga. I'm not as active as I used to be. But we here, mastering ourselves."

"I see." An anxious tickle cruised up her spine. His yoga knowledge and practice incited her desire.

"So, let's review."

"Okay."

He pulled a spiral notebook from his briefcase. He flipped through the pages until he landed on his Kendali case annotations. "So, our suspects." He turned a page. "I don't know why I am compelled to share this information with you, but here we go. In no-"

She interrupted, "Because she is my sister. You feel the love I have for her."

"That is accurate. I do feel it." His passions stirred; her demonstration of love's convictions gave him a tremor in his chest. "So," he began, reading from his journal. "I have Tasir, Wes, Hiram-"

"Whoa. Wait. Hiram? I mean Hiram is a beast, but I don't think he killed her."

"You said yourself he can't be trusted."

"That is true." She rotated her eyes toward the ceiling the soft track lighting beamed on her face. The reflection of mocha sunshine invited Geronimo to a next level of honesty.

"Tea, I know Hiram is feeding you intel. Don't let your recent relationship and common love for Kendali cloud your judgement, sweet love."

The 'sweet love' sent a hot wave of lustful wishes up her thighs. "What makes you think Hiram is talking to me?" Her face displayed a cat swallowing the canary expression.

"Hiram is a controller. He is trying to control this investigation. I know he's the one telling you what to post."

She surrendered. "Not everything I post."

"I know. Did you ever consider that he using you to angle the investigation away from him?"

"The thought crossed my mind and crossed right out. I just don't think he would do it."

"Did you know his frat brother Khai was sleeping with Kendali? And she was pregnant with his child?"

"Oh my God! Seriously?"

"Yeah."

"Are you sure?" Her bottom lip dangled around her chin, trying to find a place rest. The news knocked it out of place.

"Unless they were texting each other lies. And the autopsy did indicate pregnancy."

"She was so free giving with that snatch. Goodness, Kendali."

"I guess your informer failed to tell you that?"

"Yeah. He skipped that info."

"So, while he isn't number one on the list, he remains a person of interest. And please don't post anything we discuss."

'I won't. Who else you got?

"We have to throw Khai in as a person interest just because. And Dre. But they are very weak suspects. Motivation and intention is there, but their capability for this level of assassin hire, maybe not."

"Now Dre, maybe not. He has average pockets, but don't sleep on Khai. He makes a nice living with KD's."

"Yeah, but our cursory overview of his finances tell us he is not quite there."

"I see. How much we talkin' to hire such an assassin?"

"Bare minimum- 100K."

"Ahhh, I see."

"Yeah, so they are POI's but further down the list. Now Maceo Grant ranks higher. He has motivation-"

"Geronimo, c'mon. Maceo? Uh-huh. I don't know him, but I know him. Hired guns? Not his style. He is hands on, king of the streets type."

"Yeah, but he was imprisoned for murder and he hates Hiram."

"Right. And his type would go straight for the jugular. He would pop Hiram, one time. Bullet to the temple. Thee end. I think you can scratch him off."

"Yeah, maybe. Time will reveal. Max is still on the list, but not as strong in light of Tasir and Wes. And we gotta include Georgette."

"Georgette? Now you gonna make me cuss, detective. She adored Kendali!"

"I know, but Kendali and Hiram were having an affair. A very intense affair it seems, and I think she knew."

"Well a lotta folks knew, but didn't know. It was always a rumor. But they hid it well. How do you know Georgette knew?"

"She said so."

"She did?"

"She did and she didn't in the same way everybody seems to believe they were having an affair, but because they didn't *see* Hiram and Kendali in public, then it was just a rumor. But a rumor is an unconfirmed truth."

"Yeah. I get it. But no. I am goin' with Tasir, Wes, and Max a strong possible."

"No doubt. And that Vixen Notebook is definitely revelational. I can see why they don't want it released." He closed his journal and savored the honey liquor glowing in the tumbler.

"You been reading her series?"

"Yeah. Been skimming here and there, but I dug in deep last night. That final installment, whoo!"

"You have a copy?"

"Of course. This is a criminal investigation."

"Wow. I haven't even seen it. Dominion is very secretive with her books."

"Yeah. I see why." He swallowed the last of his elixir. "And I paid a visit to Myesha Morgan. Of course, she is happy to give me all the details."

"Well, that's Ms. M-Squared for you. You know she all about the dish."

"Yes, she is. Now. More importantly. What are we all about? What are we gonna do about us?"

"Us?"

"Yeah. You need what I have. And I want to give it to you."

"Oh really? What do I need?"

"A deep spiritual massage. You are long overdue."

In her mind, Toya readied herself to receive the gifts of Geronimo Blackfoot, but she played a lame game of hard to get for a few more minutes, the two of them going back and forth about her needs and his desire to fulfill them. "Yeah. It's been over six months."

"That is so unnecessary. Get what you need. Life is too short. And you are too fine a woman to be out here wanting for what is around you in abundance. Why starve yourself in the Garden of Eden?" She swooned as his forthright poetic mandates danced around her aura.

"Hmmm…"

"Come with me. Be my Eve. Let me take care of you."

"Okay, Adam." Toya sent a quick text to her mother, telling her she would be late and to make sure her daughter went to bed no later than 11 p.m.

They left Nina's and she followed him to his house. After about five minutes of settling in, he undressed her and bathed them both in vanilla lavender bubbles honoring her sister Kendali. Toya cried as the aroma filled her spirit. Geronimo kissed her tears, one by one as they meandered down her cheeks. His large powerful hands, deeply caressing her biceps and elbows as he pecked away her pain, stirred more tears. She cried harder, the teardrops increasing in size as the purgation intensified. Her legs tightened around his body. The water sang a sad song, splashing sounds inspired by her stored-up melancholy. He encircled his neck with her arms. "Hold me tight." He pressed her legs into his flesh and nodded. She returned the affirmative gesture and he stood up, steadying himself, raising the both of them from the baptismal pool. He carried her to his bed where he oiled and massaged her body, taking his time with every iota of delicious cocoa brown flesh as soft jazz played in honor of

Toya's rebirth. "Oh Geronimo," she murmured between touches that instantaneously healed her most broken places. "Thank you, brother. You are the sweetest...most righteous..."

"I am honored to be chosen, love." He kissed her back and she arched in response; the ambrosia dripping from her restored treasure chest made a gushing sound. His manhood rose, thickened and elongated to its full limits, corresponding with her melody. After showering her with kisses from head to toe, he ate the ambrosia of her ever-giving fruit and gave her what she needed, in waves of fast and slow divine carnality until the dawn.

Chapter Eleven
Maximized Tension

Saturday, Break Of Dawn

"What da fuck?" After waking to a silhouette sitting ominously on his man cave couch, Hiram scrambled to his feet from his pallet of purple comforters, the makeshift bed of a disconsolate pauper. He rushed to his desk to get his .45, keeping his eye on the motionless shadow watching him. He rummaged through the top drawer; his gun was gone.

The shadow announced, "I relieved you of your weaponry."

"Max?" Hiram angled his groggy head toward the dark figure.

"Hiram, I come in peace. I want to talk. That's all."

"Peace? Nigga, is you for real?" He crossed his arms.

Max sat still as a mannequin. "I am."

Hiram turned the track lights on low illuming Max's face. "Talk."

"I did not kill Kendali. I love her. More than I can express. Cliché, but words get in the way. I adored her. I-"

"Okay, okay, okay. I get it. You loved her." Hiram pushed his hands against the air shoving Max's sentiments back to him.

"No, I said love. Present tense. My love for her is burning, an eternal flame. Never ending…"

"Right, Right." Hiram straightened his posture, a difficult task as he was hungover from last night's communing with The Don J. "But why did you run? You should have stayed. Talked with the police and cleared your name."

"I guess I could have, but they would have tried to nail me for it, just because of…because of…just…how I love her."

Hiram reached for his bottle of Don Julio from the floor. "You mean your little shrine?"

"How do you know?"

"C'mon, man. You know I got my people on this case. You were not the only one that loved her." He sipped from the bottle.

"Love, present tense. For me. And you didn't love her. You used her."

"Don't tell me I didn't love her! I did love her!" He pounded Max's statements with his tequila flask in one hand and his other, a balled fist beating the atmosphere between them.

"If you say so. I just want you know. To know that I didn't kill her."

"I know. I don't think that you did. The police don't think so now either. You are still a person of interest, but a weaker suspect."

"How do you know all of this?"

"I told you. I am dedicated to bringing her killer to justice. My people are on this."

"Typical. You have to control everything."

"Not everything. Clearly. Or she would still be alive." Hiram leaned on the edge of his desk. His eyes watered as he placed the tequila on a coaster behind him. "Your envelopes...did you keep copies? Who else has the intel?"

"No need to keep copies. I am sure you have tidied up with all the recipients. I didn't send to anyone other than those that served a purpose in my plan. But none of that matters anymore."

"So, I don't have worry about any Myesha Morgan types popping up with an exposé?"

"No. That's over. The envelopes are no longer relevant and your secrets, I have discarded from my mind."

"Hmph."

"Well, Mr. Know-It-All. That's all I have. You won't hear from me again." He rose and walked toward the terrace door. He stopped and looked at Hiram. "And stop drinking. It won't bring her back and it is a repulsive display of your self-centered, self-absorbed demons. Get a more dignified way to mourn."

"Yeah, yeah. Fuck you. Nobody can tell anybody how to mourn."

"Okay. Fuck me." Max turned to leave.

"Wait. You aren't going to talk to the police? Clear your name?"

He looked back at the alcoholic publisher. "No. What for? The only woman I will ever love is dead. I have a bigger responsibility to her now. I have a mission. Maxmillian Gray is dead too. Someone else is being born."

Hiram, befuddled by his statement, watched the equally mournful man, walk down the cul-de-sac onto the main street and disappear into the sunrise.

7:30 a.m.

Georgette spoke quickly to the hostesses as she whizzed past them into the main dining room of KD's, eager to get a big breakfast takeout box from their Saturday Sunrise Buffet. She waved at Khai who was standing behind the bar talking to his bar manager. She wondered if people noticed her Sweet Kane sugar afterglow; Thaddeus had been regularly blowing her back all the way out, pushing her internal sunshine from the base of her spine to the top of her head fashioning an orgasmic halo. She felt girlishly giddy as she approached the omelet chef and placed her order. One everything omelet for Hiram and one turkey, spinach, and feta omelet for her. She never ate omelets. Her breakfast usually consisted of granola, yogurt, and a green drink, but Thaddeus changed that with their regular fuck-me-feed-me shenanigans. Patting her belly, she chuckled to herself thinking of the strawberry shortcake he fed her in the aftermath of last night's love session.

"Mrs. Rivers." The omelet chef gave her two big black shopping bags filled with takeout trays.

"Everything is in here?"

"Yes, ma'am. All the fixings. All the trimmings. Waffles, sausage, grits, and toast"

"Thanks so much." She dropped a twenty-dollar bill in the tip vase, emblazoned with KD's logo, hearing Khai in her head with his diatribe about tipping. *"I made the money to start this business on tips. And a lot of these bougie kneegrows won't even give my people a tip. All that money they got and they too damn cheap to share. Damn! Give a brother a five, preferably a twenty, and stop being so damn stingy."*

"Thank you, Mrs. Rivers." She smiled at the egg master and headed for the exit. Khai stopped her with a gentle touch on her forearm.

"I'm surprised to see you here."

"What? What are you talking about?"

"You ain't hugging me? You were gonna leave and not say anything?" He held her hand.

Georgette didn't want anyone too close to her halo, arousing their suspicions. She just wanted to get home and shower. While she wished she could have Thad's aromatics waft off her aura indefinitely, she still had a husband, children, and a circle to respect and protect. "I waved when I came in, but why are you surprised to see me? I know you haven't been here the last few times I have picked up food for your frat." She slid her hand from his grasp slowly.

"Yeah. Busy behind the scenes."

"Why are you surprised I'm here, Khai?"

"I guess Hiram didn't tell you?"

"Tell me what?"

"Ask him. I am not the one to tell you."

"My goodness. I am so sick of all of y'all. Everybody. Jeezus."

"Just ask your husband."

"Fine, Khai." She raised her breakfast bag. "On my tab?"

"Of course."

"Enjoy your day."

"You too."

8:00 a.m.

"I'm surprised to see you up." Georgette arrived home and entered the kitchen where Hiram sat in the breakfast nook drinking coffee.

"Yeah. I needed coffee."

"That hungover, huh?" She quietly grieved his living death. "What's goin' on between you and Khai?"

"Nothin'. That's KD's?"

"Of course. What do you mean nothin'?" Georgette sat the shopping bags on the counter.

"Nothin' means nothin'. Why are you askin' me this?"

"He said he was surprised to see me. And that I should ask you what's goin' on with y'all."

"Nothin' is goin' on. You know I have been here."

"Exactly! And that's the fuckin' problem! You been here and nowhere else! In your self-imposed prison."

"That's not totally true."

"Argh!" Georgette stomped back and forth along the length of the main countertop. "What the fuck?! I am so muthafuckin' *sick* of your muthafuckin' ass."

"Whoa. Hold on. Why are you talking to me like that?"

"Why in the fuck do you think? It's the same half conversation we have been having for too many weeks. Me asking questions that you don't answer and you making irrelevant small talk. I am tired of your fuckin' ass. This 'bout to be an Al Green hot grits episode."

He stumbled to his feet. The warm coffee coupled with her hot porridge threat sobered him. "You need to chill. Don't pull up on me like that."

"I can pull up on you however I want at this point. This shit has gone on long enough. You not workin'. You not eatin' Just drinkin'. You haven't seen your children. It's time for you to come back to life. To get back on your throne."

"Look. One day at a time, Gee. I will be back full throttle sooner than you think. I've been goin' to Isis meetings. I have been doin' a lot more. I set us up with Isis."

"Yeah, but there is work to do. They want *The Vixen Notebook* to be the launch release."

"I know this."

"Well, you with it?"

"I told Mustafa you would decide."

"Ha!" She wrung her hands, spinning her wedding band on her finger, the ring a little tighter these days. "We can't even decide on a cover. The creative team is so disagreeable on this project. Everybody is so fuckin' crazy. I am over refereeing the book cover battle."

"Well, Kendali *was* murdered, Georgette. Emotions are running high."

"I know. I know." She observed her husband taking in her watery eyes and sad countenance; his mouth curved downward, lips lost in his untamed goatee and burgeoning beard. "This is a tragedy of epic proportions." She pressed her buttocks against the counter. "I brought the mock-ups home. You need to look at them. One side wants a photo on the cover. The other side wants the cover to look like a high school girls notebook. Aye."

"I will look at them." He noticed her dress, office attire unusual for a Saturday morning. "Wait. Are you just gettin' home?"

"Don't change the subject. Stick to the matter at hand. These covers. This release. Our children. Our work. Isis. The launch."

"I said I will look at the damn covers."

"When? And when for everything else? Our children. Our work. When, Hiram?"

"I know. Everything is good. I will handle it. I will handle everything."

"Handle it how? The same way you handled her?"

"Handled who?"

"Hiram, you think I don't know what's goin' on? This kind of mourning is not for a protégé. This kind of anguish is for a lover."

"What? Georgette-"

"Hiram. Stop. Let's just clear the air."

"Clear what air? There is nothing to clear."

"Hiram, you were fuckin' her. Tell the fuckin' truth. Just fuckin' admit it." She pushed herself from the counter and shifted her weight to one side, hand on her hip.

"Gee, let's just leave this alone."

"Fuuuck that! I left it alone long enough. Get honest gotdammit! You were fuckin' Kendali. Admit it!"

He looked into her eyes and then turned to walk away.

"Hiram, if you walk away from me...you are...I swear to God, I-"

He stopped and turned around to face her. "Georgette, don't do this. Focus on our empire. Nothing else matters. Only us."

"Sweet Jesus, man!" Hands squeezing the counter, she roared, "Hiram gotdamn Rivers..."

His body quaked violently, her relentlessness overpowering him. "Fine! I was fuckin' Kendali. Okay? Yes! I was fuckin' her! Dammit! Yes! There you have it."

"I knew it. Everybody knew it. But I took your lying word for it. When I asked you, you told me, no."

"Well, my answer may have been true when you asked."

"You asshole." She held her forehead in her palm, clicking her teeth with rage. "You cavalier, cold son of a bitch. Are you playin' with me? It may have been *true*?"

"No, I'm not playin'. I may not have…Gee, look…"

She raised her hand at him, a gesture requesting his silence. "You make me sick, Hiram Rivers." A coolness came over her. "You are such a low life. I fuckin knew it." She lowered her voice a notch above a whisper. "I am so fuckin' dumb. Just a fuckin idiot."

"Gee, stop. You are not. It had nothin' to do with you. You know I love you."

"Our love is not the subject. At least not for me. *You were in love with her.*" She shook her head, auburn locks smacking her face. "Fuck you, Hiram."

"Is this why you are still wearing this weave? And puttin' on weight?"

"Puttin' on weight?" Thaddeus' healing buffets accompanied by his soothing smile and love spun hands appeared in her mind's eye, relaxing her a skosh more.

"Yeah. I take notes. I'm watchin'. You think I'm just a full-fledged alcoholic, drunk and oblivious. But I'm watchin'. Just like, I know you just gettin' home."

"Stick to the subject, nigga. We talkin' about you screwin' that bitch."

"Are you still wearing this hair because I was seein' Kendali?" She flashed an angry glare. "If it is, Gee, you need to stop." He walked closer to her. She stepped away from him, leaning on the counter again. "Yeah. I notice all the fat plates you bringing home. You are eating all kinds of stuff you don't eat. You haven't had a green drink in weeks."

"Oh, you clockin' my movements like that?! You liked it on that fat bitch!" Her rage returned.

"Oh my God. God forgive her." He raised his arms to the ceiling. "How can you speak ill of the dead?"

"Because she's fuckin' *dead*. It doesn't matter. Jeezus! Here you are protecting your precious Kendali. The bitch is dead and gone and you are still…"

"You are horrible for that!"

"*I'm* horrible? Me?"

"Yes. You are talkin' crazy."

"I'm crazy and horrible but I believed you and trusted you. Treated this bitch like a sister. Trusted her. Gave unto her. Mentored her. Loved her. And she, in return, fucks my husband. And *I'm* horrible? Okay." She picked up her purse and work bag and turned to go upstairs.

Hiram shrunk under the weight of her words, suspended in the despair of a truth that she screamed like a human bull horn. "Gee, I love you. It had nothing to do with us. Or my love for you. Nothing at all. I'm sorry, baby."

"It's cool. I get it. Once a video hoe...always a video hoe. And what guy doesn't love the video vixen?" She walked upstairs to the bedroom, lay across the bed, and thought about his apology. He never apologized to anyone for anything. Maybe he was changing for the better. A series of revelations about their lives encircled her mind. Heavy-hearted with the countless outcome possibilities of their current episode, she cried herself to sleep.

12 Noon

"I got your favorite." He dangled the bright yellow bag in front of her beaming round face full of delight.

"You always know how to get right to the center of my soul." She grabbed the bag of Swedish fish from his hand and kissed him all over his face smacking him with loud, noisy kisses and clutching his neck tightly. She pulled him inside the suite, and he followed excitedly, like a sixteen-year-old boy preparing for his first dose of trim. He adored her womanly power to keep everything between them anew with her vivacity and carefree attitude.

As she groped him, they stumbled to the bed. "Kenni, wait. Girl." He giggled and she kept pecking him on his cheeks and chin. "Girl, you are crazy."

She bounced back onto the fluffy comforter, naked, juicy thighs, belly, and breasts, shimmering with vanilla coconut oil laced with that intoxicating lavender she loved and he loved even more. "Yeah, crazy for you."

He stripped off his clothes and dove into her ambrosial curvaceousness. "And me for you," he replied pushing his rock hard steel into her volcanic slushiness. He explored the cool heat of her loving hollow, biting her neck as she swerved her hips into his thrusts. "Oooo, Kenni. Baby. Why? Why, Kenni? Don't you know I love you? Why did you die on me, girl? Why?"

His buzzing phone attempted to interrupt their melody making but they kept improvising the jazz of a sweet, sticky escapade. Bzzz. Bzzz. He kept up his thrust; she maintained her swerve.

"You don't wanna answer?"

"Fuck the phone, baby." He dug deeper into her core and he felt her lava bubbling, ready to combust.

"Hiram...honey. Mmmm, yes. I miss you so much." Bzzz. Bzzz. "Honey, oh, baby."

"Yeah, that's right. Gimme that juice." He burrowed into her back with his fingers on her spine and his long stroke on her A spot. "Give it to me, Kenni. Right now. Give it up, girl. Give it the fuck up! Give me what I want. All of it. You juicy mutha-" Bzzz. Bzzz.

Hiram leapt from his dream, his boxers soaked. "Shit." He rolled over on his purple palette and picked up his phone to multiple text messages from Crispus. He responded.

⬜Text Message⬜

Crispus: When we gettin' up
Crispus: You in there with the Don J. You got to come off of that
Crispus: Hit me back. Let me catch you up
Hiram: Man your timing is right on.
Crispus: What's up
Hiram: Nothing. It's time we catch up. You right. Mall lot?
Crispus: That's cool. I'm close by
Hiram: Good. Gimme 30.
Crispus: See you in 30.

12:45 p.m.

Crispus was eating a sandwich when Hiram pulled up and hopped in the passenger seat.

"My man," Crispus said as he gave him pound.

"What's goin' on? I know you good, cuz you eatin'."

"You know it. And I had breakfast at your homeboy's this mornin'."

Hiram grimaced. "Oh yeah?"

"Yeah. What's goin' on with y'all?" Crispus asked as he pulled a manila folder from his visor and placed it on his lap.

"What do you mean?"

"Yo, Hiram. I'm a detective. C'mon, bruh. Humor me. What's goin' on?"

Hiram stared out the window watching the Saturday shoppers moving around the parking lot. Some driving up and dropping off loved ones. Some parking their vehicles and strolling leisurely into the shops. And others being served lunch in the sidewalk cafe of the food court.

"We just don't see each other so much since Kendali was killed."

"And why is that?"

"I mean I just been in my own funk. You know this."

"Yeah, but why are you and Khai estranged? Or so it seems."

Hiram swung his head around and barreled his piercing eyes into the fixer's pupils. "He was fuckin' her." Venom dripped from his words as he froze his gaze on the investigator, waiting for his reaction.

"Fuckin' her?"

"Yeah. He was fuckin' Kendali."

"Damn." Eyes swirling in his head and landing on the center console in sad surprise, he murmured, "Wow." *Should I postpone this Georgette and Thad conversation*, he pondered.

"Yeah. So I ain't got a whole lot to say to Mr. Draper these days."

"I guess not. But did he know about y'all? You kept it real close to the vest."

"Yeah the nigga knew. He is the only person I ever talked to about Kendali. The only one." Hiram banged his fist into his palm. "Every time I think about...maaan..."

"I know, bruh. I know." Crispus looked to the high noon sun for answers. He wanted to end the conversation without revealing the affair. This seemed to be too much to heap upon, even Hiram's haughty head. "Look. If you wanna catch up another time-"

"What?! C'mon, Cee. Gimme whatchu got. I already know anyway. She fuckin' ain't she?"

155

"Yeah."

"Who is it?"

Crispus hesitated, tapping the manila folder packed with notes of Georgette's indiscretions. Hiram pressed him. "Man. You betta go 'head. I'm listening."

"Thaddeus. Thaddeus Kane." He dropped the folder in Hiram's lap.

Hiram gave it back, smacking him in his chest with it. "I don't need it." He scoffed, smiling sardonically, a toothy sinister grin. "I will be fuckin' damned. Thaddeus muthafuckin' Kane." He laughed loudly, almost screaming. "Ahhh. I knew it though. Wow. Thaddeus Kane. And she know this nigga can't stand me."

"Does she know about you and Kendali?"

"Damn. Your detecting ass. We just had it out about Kendali. She forced me to admit it. The affair."

"Forced *you*?"

"Yeah *me*. She *is* my wife. You play chess, Cee, so you know. The queen goes where she wants and does what she wants and the king is relegated to not even a two-step. His one step groove is all he's got."

"True enough. Just hard to see anybody forcing you to do anything." Crispus chortled at the impossibility. "What do you wanna do about this? I mean you know Chris Rock say she gets a free fuck card and she been gettin' hers stamped regularly by Thaddeus."

"Yeah. Uh-huh. I'ma handle it. You just keep tabs on her."

"Think before you act, bruh. You been on that sauce so I don't trust you."

"Trust me; you can trust me. I ain't that sauced up. I got it. Everything is under control."

"Alright then."

"We will get up again soon." They dapped each other up.

"Alright, Hiram. Lay off the Don."

"I will. Sooner than later." Hiram exited the car and jumped in his Range Rover, feeling renewed and ready to return to his throne. *These muthafuckas got me mixed up.*

9:00 p.m.

Numbed by pain and drunken with confusion, sadness, and honey whiskey, he knelt before his sacred prie dieu, set up in a new abode far away from searching eyes, but close enough to those who owed their blood to the debt issued by the last breath of The Amazing One. His eyes welling with tears, his heart pounded deafening throbs as he gathered his thoughts. "How dare the police make me a suspect," he growled. "Forthwith, there is no turning back. I accept this mission and I will execute with sincerest conviction. I am dedicated to its end, until the end." At the crossroads of his new birth, he was humble and determined. The living needed protection and the fallen needed vengeance, for they shared a common enemy, and now, a common protector.

"I will avenge your slaughter, my beloved Grace. I will be forgiving in justice but lack mercy in compensation." He wept for several minutes while lighting lavender vanilla candles and inhaling the intoxicating smoke of frankincense. Her life sized poster came alive for him. He touched the paper feeling the flesh of her arms and thighs under his fingertips. He closed his eyes and immersed himself in a vision where he tasted her soft cheek, buried his face in her fragrant auburn locks, and sunk his manhood into her succulent peach. An erection was upon him. "Oh, Kendali!" he bewailed. "You were too good for this world! They defiled you! Why, Sweet Grace? Why did you..." He wiped his tears with a purple handkerchief and dug his hand in a crystal candy dish filled with Swedish fish. He sucked and chewed the candy, pacifying himself until his weeping subsided. "You needn't be here in this madness. You did not belong here!" He stroked his hardness. "I will avenge the wrongs inflicted upon the innocents, all of them. Their families. The ones you sought to free and heal with your loving heart. And those still lost, I will find and free, for thee." His voice boomed from a fierce and fiery storm within his soul. "I hereby forsake the world, for my dear Grace." He reached for the pearlized bone handled tribal knife that belonged to his father. He breathed deeply and began cutting, slicing one long opening along his left side and then one long opening on his right side. "You are my Isis, resurrecting me, birthing me into Osiris, the Grand Supreme Sword Wielding Warrior of The Cosmos. You heal me. You purify me. You sanctify my soul for the sake of our mission, the mission for The Greater Good. I am born again, more powerful, more loving, more daring, more forceful. The Invincible One, I am. Because Of You. I will scorch the earth, ridding our sacred planet of all evil, of all wickedness. All of those that defile thee. That ravage thee. They will pay their debts and their generations will be snuffed out, destroyed eternally. And LOVE, the Love that sparked you, the Love that sparked me, the Love that is the center of our galaxy will be restored forevermore. With Grace."

Chapter Twelve
Brother After Brother After Brother...

Monday, Break Of Dawn

"I'm so sorry."

"You don't need to apologize. And don't feel sad. I'm okay here. It's beautiful."

"I'm so angry, sis. I wish we had known each other better. I cry too much. You didn't deserve this."

"Butterfly, it's okay. I lived the life I was supposed to live."

"But snuffed out, Kendali?"

"Yeah, but Karma spins her wheel. And it was my turn." She pointed at the bullet hole in her chest, dried blood flaking onto her white sundress. *"You see this? I didn't even feel it. Just a sting and a pop! Poof! And I was gone."*

"Yeah, but who killed you? Who killed you?"

White, gargantuan, feathery angel wings with purple streaks at the tips, appeared from behind her back, rustling in the breeze of an unnamed netherworld. The angel butterfly raised her arms and lifted her body from where she stood. She hovered two feet off the ground and waved her wings; silvery dust sprinkled the air between them. Her soft brown curls swirled around her cherubim face and her eyes glimmered a kaleidoscope of violet, indigo, white, and pearl.

"Wait! Kendali! Who killed you?"

"It doesn't matter. The evil doers cannot help themselves especially when you stand for good. It was a nasty business, but I loved the music. I sing in the choir here."

"Wow. Really?" Lesli clapped her hands joyfully and then inquired, *"But, who did it, sis? Who killed you?"*

"It doesn't matter, Butterfly. I'm happy now. Go flutter. The world needs the soft, beautiful power of butterflies. Bye, bye, Lesli Love."

"Wait, sis! Wait!" Kendali flew away, leaving a trail of purple tipped feathers floating around her pen sister.

Lesli tossed and turned, her arms and legs flapping around like a butterfly attempting its first flight from the cocoon. Her body jerked up and down as she moaned incoherently, waking her fiancé.

He wiped the perspiration beading at the edges of her hair. "Fly. Babe. C'mon. Wake up, babe." He stroked her cheek and squeezed her hand gently pulling her back to the earth realm. She threw her head back and forth, side to side, in slow motion. As her puffy coils brushed the navy blue satin sheets, they made a silky sound.

"Mmmm…Mmmm…Www-ait…Ken…Kenda…li…"

"Fly, c'mon." He kissed her forehead, shook her torso softly, and brought her body close to his bronze, sinewy nakedness.

She slammed her head into his chest, thrusting herself from dream world. "Ahhh."

"It's okay. I gotchu." Rocking her affectionately, he sang. "Girl, you know I love you. No matter what you do. And I, hope you understand me…"

"Oh, T. Why did this happen? Why, T?" Her tears dripped onto his chest.

"I don't know, Fly. But you are gonna be okay. *We* are gonna be okay. Let's sleep at my house this week. You seem to sleep better there."

"Okay," she whimpered.

He finished the song, "…and every word I say is true…cuz I love you…"

Titus' rendition of Lenny Williams' classic lulled her into a more peaceful rest for a little while until the delightful aroma of sausage, eggs, and waffles aroused her from slumber.

"Have your breakfast, love. I'm gonna take off." Titus nuzzled her nose with his fingers and pecked her earlobe.

She blinked open her eyes and smiled at his professional attire-navy blue linen cotton blend suit, with a light blue shirt and navy Docksiders. Her smile grew wider as she admired the tray table he set up at her desk on the far end of the bedroom. "I am the luckiest woman in the world." She gave him a loud lip smack on his face and caressed the back of his neck. They stared at each other; love's sincerity dictated the tender moment.

"You make me blush, Fly." His cheeks rose up to his eyes and his teeth sparkled at her fresh face.

"Yesss! Blush on, brutha!" She kissed him again and released her hold on his neck. "I love you, Titus Dixon."

"And I love you, Mrs. Dixon." They sealed their exchange with more kisses. "Eat, Fly. I will see you later."

"Definitely! And I am extra hungry. These damn dreams are exhausting."

He walked to the bedroom door and stopped. "Well, at least they are not as often. You gotta let it go, Fly. I know it is devastating, but we gotta release the bad. Keep the good. That's all."

" I know, babe." She sat up on the bed. "I know. Take care of the kiddies, Mr. Math Teacher."

"You know it. Bye, babe."

"Bye."

Lesli slid into her bedroom slippers and beamed along with the sunlight filling her loft townhouse. "Joy *does* come in the morning," she said. Her future husband was correct; it was time to let it go. She was ready for the dreams to cease. Kendali killed in front of them was soul shattering enough but people blaming her for the murder and shaming her for writing three-star reviews of Kendali's work shook her deep inside her wings. As she washed her face in the bathroom sink, she cleansed the fearful, guilty thoughts heaped upon her by the sorrowful followers of Kendali Grace, international bestselling author of the award-winning Vixen Notebook series. While she brushed her teeth, she scrubbed away the evil words and angry diatribes of all the fans, friends, and foes within their ranks. After finishing her wash up, the lovingly prepared breakfast smelled more inviting and positive thoughts of Isis Comm and her empowerment books took the helm of her mind.

She powered on her computer, prayed over her food, and began to eat. Savoring the homemade blueberry waffle dripping with syrup, she scrolled Zing and took notes for her next post and blog entry. All of her Zing posts and Mahogany Magazine blogs were the same these days; whatever she posted on Zing was the same thing she posted on her blog. Prior to Kendali's death, they varied. No more. Her rule of thumb for writing was simple and succinct communication. She easily adopted her new regulation having tired of the ebb and tide of the post tragedy mayhem. She finished her vittles, showered, dressed in a purple Puma sweat suit with matching kicks, of course, and returned to her desk to post her commentary before leaving for the office. Thankfully, Meade Comm was an office abuzz with the hum of new beginnings and great works. It was time to manifest her divine destiny and celebrate the festival of accomplishment.

☐Zing The Kaleidoscope☐

Butterfly Brooks (Lesli Lyn) (post):

Beloved Butterflies☐☐
I greet you in silky, soft-winged peace and the spirit of the angel butterflies especially Kendali Grace.

All the rumors are true! Isis Communications is real! The brothers and sisters have come together and created a multimedia publishing conglomerate ordained by The Most High Divine. You have never seen anything like this before. Isis is historical, the first completely Black owned multimedia corporation that publishes books, music, and film. Isis is the only place for everything artistically motivational, inspirational and BLACK! Tune in with Mustafa Akeem on Planet Radio for his daily podcast Osiris Rising at 8 p.m., as he takes you on the final leg of an extraordinary journey to the culmination of an ancient Love story, the Isis-Osiris mystery materializing right here on earth in the literary world. And in the words of my beloved brother, Mustafa: We Back To Black!

Reactions: 1,208 Comments: 365 Shares: 2,461
(Load previous comments)

Gloria Jenkins: OMG! I have been seeing the ads. I love them!
Shannon Gee: Yaaaaaaaas! Finally! I am so excited for everybody. Back to Black☐☐
Asa Banks: That's what's all the way up☐☐💯
Black Sunshine: I love that you named it Isis☐
Natalie Bates: This is awesome! ☐☐We in there!
Athena Black: ☐☐ Yes yes yall!☐
Butterfly Brooks: @Athena Black Oh sis, you gonna get a call super soon! Your expertise is required☐☐✔☐
Athena Black: Looking forward, Ms. Butterfly☐
Phoenix Ash: So dope! This is what's needed. I love it

Fonte Stanford: Now how Muse reacting to this? Y'all tighten up. Protect ya neck!

Butterfly Brooks: Yes, brother. They are on it! Check out Bradford's editorial in our most recent Mahogany Magazine issue.☐

Fonte Stanford: Will do, sis. Back To Black!☐☐

And then she wrote…

☐Zing The Kaleidoscope☐

Butterfly Brooks (Lesli Lyn) (post): I had nothing to do with this murder. I write critiques on a whole lot of authors and they are all still living and selling a whole lot of books in spite of my constructive critique. If you honestly think one bullet straight through the heart was executed by some delusional fan of mine or Bree McDee's or anybody else of our ilk, YOU ARE DELUSIONAL!!!!!!!

Reactions: 400 Comments: 127 Shares: 360
(Load previous comments)

Tanika Thomas: Girl. Don't listen to these fools. They stooopid!☐
Gina Hayes-Fife: We love you. We know better. Just waiting for you to drop that empowerment book! I know it's going to be the bomb! ☐☐☐And on Kendali, God rest her soul. I just wish everybody was nicer.
Vanessa Peyton: ooooo☐ I am waiting too! You betta flutter, Butterfly!
@Gina Hayes-Fife: What do you mean nicer? You trying to say something about Kendali?
Deena Deen: ☐You certainly didn't help with all that critiquing as you call it. Ms. hyper critical.☐ RIH Kendali G!☐☐ @Gina Hayes-Fife: Yeah, you saying what about Kendali?☐
Gina Hayes-Fife: I am not trying to say anything. I am saying that there was so much ugliness surrounding her, this book business, other authors, publishers, the fighting. And she was in that nasty music industry. I am saying everybody's hands are dirty. No one is innocent, least of all Kendali, God rest her soul.
Deena Deen: Wayment! Wayment! You tryna say she deserved to die?!

163

Gina Hayes-Fife: I am not saying that at all! That is not for me to say. I leave that to those who do really feel that way. She had her share of enemies, clearly. She is dead. Killed. Murdered. So…I am just saying, I hope we can all learn from this, from her tragic death. Everyone needs to be kinder to each other, including Kendali. She could have been more thoughtful, kinder. That's all.

Odessa Williams: @ Gina Hayes-Fife WORD!!!!!! I agree!

Kathy Kay: Yeah probably not a help. BB goes in. Sometimes too much. ijs

Akilah Butterfly: But she izzzzz a Butterfly and that's what we do! □□Certainly, there is a conspiracy much bigger than some damn book reviews that has an author dead. C'mon people! Stop it already! And yes, B Fly Brooks! Drop that book!□□□

Butterfly Brooks (Lesli Lyn) @Akilah Butterfly: Sooooon, Butterfly. Real soon! I am hugging your wings□ □#WingTaps Thank y'all so much!□

Calvin Spriggs: 💯on that, sis! Y'all tripping. Stop puttin that out there, on BB. Stay true, Ma!

Butterfly Brooks(Lesli Lyn) @Calvin Spriggs: □□□□

Her seven-minute walk to Meade Comm refreshed her with new vigor and motivation. She felt empowered, elevated, and enlightened. The birds sang an ancient song as they roosted atop the one-hundred-year-old oaks standing royally on the sidewalks of the townhouse landscape of downtown Seminole City, a song ringing in her head like ancestor-speak, "Oooo chile, trouble don't last always." Upon arrival, she made her prayers in Meade Comm's pagoda and entered the building, feeling the force of the dragon door handles for the first time in many weeks.

"Good morning, Sam! The official bright-eyed and bushy tailed one!"

"Well, hel-lowww, Lesli Lyn-Lyn! You sound like the Lesli Lyn I know."

"Yes, Sam. It's a new day."

"Yes it is, Butterfly."

"I am a butterfly. I have lived several lives these past few weeks and now this new life, I am living with a new design."

"You betta, girl."

"Yes. I am in full acceptance of all that The Most High has in store for me and all the love and life lessons I am learning even inside great tragedy. It is well with my soul."

"So righteously stated, L-Double. Just like your Zing posts! Always bullseye, baby! Right between the eyes."

"Awww, Sam. You love me too much."

Sam giggled and blew Lesli a kiss as she stepped onto the elevator. "And I am gonna love you more, Butterfly."

Lesli returned the high-flying kiss just as the elevator doors closed.

It was 10 a. m., and the upper chamber of the building was still, quiet with the first round of real work getting done. Lesli skipped greeting any of her co-workers and made a smooth beeline for her corporate sanctum.

She immediately kicked off her purple suede Pumas, dropped her bags next to her desk, and logged onto her computer. Diving into her task list, three hours flew by without her noticing, until Bradford's daily show up. She was admiring her book cover when he popped in.

"L-Double." Brad appeared in her doorway.

"Yes, Mr. Meade." She gave him a comedic salute.

He followed suit. "As you were." He sat across from her and she continued typing. "You look a lot better today. Brighter."

"I am letting go. And letting God."

"And that is the best practice. Trouble don't last always and this too shall pass. All the elder wisdom applies."

"So true." Lesli smiled at Brad unwittingly confirming the ancestral song that whispered their heavenly promise to her on the way to work. "How are you faring, brother? Charlene still aggravated with the security detail?"

"You know it, but she just gon' be aggravated. I am not playing with these Muse assholes."

"Are they still making their so called offers?"

"No. They stopped. I think our editorial did the trick. Combined with the social media buzz about it. That's one thing Zing and the other social platforms are good for."

"I told you, Brad. It is all about how we use a thing."

"You are right, Empress Butterfly. I think the Muse issue is subsiding for now. There will be more to come when we take a bite out of their sales, but we are prepared for it."

"Yes, we are!"

"Your empowerment books, they are going to be the headlining nonfiction releases exclusively available on Isis. Alongside Kendali's final Vixen Notebook as the headlining fiction release."

"For real?"

"Yes, for real."

Lesli teared up at the news of debuting next to Kendali. "This is the best news. It is so on time! My day is made." She swirled around two times in her office chair like a child enjoying her favorite carnival ride and stopped abruptly to face Brad. She stared at him in the eyes, released a long excited cackle and banged her fists on her desk in a concomitant rhythm. "And I am so in love with my cover!"

"Good! I am glad to make your day, sis. And yes, your cover is fly. Just like you." He stood, caressed her fist, and left.

She couldn't wait to tell Titus. She sent him a text.

☐Text Message☐

Fly: T! Guess what!☐

My Hero-T: What?☐

Fly: My empowerment series is the headlining release for the Isis launch for nonfiction and Kendali's final Vixen Notebook is the headlining release for fiction! Headliners! Side by side with my sister butterfly in heaven!☐☐☐☐

My Hero-T: Yes, Fly! Congrats, babe.☐I Love You! ☐I told you, everything is gonna work out.

Fly: Yes, it is. I love you, Mr. Dixon. My hero!☐

My Hero-T: Yes, Mrs. Dixon☐

And then she made her Zing appearance, using Zing as a thing.

☐Zing The Kaleidoscope☐

Butterfly Brooks (Lesli Lyn) (post):

Beloved Butterflies☐

I greet you in silky, soft-winged peace and the light of Love❤

Question: What is going on with these bad covers?

Distorted images, illegible fonts, misspellings, incorrect punctuation, and even watermarks are appearing on these covers. And I am talking all kinds of authors and all kinds of genres inside so called urban fiction. Top sellers, mid sellers, and no sellers are doing this. So now y'all not gon' edit the damn covers?

You are out of control and out of line, good people. Get right or get left! The day of this disrespectful sacrilege is ending! Roll out or get rolled over!

#ReadersRebel #ReaderRevolution

This is the BB. I am silky, soft, and signing off. Float On. Especially Kendali Grace Butterfly.☐☐☐☐

Reactions: 563 Comments: 592 Shares: 764

(Load previous comments)

Amber Alise: Gurrrrrrrl☐

Akilah Butterfly: I am a reader and I am rebelling.☐☐☐☐

Zenobia Jones: As an author, I feel embarrassed when I see this. I wish they would just go away. Muse has no standards. They should reject more of this junk.

Troy Wright: Yeah. It's bad.

Candice Dodd: I guess they just trying to figure it out.

April Thomas: Well figure it out on your own time, not on my mind. I stopped reading books from some publishers because of this. Hey, Butterfly☐

Butterfly Brooks (Lesli Lyn): @April Thomas Hey, Supah Star☐I am glad you fluttered thru.

April Thomas: @Butterfly Brooks (Lesli Lyn) ☐

2:00 p.m.

"…And in the words of my beloved brother, Mustafa: We Back To Black!" Mustafa read the words of Lesli's Zing post out loud. "My sista!" He smiled and pumped a fist. His ringtone sounded Stevie Wonder's Master Blaster. It was Bradford.

"Big B! What's goin' on, my man?"

"You, big brother. How are things goin' for us?"

"You know we are completely on track. Everything moving forward with very few challenges and very few kinks. All praises to The Creator."

"Yes. Amen, brother." Bradford walked to his office window to absorb the vibrations of the pagoda garden. "I just gave Lesli the good news about her headlining the Isis launch."

"Right on. I just finished reading her Zing post about Isis. She is a gem of a butterfly."

"She is."

"Is she excited?"

"You know it. Especially since she will headline alongside Kendali. You know that murder took her down. Clipped her wings, man."

"Yeah. That goes for all of us. May Kendali be at peace. You heard anything about the investigation lately?" Mustafa sorted through a stack of paperwork on his desk.

"No more than what everyone is talking about. They have about four suspects in the music industry. I heard Hiram, Maceo, and Georgette have been questioned. And rumors abound about Hiram being the target. I heard Dominion gets all her publishing rights."

"Yeah. I heard all that too. We have seen Hiram in action. You never know." Mustafa thought about Hiram's suspected sabotage of Thaddeus' TV show.

"We sure don't. It's like Brother Malcolm said, 'I don't trust myself.'" Brad popped a breath mint in his mouth.

"Word. That Max dude still seems to be a likely culprit."

"Yeah," Brad concurred. "Sometimes it is the obvious. They say dude was crazy for her. He looked like he had 'snap out' proclivities."

"He definitely got some issues."

"No doubt."

"What's going on with Muse? Still harassing?"

"Nah," Brad answered. "It's quiet for now. I still got security for the family. Nobody else heard from them?"

"No more than usual. You know they been on Hiram's ass for a minute. Wanting him to do a merger. But we know what that means."

"Yeah. Run through you like a two-dollar trick. That's all they know. Pure savages."

"Deep in their souls. But we ready for 'em."

"Yes, we are." Brad lifted his head victoriously, loving the sun-drenched sky raining light onto the beauty below.

Mustafa's phone beeped. "That's Georgette, bruh. Ready to finalize some things on the Kendali piece. They keep her stuff on some covert type time over there at Dominion."

"Yeah, I heard. Alright, Mustafa. Handle our business. I appreciate you. Make it a great night."

"True indeed. We will catch up. Peace."

"Peace."

Mustafa answered Georgette's call. "Hey, sista. How is your day goin'?"

"It's goin'. How are things at our new home, Queen Isis?"

"All is well. Going smoothly. Give thanks to the ancestors."

"Yes. Yes." She sipped her green drink. "Well, everything's a go for Kendali's Vixen Notebook except for the cover. Our creative team is at odds which rarely happens, but tensions are high since Kendali was killed. You understand?"

The anxious melancholy in her voice was apparent. "Of course I do. I know this is the one transfer we are handling CEO to CEO because it is a tragic delicate situation. I'm clear, sista. No worries."

"Good. I thank you, Mustafa."

"And I thank you, Georgette. You and Hiram joining us means so much to all of us."

"And the inclusion means even more to us."

"Alright then. I look forward to wrapping this up shortly. The launch gala logistics are being finalized. Ms. Toni G got us covered."

"She is the best. We are going to have a blast! In the name of Kendali. In the name of love."

"Absolutely."

"Alright, Brother Akeem. I am back to work."

"Have a good evening, sista."
"Thanks. You too."

3:00 p.m.

Arranging his files proved a more daunting task than he anticipated. Mustafa rang his assistant. "Camille, I am gonna take you up on that offer."

"I'll be right in, boss." She entered his office, scooped up the pile of paperwork and dropped her shoulders, giving him a chastising head shake. "I told you, Mr. Akeem. You gotta delegate. Stop being so persnickety."

"You are correct, sista love. I am learning."

"I got this. You go and do CEO stuff. You need to review the reports of your department heads. And the agenda for next month's financial meeting with Mr. Green."

"You are right. Aminah and my former assistant used to tell me this constantly."

"It's time you listened."

"I got it!"

She left and he loaded his department reports. As he scrolled through the presentations, his phone buzzed repeatedly; notifications popped up in rapid succession. "Whoa. I guess I need to get used to being more in demand too." There were several texts from Hiram and Maceo.

▢Text Message▢

Hiram: Hey brutha.
Hiram: You in?
Mustafa: Hiram. My main man. What's up? I'm here. Working.
Hiram: Working of course. Need to talk.
Mustafa: Come thru
Hiram: En route. Five minutes away.
Mustafa: See you when arrive

▢Text Message▢

Maceo: What's happenin' Mustafa?

Maceo: need to swing thru.

Maceo: I have some things for you.

Maceo: Need to hand deliver.

Mustafa: Maceo! Hand deliver? Word? Bring it!

Maceo: Cool. I will see you in about an hour. You will be in your office?

Mustafa: You know it. All work, no play. I am a dull boy.

Maceo: Hardly dull

Mustafa: lol. I will see you when you arrive. Peace

Maceo: One

Mustafa managed to read through half of a presentation by the time Camille alerted him to Hiram's arrival.

"Mr. Rivers is here to see you Brother Akeem," she said into the Bluetooth headset sitting in her ear.

"Send him in, sista."

She disconnected the call. "Go right in, Mr. Rivers."

"Thanks, baby girl." Camille blushed at the words floating from his lips adorned by five o'clock shadow.

Mustafa complimented Hiram's afro, making patting gestures around his own head. "Man, you joining the Black power ranks I see." Mustafa gestured for Hiram to sit on the lounge sofa by a window while he eased into an armchair facing his colleague.

"Ha ha, man. Not intentionally. But it seems so. The women love this hair." Hiram rested his arm on the back edge of the sofa.

"They do. The lion has a mane. It's our mark of beauty. Like the beard, mustache, goatee."

"Apparently. When I do go out, they stay in my face. Lovin' it. Georgette hates it."

"Well, she will come around."

"I don't know. It may not matter to her. Which is what I want to talk to you about."

"What? You need Aminah to talk to her? She loves Aminah it seems."

"She does. But no, bruh. That's not it."

"Oh, yeah. You ready to tour the headquarters? You haven't yet."

"No, but I will. Some other time."

"Alright." Mustafa chortled at his failure to figure the reason for Hiram's visit. "You talk. I'm listening."

"Right to the point. You know that's where I live." His voice lowered an octave, and he inclined his upper body toward Mustafa. "In order to keep the peace and because I know Isis is bigger than any of us, especially me. I am asking you to talk to Thaddeus. I need you to reason with him. And tell him for the sake of the greater good, to stop seeing my wife."

"Seeing?" Mustafa gradually sat up, his locks dangling forward about his shoulders. "What do you mean seeing?"

"Ya' boy is fuckin' my wife."

"Git da fuck outta here?! No way." Mustafa dropped his foot on the floor and shifted his body forward. He placed his fists on his thighs.

"Yeah. He is. Now the old Hiram would have just stepped to him, straight up. Or had him handled, served up. But the new Hiram wants peace, love and understanding. Because for real, I ain't even really mad about it." He slapped the arm of the sofa. "I mean I am, but I understand it. Georgette needs what she needs. She has endured a lotta my bullshit. But this setup is bad for business."

"You damn right it's bad for business. Are you sure they fuckin'? I mean *sure sure*?" Mustafa crossed his legs and folded his arms. His eyes narrowed and he beamed in on Hiram's countenance.

"You forget why you asked me to join the team? Security. Recall?"

"Well, yeah." Mustafa lifted his arms and crossed them behind his head, cradling his anger.

"So, yes. I know for sure. My people have been following her. Confirmed my suspicions." He stroked his beard. Its oils sent a calming flavor into his nostrils. "Like I said, I'm enraged, but I ain't mad. I get it. But I need Thaddeus

172

to check himself if we all gonna be working together. Isis is most important. I wanna move forward without incidence or consequence."

"Look, akh. I got it. I will take care of it."

"That's all I need to hear." Hiram stood and Mustafa followed suit. They shook hands and embraced. "Alright, brother. You keep working. We will catch up soon."

"Definitely."

Hiram left the office and Mustafa returned to his desk. *Thad. Nigga. Have you lost your fuckin' mind?!* He texted his comrade.

🖤 Text Message 🖤

Mustafa: Good day, Thad. Wyd
Thad: Ain't nuthin' Working on your book
Mustafa: Good. Let's meet later. You up for some one on one?
Thad: You reading my mind.
Mustafa: Bomb Body. 7pm?
Thad: I'm there
Mustafa: Peace
Thad: One

The financial department's pleasing presentation and report eased his mind. The numbers were better than he expected. Expenditures were lower than projected and potential profits were higher than initially calculated. He chuckled to himself. "We still underestimate the Black dollar." He winked at the original oil on canvas of Malik El Hajj Shabazz. "One day, baba. We will get it one day real soon."

4: 30 p.m.

Maceo observed Hiram leaving Isis headquarters, cruising past him as he collected his thoughts and his leather portfolio before meeting with Mustafa. "I wonder why he here?" He sighed with his eyes closed thinking about his love-hate relationship with Hiram. He forgave him but he still could not forget

Hiram's nature. "We are who we are," he preached to himself. More importantly, Nikki was right- he could not forgive him for hurting Bree. Bree was family and mistake or not, for that, Hiram was better off dead.

Walking to the entrance he enjoyed the view of the building in all of its rehabilitated glory. The natural brick had been restored to a rich crimson with an amber sparkle. The mirrored rectangular windows reflected the beauty of Hamer Hill Park's southern edge, still verdantly beautiful in spite of its new tragic history. Three tiers of white marble steps glistened a regal welcome to all visitors, flanked by red, black, green, and gold painted lion and lioness statues on each side, Isis and Osiris, redeemed and resurrected to their rightful thrones. He waltzed through the double glass doors etched with the goddess logo, Isis Communications, One Vision, One Purpose, One Love. After taking the elevator to the third floor, Camille greeted him with her soul sister charms.

"Brother Grant! Good to see you."

"Good to see you, Camille. Lovely as always."

"Awww, thanks so much."

"Mustafa is expecting me."

"He is. You can go right in."

"Thanks, love."

Maceo found Mustafa buried deep in thought, thumbing through a binder of presentations and scrolling his computer.

"Akh! Brother!" Mustafa gave Maceo a bear hug and dapped him as they unlocked their embrace.

"I am glad you had time today, Mr. CEO of the only completely Black owned and operated multimedia publishing conglomerate, books, music, *and* film."

"Maaan. You know this is *all* of us. All of our doing."

"Yeah, but you had the force, to force it. And I'm so glad you did."

"Me too, Mace. Me too." Mustafa motioned for Maceo to take a seat and parlay in the lounge area of his office. "You want anything? Water? Snacks?"

"Nah. I'm cool, bruh." Maceo placed his portfolio on the coffee table and pulled out a flash drive. "This is all of Isaac Cole's books." He slid a thin packet of papers next to the drive. "And this is a contract that turns all of his books over to Black Butta. All rights, royalties, everything. In perpetuity."

"Say what?"

"Yes. He doesn't want the books and nothing to do with the books."

"What? I thought his books sold fairly well, right? Or are they duds?"

"Nah. No duds here. I mean they ain't million sellers, but they earn a living on Muse. About 75 K a year. Sometimes more." He stretched his legs and pushed back in the armchair.

"Is he crazy? He don't want none of that cheddar?"

"No cheddar. Just a Pearl is all he wanted. So now, yes. He crazy."

"A pearl?"

"Yes, *my* Pearl."

"Aw shit. It's like that? Poor Ike."

"Well, he is far from poor. Ike made out big time in the streets. Really, for him, the books was just a way to get next to my wife."

"Ahhh. I see."

"Yeah. So, he all broke up. This is his dramatic finale. For real, I don't give a fuck. He just knows he gotta stay away from Nikki. Thou shalt not cast Pearl before swine."

"Maaan…" Mustafa chortled.

"Pun intended." Maceo winked. "We won't see or hear much from him anymore."

Mustafa shook his head. "Man! What is goin' on today?"

"What do you mean?"

"Hiram just left here with similar woes. Well, let me just…"

"What's goin' on with Hiram? He always bringing some bullshit."

"It's not really him. I don't even wanna say. But I will tell you. Just between us."

"You know that, bro." Maceo thumped his heart two times with a peace sign.

"Thaddeus is seeing Georgette."

"Whoa-ho! Ha ha ha! I don't blame her."

"Damn, man. You ain't got no sympathy?"

"Hell no."

"I thought y'all were cool now."

"We are. I just know what he is. Regardless of all his tears and his epiphanies and revelations. Hiram is an asshole. Period. And he roughed up baby sis."

"Yeah. I remember you telling me about the incident with Bree. That was some bullshit."

"Kill worthy."

"No doubt," Mustafa concurred. "Leave the women out of men folks business. That's what my granddaddy taught."

"Precisely."

"So you think the rumors are true? The bullet was for him?"

Maceo's expression turned stern and stoic, concrete chocolate. "I can't speak on that."

Mustafa noted Maceo's change in mood. Questions, answers, speculations, conclusions, and second guesses flooded his mind. "Okay. Can't speak. Okay."

"Bruh. The police jive interrogated me about the murder. So, I don't talk about it."

"Word? You a suspect?"

"Everybody's a suspect. That's how this works when they have no idea and no evidence."

"True. I gotcha." Mustafa went to his fridge and grabbed two bottles of water and returned to the sofa. The two men hydrated their conversation. "No worries here, bruh. We gotcha back. Ain't no railroading goin' on. Fuck that. Not on this watch. Osiris has risen." Mustafa raised his water bottle.

Maceo toasted his comrade. "By the power of Isis."

"Indeed."

7:00 p.m.

Monday nights at Bomb Body Fitness were generally slow. Mustafa relaxed on the bench of one of the outdoor courts. Twilight still shone brightly in spite of the LED flood lights. Watching the sun pass his torch to the moon, he thought of the empire he and his brothers were building. He smiled and patted his chest, feeling his heart patter a festive beat. He ambled over to a nearby tree and poured libations, whispering gratitude to the ancestors with his head pressed into the bark and his eyes studying the grassy earth under his feet. All was wonderfully well in his world and he was thankful. Thad's voice concluded the ritual.

"Mustafa! Bro!"

Mustafa turned around to see his friend standing next to the bench where he had arranged his belongings.

"Blessings, brother." He waved and walked to the court where Thaddeus was prepping to play, stuffing his jacket in his duffle bag and lacing his sneakers.

"You fuckin' Georgette Rivers?" Mustafa rested his fists on his hips staring Thaddeus square in the eye, his own right eyelid twitching slightly.

"Damn, you jumped right in with both feet, yeah?"

"Uh yeah. We have come too far with Isis for any fuck-ups, especially not some where you stick your dick bullshit, yo."

"Whoa, whoa, wait up." Thaddeus swerved his body around so that he and Mustafa were toe to toe. In full defensive posture, he towered over his publisher by six inches.

"Look, Thad. You are my brother and I love you. And you know I respect you. But c'mon, akh. We can't do this. You gotta end this thing."

"Maaan, check it. She was mine *first*." He slapped his chest. "She should have been *my* woman. So fuck Hiram. He doesn't appreciate her anyway."

"I am no fan of Hiram Rivers. But he has come around. And we have to let bygones be bygones. He brings a lot to Isis."

"Bro, I ain't tryna hold up progress, wreck what you are building. And I hear ya' bygones, but you betta watch that muthafucka. He is not to be trusted." He placed his hand on Mustafa's shoulder.

"I gotcha. And it's we, bruh. What *we* are building. What *we* are building, bruh."

"Right. I'm just sayin'. I will not stop seeing Georgette. She is gonna have to tell me that. Not you. Not Hiram. Not Jesus. Nobody."

"Bruh, I get it, but…"

"No, but's akh. I'm not gonna stop until she says stop."

"What about Isis? Can we all be at a meeting with you fucking his wife? Meetings, events, roundtables?"

"I can step back from Isis."

"Step back?" Mustafa sat on the bench and arched his neck, eyes to the sky.

"Mustafa, I am just an author. You don't need me like that. I am more a silent advisor anyway." Thaddeus picked up the basketball next to Mustafa's feet.

"Yeah, bruh. But I just-"

"Man, I am always here. Always here for you and with you. I am here for Isis. For all of it."

"Damn. It's like that with you and Georgette?"

"I don't know what it's like. I just know I dig her. I been diggin' her and ain't nobody, least of all her jive ass husband gonna tell me to stop seein' her. It's the man principle."

"Alright, bruh. Just be careful with this."

"I know he mad about it, but I ain't got nuthin' to do with that. Those are his feelings."

"Well, he is and he isn't. Believe it or not, he is actually real cool-headed about it. He gets it. He understands Georgette. So he' s not really mad, but like you said, the man principle is in play."

"I get it. He just gonna have to deal with it. I stay outta his way. He stay outta mine. It's all on her. Georgette gets to pick and I'ma roll with it."

"Yes, Isis dictates. The pick and roll. Ha ha." Mustafa jumped up from the bench feeling invigorated.

Thaddeus bounced the ball to him and he caught it. "Yes, she does. Always. And on that note, let's ball."

9:00 p.m.

"I think I like us having separate houses." Nikki curled up under Maceo on the fluffy bearskin rug spread out in front of the TV. The lush moonlight beaming through the warehouse windows drenched the living room in a warm, sensuous glow. They had been watching movies, playing video games, and eating snacks.

"Oh you do, do you?"

"I like you and the boys having your masculine space. Where the boys can be boys. That's the only reason."

"It betta be the only reason." Maceo smacked her hip and snuggled her into his side.

"You know that, Mace. One thing that's always held true; we love being around each other."

"No doubt. You my nigga wit' a betta figga."

Nikki giggled at her husband's comment. "And you my favorite chick wit' the good dick."

"Ahhh, ha ha! Pearl, you crazy." He kissed her forehead. "I can't believe you just beat me in Minecraft. Who taught you? Cam?"

"No, Canaan. Cameron thinks he's too good to teach anybody."

"Yeah. He thinks everything he knows is top secret. Dat' boy is stingy with the info."

"He is."

"That's your son."

"Now, he my son?"

"You know it."

She playfully punched him in his side. "I am over the moon that y'all are setting up a royalty account for Isaac's children."

"Yeah. It's only right. Nigga ain't thinkin' straight right now."

"No, he's not."

"I can't blame him. You are a Black Pearl. Exquisite. Rare. Precious. To have you in his grasp and you slip away..."

"Awww, honey."

"It's true. I could almost feel sorry for dude if he wasn't such an asshole."

"Honey, you are the sweetest. Making sure the children will get the royalties in spite of how you feel about Isaac." She played with his fingers and fondled his palm.

"Not even sweet, Pearl. Just right."

"Right," she sang and kissed his left cheek, sitting up next to him. "And sweet." She held his face and kissed his right cheek.

"You are such a luscious, delicious fantasy, Pearl." He sucked her bottom lip. "Poor Ike."

"Mmmm. Yeah, poor Isaac." She closed her eyes and returned his suckling affections. Her legs encircled him easily as she mounted his lap. Her robe dropped open, mocha medallions atop black coffee teardrop breasts kindled his inner desire. He stretched his mouth wide, ravenously attempting to devour her entire fruit. "Ah, Mace!" she squealed in pain filled delight. "Honey." She gripped his flexing biceps tilting her head back, relishing every second of his feeding.

"Yes, Pearl," he whispered. He pressed his fingers into her spine massaging her flesh vigorously. "My chocolate milk...tastes...so good."

"Ooooo, honey. I love you so much, Maceo."

"Yes, you do, luscious. Show me, baby." He bounced backward against the edge of the sofa and laid his head on the cushions, his neck fully exposed for her taking. And like a predatory lioness she attacked his Adam's apple lovingly licking and sucking his Black skin causing him to tremble. She bit the tops of his shoulders slowly nibbling her way to his ears and all around his neckline.

"Nikki. Ooo, Nikki." His erection thumped between her thighs as her carnal cocktail trickled down the shaft. "You so ready," he hummed into her ear.

"I am."

"I love you, Pearl." He pushed into her intoxicating canal, already drunk from the funk of her wetness.

"Yes, you do, Mace."

"Shhh," he ordered. "I need the silence. Just the soul of your succulence…." Her juiciness lulled him into a poetic space. "You are my Great Goddess, Nut, The Ever Black Of All. Mmmm…" Their balanced even stroking made his thrust more powerful. "My Magic Goddess of Majestic Midnights. You are The Isis, The Iridescent One. I am Your Osiris, The Omniscient One." For a longtime, they made love in the quietude of their souls binding together and as they slowly arrived at the peak of their orgasmic ecstasy, he issued his final mandate. "Pearl, never, ever desert me again. Ever. We are forever. For always. The Great Divine Supreme Eternal Infinite." One teardrop fell from his eye onto her cheek, opening the floodgates of her emotions. The waters that flowed from them were no longer guilty, angry rivers of past transgressions, choking fears, and poisoning regrets. This was a regenerating, redemptive christening of their two souls into a deeper, higher, stronger love. Amen.   Ameen.   Ashe.   Ah-Ho.

Chapter Thirteen
It's More Than A Notebook

Wednesday, 12 Noon

Georgette's fling with Thaddeus challenged the sovereignty of Hiram's ego, pride, and emotions. Though he understood why his wife would step out on him, he wasn't particularly fond of her choice to do such. Even so, he afforded her a pass due to his own transgressions. "This nigga is fucking my wife who ain't even fucking me. Damn, Gee."

He mumbled as he grit his teeth while images of his naked wife frolicking with his Isis colleague live-streamed through his head without escape. Sharing the table of a rising media conglomerate with Thaddeus proved a double edged sword. While the one bloody, cutting edge was obvious, the other edge was a disguised blessing-Mustafa as a voice of clarity and reason keeping the peace. If not for Brother Akeem, he knew the irrevocable outcomes of his actions and reactions would have been life-altering. As he dressed to go to Nina's, his phone rang.

"Detective. What can I do for you?"

"Mr. Rivers, good day. I have a bracelet for you. If you can meet someplace, I would like to give it to you."

"Oh wow. That's alright, brother. I appreciate that." Hiram was moved by Geronimo's remembrance of him and the amulet. "I'm actually headed to Nina's. Can you meet me there?"

"Surely," the detective returned. "Thirty minutes?"

"Thirty it is."

Pulling into the parking lot of Nina's, Geronimo observed Hiram at the bar, stirring his drink. His hunter's eyes need not search too hard to see the mogul's brokenness; his rounded shoulders softened his posture and his eyes glowered with sadness. Once inside, they approached each other and shook hands. The detective handed Hiram a small wooden box.

"From grandmother's hands to yours, good brother."

"That's a beautiful move, detective. What do I owe you?"

"Nothing at all," Geronimo said as he raised his hands. "It's a tribal gift, but I would like to ask you a few more questions, if I may."

Hiram gestured for the detective to have a seat as he responded, "Sure. Would you like a drink?"

"Nah. They don't have my particular brand in stock. Besides that, I'm on the clock. Thank you, though."

Hiram opened the box as Detective Blackfoot sat next to him. "In stock? What's your drink?"

Geronimo laughed. "Moonshine, brother. Mountain distilled."

"Ah, yes. Indigenous spirits." Hiram removed the bracelet and put it on his wrist. "This is perfect, detective. Thank you." He admired the arm piece and grinned with delight.

Geronimo was warmed by Hiram's happiness, but not swayed in his investigation. "So, Mr. Rivers."

"Yes, detective. How can I help you further with the investigation?"

Geronimo removed his phone from his briefcase and scrolled to his notes. He wasted no time getting to his most important question for the famous publisher. "Mr. Rivers, have you ever considered the bullet may have been meant for you?"

"I heard the word on the street. It is definitely plausible. A lot of folks don't care for my brand of passion. Determination. It comes with the territory." He guzzled the last of his cranberry juice. "Braxton!" he bellowed for the bartender's attention. He shook his glass in his direction. "More lime this time."

"Yes, sir, Mr. Rivers."

"So, yeah, detective. It could have been for me."

"Who wants to kill you?"

He roared with laughter. "Every damn body! Ha ha ha!"

"What about your wife?"

"Oh absolutely! She always wants me dead." He danced in his chair bouncing to the beat of the band, laughing to keep from crying.

"You think your wife wanted to kill you?"

"I am saying everybody wants me dead. Are you listening to me, Geronimo?"

"I am. I am."

"Now would she hire someone to kill me, probably not. I imagine she would want the joy of watching me die all to herself. Ha-ha!" He drummed the bar with the palm of his hands. Geronimo listened attentively as Hiram shared his most sober thoughts on the situation. "Yeah. My baby, Gee. Mama to my children, co-founder of my dreams. I told you, detective. Max. Those music industry people. That's a dirty bunch. Tour that rabbit hole."

"We are. I just want to feel where you are on you being the possible target."

"Well, that's where I'm at. It is highly possible. Those assholes are worried about that final book. And they should be. With the current state of crackdown in our country, our little book will pique the interests of many. Many authorities. People who have the power to enact justice, like yourself, detective. Our caped crusaders."

"Yes, true enough. True enough. We are studying the music industry folks, definitely. Without a doubt." Geronimo pushed away from the bar and replaced his cell phone in his briefcase. "What about Maceo? And Khai?"

"Like I said to you before detective. We never know what's in the hearts and minds of men, or women."

"Indeed, my brother. Indeed."

4:00 p.m.

After having a few vittles at Nina's and chatting with Hiram about life, liberty, and the pursuit of happiness, he returned home and laid out all of his notes and evidence on his work table. Georgette and Hiram fed his suspicion just as much as anyone else including Dre, Khai, Max, Tasir, Wes, The Eisenbergs. And deep down, as far-fetched as it may have been, he could not completely discount the social media mob rule that accused Lesli Lyn and Bree McDee. Did Bree really leave on a sabbatical? And their fans were so...fanatical. Twas possible a crazed fan had her killed. Unlikely, but still possible. Geronimo reflected on his second interview with the publishing mogul, making special notes about his peculiarities. Hiram was undoubtedly trying to control the investigation. "What are you trying to hide? Why are you so involved, Mr.

Rivers?" Geronimo mumbled his train of thought as he reached for his glass of moonshine.

Geronimo sat on the floor and perused the pages of evidence that lay before him. It was as if Kendali Grace had sacrificed herself so that her book of truth would come to light. She didn't have to mention any suspects or transgressors by name, for one knew exactly who these people were had they been fans of The Myesha Morgan Show. Thus far, The Vixen Notebook had been an enthralling read, but it was equally tormenting. His stomach turned as he continued his investigation into the pages of Kendali's unpublished tell-all weapon, pages filled with the debauchery of Tasir, Wes, the Eisenberg brothers and many others. "Anyone could've killed her," he said as he scratched his head. The motives, the shapes, sizes, colors, and numbers of his cast of suspects ticked in his head like the stock market ticker. His soul ignited a fire inside him, a flame seeking vengeance for all the fragile spirits crushed under the evil weight of these demons she so eloquently revealed.

So much was loud and clear to him with so much more being inaudible. He listened to what the pictures were saying; what the videos conveyed; what witnesses shared; what the evidence was trying to make plain. The Wolf sensed that he was missing something, that he needed more. In a moment of mental tension and emotional frustration, his psyche called out for comfort and ease. Toya's passionately feminine voice reverberated in his head. His phone rang. It was Chief Dempsey.

"Chief Dempsey. How goes it?"

"It's going, Wolf. Rather, now, it's gone. I don't know how to tell you this."

"Tell me what, Chief?"

The leader of Seminole City's police force could find no easy way to communicate to the news. "You have to back away from the Grace investigation, particularly along the lines of Tasir Samaan."

"What? Wait. Don't tell me. Fed shit?"

"Yeah, Wolf. Feds. Tasir is their puppy and apparently they've caught wind of the murder investigation. So...we gotta drop it."

"I'm so sick and tired of this bureaucratic and political bullshit!" the detective spat with fury. "Do you have ANY idea of what I've invested in this? And I'm sure that I will have someone dead to rights on the murder soon."

"I believe you, Wolf, but this is out of our hands. And if it's any consolation, the feds are highly impressed with your skillset and your reputation. So much so that they've invited you out with them tonight. As a courtesy."

"Invited me? Invited me to what?"

"To see them take down Tasir tonight. You interested?"

Geronimo laughed at the insult. "Is that supposed to be an extended courtesy, Chief?"

"Damned right it is. Take it, Wolf. Go see 'em nab that diabolical piece of shit, but this investigation is over for us."

The detective huffed. "Chief, this is bullshit. I mean, I don't even know if I really like Tasir for the murder. There are other suspects, and how did the feds narrow it down to just him? Wes left town in a hurry and some of my other suspects could very well wear the murder. I'm not feeling this. At all."

Chief Dempsey exhaled his displeasure with the outcome of the investigation. He didn't particularly like the idea that his top grade detective had spent numerous man hours on an investigation that he now had to surrender to the FBI. "Look. The Hoover boys not only like Samaan for the Grace murder, but they love him for it. Their evidence is apparently rock-solid. He had his own murder squad. There are sex crimes. Narcotics. Racketeering. Trafficking. Public animal number one. Let them deal with it from here. If I had known, or even had a clue, we wouldn't have touched it, but here we are, Wolf. Not the ending we wanted, but one that's outta our hands. Great detective work though."

Shaking his head in disappointment, Geronimo took in the praise as he tossed the pictures that he held atop the footstool next to him. "Well, if nothing else, I'm going to watch them arrest his ass. I want him to know that I was on to him too. Shit. Maybe I'll even dress up for the occasion."

The chief laughed. "Dress up as the executioner. They're staging outside his home in two hours. I'll let them know that you're on the way."

8:00 p.m.

The Oasis, Tasir Samaan's estate, beheld a completely different air at night. The full moon and the colorful decorative lighting cast from different angles, gave the mansion and its surrounding acreage an eerie haunted quality. As the detective neared the gate, he could see where the FBI had staged personnel and equipment for the night's takedown. He parked, exited his car, and approached a group of agents who were standing next to a tactical vehicle checking their gear.

Geronimo flashed his badge. "Detective Blackfoot. I'm looking for Agent Bartholomew."

"That would be me," replied one of the only two women in the group. She was tying her locks into a ponytail. "Erica Bartholomew," she continued with an extended hand. "I'm the agent in charge. Your reputation precedes you, detective. You solved some phenomenal cases."

"Thank you, Agent Bartholomew."

She laughed as she held up her hand. "Please, detective. Either Erica or Bart is fine."

"Okay, Erica. And thank you for allowing me along with you on this raid and arrest. I had no idea you all were looking at this guy."

"Yeah. It was hush-hush. Under the radar. Didn't want any leaks, so we monitored him and any law enforcement agency who had him in their scope. When you got too close, we had to move in, especially since we had learned that he was planning to leave the country for a few months. We had to act immediately."

Geronimo nodded his head. "I understand the urgency. Just wish I could've worked on this a little longer."

Erica led her guest to the open tailgate of a black Chevy Suburban. "I'm sure you did. I don't have to tell you how much of an animal this guy is."

"Not at all. He's a bona fide scummy piece of shit."

"Tell me about it." She handed him a bulletproof vest. "Put this on." Geronimo accepted the protection. "I'm not sure what we're going into. Our early intelligence told us that he'd be here alone. That would've made for an easy extraction. Our latest intelligence is singing a different song."

"What do you mean?" he asked as he tightened the Velcro strap of the vest. She pointed at him. "Do you have your weapon, detective?"

Geronimo instinctively guided his right hand to his nine millimeter. "Yeah, but I thought that I was invited to simply observe."

"Oh, no. I mean, if you just want to sit back and watch, cool. If you want a tangible part of this, suit up, lock and load." She chambered her gun. "Our latest intel indicates there are six vehicles here that are not Tasir's. So, we're probably crashing a party of some sort. You game, detective?"

"Of course, and Geronimo is fine," he returned.

"Cool. Now, let's go nab ourselves an international criminal."

"International?"

"Yep. Welcome to the rabbit hole."

After successfully breaching the perimeter of The Oasis, the agents, with Detective Blackfoot bringing up the rear, advanced to within fifty feet of the home. Moving stealthily around the house, they surveyed the windows and doors checking for escape or surprise attack possibilities.

Erica keyed her headset. "What do you see in the rear, Mills?"

"All's clear in the back," the agent responded. "No activity. Not a creature is stirring. Not even a mouse."

"This is no mouse we're catching here," Erica mumbled. "It's a filthy, evil rat." Looking through the windows at the front of the residence, she noticed a man walking towards the great room. "I've spotted the help. I need everyone in position at the doors. Remember, this is a silent breach."

"I've overridden the security system," a tech support agent transmitted from the staging area.

"Copy," Erica replied. "Okay, guys and girls. We enter in three, two, one..."

Once inside, an agent quickly and quietly subdued the butler, pushing him against a wall and pressing his forearm across the startled servant's chest. "Shhhhhh," the agent commanded with a whisper, his weapon hovering at the side of the butler's face. "Where's Tasir?" he asked.

The butler croaked with bulging, fearful eyes, "Lord Samaan is absent at this time."

"Don't you fuckin' lie to me," the agent growled as he cocked the hammer on his weapon. Terrified by the aggressive agent, Tasir's butler wept and urinated on himself. "Shit, man," the agent spat. He stepped away from the shaken captive, avoiding the pool of pee forming on the floor.

"The lord is not here," the servant wailed with snot-curdled speech. "He is absent from The Oasis." Hearing the tearful voice of the distraught prisoner, Erica went into the kitchen with Geronimo heavy on her heels while the other agents searched the remainder of the house.

Agent Bartholomew holstered her weapon as she approached the captive. "Ramon, listen," she began. "I'm not going to play games with you. Either you tell me where your boss is or shit's going to get real bad for you real quick."

Ramon's uncontrollable weeping ceased abruptly when he heard his name. "You know my name?"

"Of course we do. We know everything about you." Erica took two paces toward Ramon. "So, I am telling you. It will be best for you to cooperate."

"Please!" he pled cowering in front of Agent Bartholomew.

"There are more than half a dozen cars outside," she said looking squarely into his eyes. "And judging by the looks of this kitchen, you have prepared a banquet for an empty house?" She stretched her arms outward. "Don't fuck with me, Ramon. Where is Samaan?"

Geronimo exited the kitchen to conduct his own search. His instincts summoned him to the parlor with a mural of a merry-go-round above the mirror. Two agents were searching the room as he entered. "Something is happening in here," he mused. "Bring the butler in here," he shouted.

"What's up, detective?" Erica asked as she crossed the doorway, holding the distraught domestic.

"Not sure just yet. But something is going on in this room." He heard the cartoon voice reverberate in his head, *Follow the merry-go-round.*

"All agents have checked in. No one's here. All floors are clear."

"Uh-uh. Not clear. We know someone is here. The cars. The food. We know this."

"Hmmm. Yeah, we do." Agent Bartholomew tugged at Ramon.

"I am telling you The Lord is absent at this time."

"Then what's with the food? The cars?" Erica pressed him.

"Those are visiting friends, but they are not here. No one is here. The Lord is absent at this time."

"Pshhh! Bullshit!" she yelled. "One last time, Ramon. You wanna cooperate?"

Ramon dropped his head, his eyes watering as he gazed at his soiled uniform.

Geronimo, Erica, and the other agents browsed the room and its contents. Ramon watched their movements. Detective Blackfoot studied the butler from the corner of his eye. Every time an agent was close to the fireplace adorned with the colorful 'horsies', Ramon winced, his eye twitching automatically. Geronimo toyed with the small figurines on the mantel, various depictions of the childhood equine delight.

"No, please. Careful with those. They're expensive. Very expensive."

Geronimo ignored Ramon, browsing the fantastical stallion knick-knacks. He felt a slight draft and stopped. He turned his weapon on the butler. "Open it."

"Whoa, detective hold up!" Erica commanded.

"Open it!" Geronimo ordered again.

"Detective!" the lead agent yelled. "Holster your wea-"

Petrified, an overwhelmed Ramon screeched, "Spin the merry-go-round! The big blue one! Spin it! Spin the merry-go-round!" as he pointed at the sky-blue carousel, the largest, most ornate piece in the menagerie. One of the agents nearest the toy ceramic spun its top. The mantel receded into the wall revealing a passageway with a descending staircase. Silence fell upon the room.

Erica looked at Geronimo. "The Wolf!" she exclaimed. Geronimo blushed unconsciously and humbly bowed his head to her.

The team descended the staircase and entered a long hallway. Detective Blackfoot led the way with Erica behind him. Two minutes into their journey, they heard strange noises resonating off of the concrete walls. The deeper they ventured into the bowels of Tasir's mansion, the odd sounds became faint voices, a crescendo that unsettled Geronimo's spirit as they neared the suspect. The musty, humid dungeon air choked him with confirmation of the rumors and validation of Kendali's Vixen Notebook. He felt queasy as rage filled him up to his watery eyes, overflowing with the emotions that come with the truth about the ungodliness of the world.

The detective turned to the agent in charge as they arrived at another long perpendicular hallway lined with rooms. "Do you hear that?"

"Hear what? The voices?" she replied.

"Yes," he said as he readjusted the grip on his weapon. "Children's voices."

"Damnit!" she murmured as she keyed her headset. "Command, we are going to need some medical assistance here. Probably lots of it." She turned around, eyeing her fellow agents, who had been following her closely into the multi-million-dollar sewer. She raised her hand, giving silent instructions for some of her team to make a left turn down the hallway and the others to go to the right. The lead agents nodded and then turned to their subordinates iterating Agent Bartholomew's instruction. After they all quietly agreed to the strategy, she raised her hand and began counting down on three fingers. She dropped her arm. "Now!" she bellowed.

The agents rushed the area. "FBI! Freeze! Don't move! Federal agents! Don't move! Don't fucking move!" They burst into the rooms, kicking in the doors and exposing prominent, influential adult men and women in various states of undress with children ranging in ages between five and twelve. All the rooms were lavish, vibrantly decorated cells, abundant with toys and games, enticingly reminiscent of Hotel Disneyland. The children screamed and cried cowering in corners as agents swooped in for their rescue. The savage pedophiles held up their arms, surrendering and yelling "Don't shoot!", "My God!", and "Don't hurt me!"

In the farthest cell, at the very end of the hallway, was the wicked catch of the day. Geronimo was inflamed when he found Kendali's subject with two naked boys, one being an unconscious nine-year old with needle marks on his arms. Lying next to the intoxicated minor, an incoherent Tasir mumbled in a drunken haze.

"Come on, little one," Geronimo directed as he led the other conscious boy out of the room. "I need an agent in here!" he shouted into the hallway. An agent appeared and took the unconscious boy out of the room. Geronimo pointed his weapon at the sand savage and cocked the hammer. "You monstrous, devil piece of shit! I wouldn't mind losing my career over you!"

Tasir slowly raised his head, still unaware of the takedown. "Detective, come lay with me." He reached for Geronimo's crotch. Tasir's advance was met by Geronimo's fist knocking him out cold. Geronimo pounded the pedophile into the bed until he was breathless.

Agent Bartholomew interrupted the beating. "Detective!" She grabbed his arm as he was about to land the death blow. Geronimo resisted, heaving breaths of weariness, exhausted by his rage. "Detective, please!" she screamed as she was losing the battle with his strong arm. "Geronimo! Let him live. And suffer!" He dropped his arm; her words returned him to his senses.

"Yes, suffer. Suffer he will. He must." Detective Blackfoot stumbled backward and straightened his posture comforted by the thought of Tasir's infinite misery. "Dammit. I got this low life's blood on me." He arched his back and chanted for a few seconds wiping the blood onto his pants. "Ancestors! Purge this scourge from our world, from our universe forever. For all eternity."

"Amen," Erica concurred.

"Let's go, Agent Bartholomew. Our work is done. At least for tonight."

Chapter Fourteen
Isis The Killer

Friday, Sunset

⬜Zing Post Tea Thyme Group⬜

Latoya Tea Thyme Mitchell (post): Yes! Tasir is going down! We have the victory, family! This low life savage is being hammered by the gavels of justice as I type! Kendali, my dearest, sweetest sister, you can rest now, Beautiful. For all the fights you fought, the lives you changed, especially your own. For every tell-all book~ you have won, my sister! Rest sweetly on your heavenly throne. Oh, I hear the last installment of The Vixen Notebook will be available only on Isis! I hope this is true! How on point is that?! #Queenin⬜

(Load previous comments)
Reactions: 8,452 Comments: 3,665 Shares: 10,459

Calvin G: Down with the savages! I'm glad. She can rest now!

Sherron Diamond: May she be at peace. I miss her so much.⬜⬜⬜❤

Sarah May: Yassssssss! They need to burn Tasir's ass. Rotten low life child molester!⬜Rest In Heaven, Kendali!⬜⬜

Shannon Gee: Take rest, Kendali G!⬜⬜ I don't even have anything to say about that monster

Elisha Durham: I am so glad they caught this fool. My people used to work for one of his businesses. He told me about the rumors and always said he thought they were true. I hope they give him the death penalty!

Sandsuhray Hawkins: It took long enough! So sick of these awful people getting away with murder. Now! Burn him at the stake!⬜⬜⬜⬜

Gina Hayes Fife: Show him no mercy is all I can say. And I can't wait for the final book! On Isis exclusively-I love it!⬜⬜

Lesli Lyn (Butterfly Brooks): Tasir will burn in hell ⬜⬜Shout out to Detective Blackfoot and Chief Dempsey and Seminole City's finest! Even though the feds took over the case, we know that you all work hard to keep our city one of this nation's best kept secrets. We have our problems and issues but we are still an

urban oasis. Kendali Butterfly, keep fluttering those heavenly wings- I feel the effects□□□□
Latoya Tea Mitchell: @Lesli Lyn (Butterfly Brooks) You always bring us home, BFly. I Love you□
Lesli Lyn (Butterfly Brooks): I love you too, Tea□□

Toya finished her posting, packed away her tablet, and found her lover man outside at the grill.

"It is so tranquil out here. You make me want to move to the country." Toya swished Geronimo's homemade moonshine slushy in her mouth and imagined herself dancing through the forest 200 feet beyond the labyrinth that bordered the farthest edge of Geronimo's backyard. "My God, this is so good. You are workin' your voodoo on me."

"No voodoo, my sweet. Just love." He spoke to her through the screened porch, where she stood, as he turned their kabobs and burgers on the grill.

"I just love being outside naked."

"Yes, you do. And you should." He sucked his bottom lip and winked at her.

She blushed. "Ger-ron-nee-moh," she gurgled.

"That's me."

"You said this was your grandfather's house?"

"One of them. He built houses for all four of his children. My father gave it to me when he and my mama moved to Florida."

"Hmph, they must have something truly awesome in Florida to leave this Shangri-La."

"They have each other."

Latoya beamed at his poetic pronouncement and stretched out on the wicker chaise watching her indigenous Black American knight prepare their provisions. The one-acre lot was a rolling field of electric green flanked by two ancient oaks with a path between them leading to a clearing where Geronimo arranged a labyrinth accentuated by bamboo torch lights made by his cousins and benches crafted by a local stonemason. Flowers of many varieties grew naturally around the holy space. The orchids held Toya's attention the longest and urged her from her resting place. She accepted their invitation and bowed to each oak before entering the labyrinth path, a gesture she learned from her new lover. *The trees are our ancestors. They hold great wisdom, keys to the mysteries of our universe. We must always honor them.* Her lover was excited by her graceful movements as she made her way into the sanctuary. The flowers called her directly to them. The warm concrete of the bench in front of the garden, welcomed her supple bottom. She prayed and cried in the name of her sister-friend. "They got him, girl. Now, you take rest, sweet sister." She kissed the petals of the orchids and returned to Geronimo. He admired her figure as she sashayed toward him. Over the past several months, Toya's sensual reception of his spirituality and her passionate adherence to the principles of friendship and sisterhood had him spellbound.

"This looks so yummy, detective."

"Not as yummy as you, love." He squeezed her body and snuggled her under his bulging bicep, he too indulging the freedom of nudity allowed by the rural dwelling. They sat at the picnic table, birthday suited, enjoying each other and discussing the recent arrest and solving of the murder case.

"I am so glad this is over. I knew he was the culprit. Can you believe he was having all these people killed?"

"I can believe it, but I am not satisfied that he had Kendali killed."

"Really? You said that before. That you weren't so sure it was Tasir. But I just don't see why."

"Tasir definitely had motive. But so did other people. And I am not ready to discount the possibility that the bullet could have been for Hiram."

"Well, I am satisfied. Tasir is a low life pig. A savage. All those poor children. He is horrible. And he still caused Kendali and too many others all kinds of grief, strife, pain, and suffering. He is wicked."

"Oh, no doubt. But this thing reminds me of how they lumped everything onto Wayne Williams with the Atlanta child murders."

"I read up on that a little. What do you mean?"

"Wayne Williams was convicted of murdering two adult males. The police, media, local politicians attached the child murders to him based on a set of circumstantial evidence. He was not tried or convicted of any murders of children. You see?"

"Riiight. I do see. I remember that."

"Right. So. Truly, the Atlanta child murders, those cases were closed, but not solved. No one was ever convicted of those individual murders."

"So, you don't think Tasir ordered the hit?"

"I don't. But everybody including Chief Dempsey is accepting that it is Tasir. He ordered me to cease investigating and close the case.

"Hmmm."

"Yes."

"Well, who do you think is the killer?"

"Not sure. But Wes is a good suspect. I mean where is he? He skipped town. Why?"

"Yeah. That is definitely suspicious."

"Again, could the bullet have been for Hiram? And then that makes Maceo a strong suspect. He hates Hiram. Especially because of what happened to his friend and author Bree."

"Yeah. I heard about that."

"Yeah. And everyone wants to say Maceo is a street guy. He is hands-on. Yeah, but not anymore. Maceo is a businessman now. And he knows this. He is changing his movements accordingly. He is no fool."

"Hmph. I will go with that."

"Yes. And I am still not satisfied that Hiram and his wife are so clean. There is a lotta dirt there. The affairs. The pregnancy. Do we really know how much Georgette, Hiram, or Khai knew about the relationships amongst all of them? You see?"

"I do." Latoya twirled her kabob on the plate.

"Hiram gets all of Kendali's royalties. And she was fucking his friend. His frat brother."

"Yeah, but he is so devastated. So sad. So broken."

"Yeah, but is his state of being about the death and sadness or his guilt and culpability?" Geronimo bit into is burger and wiped its juice from his chin.

"Well, he *is* a shyster. And as cool and cavalier as they come."

"Right. Which makes him a helluva actor. We don't know what his tears are made of. Do you know how much money Kendali's books are going to generate now? Do you have any idea?"

"Yeah. I get it. Worth more dead than alive. Sheesh!"

"Precisely. And I am sure they are going to make a movie and a biopic about her life. Are you calculating this? All of the monies from royalties, merchandising, endorsements, and publicity rights that are going to flow from Kendali?"

"Like the mighty Mississippi."

"You got it. And what a motive for murder."

"Damn."

"Now, don't go to Zing with this, babe. Just leave it. This is me and you talking."

"I won't. I am going to take Tasir as the victory. Let Karma handle the rest of them kneegrows."

"Good, love. Now. Let's finish what we started."

He scooped her up, tossed her over his shoulder, and carried her inside, Toya giggling and creaming all the way to his bedroom.

9:00 p.m.

Hiram had moved from his pauper's palette to the sofa and was drinking less. Outstretched on his man cave sofa, contemplating the universe and his place in it, he quoted Fredrick Douglass, "Of the meaning of progress." His buzzing phone interrupted his thoughts. Still reclined, he snatched it from his desk and prayed the notification was not Khai who had been texting him intermittently since their fight. His messages were always the same, "Let's talk." "You are my brother. I love you." "This will pass. Kendali wouldn't want this...blah blah blah..." Hiram didn't have the inclination to talk to him. He was not ready to forgive him for his transgression with Kendali, even though deep down he was not surprised that they were having side relations. If he dug even deeper down, the truth was, he was really upset about the pregnancy, not so much the sex. The idea that someone else other than he had fertilized the soil that he had been cultivating, tilling and toiling so meticulously and passionately made him cringe in the pit of his gut. Thankfully, it was Toya checking on him.

☐Text Message☐

Toya: You okay?

Hiram: I'm cool. How about you?

Toya: I'm okay. I am glad it's over. I am emotionally exhausted. Now, I can really grieve.

Hiram: Yes. You can.

Toya: You too.

Hiram: Maybe so.

Toya: ?

Hiram: My grief is becoming a part of my existence. Like growing another finger. It's right there. A part of me.

Toya: ☐ Things will get better.

Hiram: Yes. I'm glad Tasir has been taken down. Trifling low life mongrel.

Toya: Yes. I'm celebrating!☐☐ To Kendali!

Hiram: To Kendali

Toya: We will get thru this. Take it easy. God got us and definitely got Kendali

Hiram: Definitely! Cheers, sista. Thx for everything☐

Toya: Of course☐

Hiram sat up, reached for his bottle, and started to pour. As the intoxicant splashed into the tumbler, his taste for the alcohol left him. He inventoried the room- the palette's rumpled purple and gold comforter stained with his tears; his socks strewn around its edge, a pile of dirty laundry consisting of worn jeans and t-shirts, long overdue for washing; his TV caked with dust, a result of his mandate to the cleaning lady to remove his man cave from her dailies; empty bags of Swedish fish dotted the floor; KD's take out boxes stacked inside the signature takeout shopping bags; empty bottles of Don Julio and Patrón assembled in a semicircle around a photo of him, like a medical team standing around their patient's hospital bed. His desk was sloppy with heaps of unopened mail he collected on his one assured trip outside of the house for the past few months, a stroll to the mailbox. He snapped into action, accepting the truth that Kendali was gone forever and he had to design a new life without her. The first step was cleaning up his space. He gathered his laundry and went to the first floor washing suite, glad that Georgette convinced him they needed a mini laundromat. After he loaded all five machines, he returned to his man cave with several trash bags and recycle bins. As he discarded the empty glass bottles and recyclable paper goods, tears clouded his eyes thinking of love lost twice, Kendali dead and Georgette falling into Thaddeus' welcoming arms. He resolved to win her back and fortify their family with the renewed dynamism of the love between them, the love that built an empire called Dominion. A love that was evolving in spite of himself. A love so powerful that it created love for others and taught people how to love and why they love. The books. The authors. The readers. A galvanizing love. A higher understanding engulfed his soul, pushing aside his feelings of guilt and regret; he declared Georgette was unequivocally his Isis.

As he continued cleaning, he pulled out some vinyl favorites and stacked them on his refurbished customized turntable, enhanced with a Bose sound system. The Stylistics, Aretha Franklin, Michael Jackson, and Earth Wind and Fire provided the soundtrack for his transformation. He took all the trash out to the trash cans and recycle receptacles lined up in the garage, filling each one to its brim. After, he dusted and polished every inch of his domain-his desk, end tables, coffee table, the bar, the display case and credenza, the television, his computer, laptop, tablet, and his library and its books. His breath expanded fully for the first time since her murder and he unexpectedly felt good. Earth, Wind, and Fire's *Love's Holiday* sealed the newfound feeling and he danced upstairs to the bathroom to shower. The ginger orange blossom body wash permeated his pores and his spirit elevated more. He reminisced on walks in the garden with Kendali at Tatanka resort and smiled for the first time in many weeks. To his surprise, thoughts of how much he enjoyed Georgette and how much she inspired him overtook his visions of Kendali. The spray of warm water invigorated him further as he patted his Patrón bred paunch and reminded himself that he needed to start jogging again sooner than later.

After his ginger flavored baptism, he dressed in a collared shirt, blue and green plaid button down, light blue khakis, and grabbed a pair of green bucks. A welcome hunger rumbled in his stomach, making him realize he had not had an appetite for food during his mourning. Only the clear distilled liquor satisfied his cravings. He descended the staircase, dropped his bucks by the door, and bounced into the kitchen. To his delight, there were several pans of KD's in the refrigerator. He smiled that Georgette still took care of him in spite of himself, even though he knew, at that very moment she probably had her ass in the air for Thaddeus Kane. He shook off the thought and made himself a plate of honey garlic salmon, curry coconut shrimp rice, and sautéed asparagus. He returned to his man cave and placed his vittles in the microwave. Propping himself up in his plush office chair, he tackled his final task, the mail heap. Aretha Franklin smoothed out the challenges of the task with her soul searing vocals, "I-I-I sparkle...loving the way that I do..." A curiously elegant nine by twelve black envelope with gold trim caught his attention in the middle of one of his piles. He slid it to the center of his desk.

"Smyth & Smyth Furrier?" He jibed, "As if she needs another coat? Is she for real?" The name was new; she had always purchased her furs from Mertz & Sons. He opened the envelope and read the note:

Mrs. Rivers:

As a platinum tier client, we invite you to explore our inventory during a private gala. We look forward to your RSVP. If you cannot attend please make a donation to our charity beneficiary, Open House Missionary. We thank you for your business.

There was a donation envelope and a membership package one sheet with details of membership tiers.

"$100,000 or more?" Hiram did a double take of the tier descriptions. "Whoa. What the..." He reread the gala invitation. "No she did not spend a hundred g's on a coat. Seriously?" The purchase seemed strange to him. He raced upstairs to her closet hoping she had not sent them out to cold storage. The area where she stored coats was just as big as her area for clothes. Georgette was a fashion whore, for sure. He walked up and down the aisle looking for anything unfamiliar. He recognized all of her furs. He didn't see anything new. "What the hell..." One more round of perusing hit the jackpot, an unremarkable rum colored full length fox. He pulled it from the rack. After looking at its quality, craftsmanship, coloring, lining he began to worry. Something about the coat and the envelope was bizarre.

He went back to his dominion and kept cleaning. He finished the mail and tucked the Smyth & Smyth items in a folder and placed it under his keyboard. An inquiry about the extravagant purchase, he noted as the next point of conversation for them. He set up a fresh stack of wax, reheated his food, and ate. After washing everything down with a sparkling water, his phone buzzed.

🔲 Text Message 🔲

Crispus: You want to meet
Hiram: What's up?
Crispus: Nothing much. Just a check in and check on.
Hiram: Cool. Nina's?
Crispus: I'm already here.
Hiram: Leaving now

12:30 am

"My brother." Hiram opened his arms to receive Crispus and Crispus accepted the embrace.

"Man, you lookin' like yourself! Celebrating the take down of that low life, huh?"

"That, and it is time for me to move to the next level." The two men settled at the bar. "Still grieving, just not mourning with guilt...and alcohol."

"For real?"

"For real." Hiram gestured for the bartender's attention. "Tony! My main man!"

"Mr. Rivers! Whatchu need? The usual?"

"Nah. Just a cranberry juice."

"I gotcha." He turned to Crispus. "Mr. Adams?"

"You can bring me another beer."

"You got it."

Tony left the gentlemen to continue their conversation.

"Man, I am so glad to see you looking like the Hiram I know." Crispus ate a chicken jalapeno popper.

"Yeah, bro. I actually feel good. I am surprised and glad."

"Of course you are."

"So. Whatchu got for me?"

"Same ole. They gettin' it in...and on."

"I know. I mean, she gettin' what she needs and I certainly have not been available to her."

"You really taking this in stride?"

"Hell yeah." Hiram tipped Tony after he placed their drinks on the table.

"Thank you, sir."

"Of course, youngblood."

"I gotta take it in stride or I will be in a cell next to Tasir."

Crispus chortled at Hiram's assessment. "Man, you really being grown up about it."

"I have to." Hiram swigged his juice. "But I *am* gonna ask her about this new fur coat she bought to the tune of one hundred kay."

"A hunnit kay?"

"Yeah. And from some company I haven't heard of. Smyth & Smyth."

"Smyth and Smyth? Are you sure?"

"Yeah, I'm sure. I just looked at an invitation they sent to her for some gala since she spent a grip with them."

"Smyth & Smyth…" Crispus took a long drink of his ale, gulping loudly. He leaned back in his chair, his face contorted with disbelief and concern.

"What is it, bruh?"

He leaned close to Hiram. "Now look. Just listen. And don't make any assumptions." He peered over both shoulders and then looked up and down the bar. He spoke just above a whisper. "Smyth & Smyth does sell furs. They have been furriers for over a century. But they make their real money doing murder for hire. The cleanest, most untraceable, well-orchestrated assassinations you ever wanna see." Crispus watched Hiram's eyeballs bubble up past his lids. "Word is, they are on the CIA payroll. And many others. They have their clients buy a fur, and the client does receive a fur coat, but it is not the real purchase. They generally send out furs that are farm raised, lesser quality because the money is really for a murder. Not a fur coat. All the arrangements are completely stealth. You buy the fur through the company. They have a series of coded transactions for the client and then they will usually confirm everything with an invitation like the one you saw. But it is not an invitation. The RSVP is used to let Smyth know to move forward with the execution. Or something like this."

"Oh...my...god." Hiram hunched over, his mouth agape with devastation.

"I don't know every detail, but it works somewhat the way I described."

"What the..." Hiram snapped his body upward, pressing his back against the chair with squeamish aggression.

"Now, don't jump to conclusions. They do sell fur coats. I am just telling you what I know about them."

"Yeah. And why you telling me bro? Why?"

"Hiram, listen."

"She wants me dead." Hiram rubbed his afro. "Ahhh shit! I mean she all but said it. Damn! Georgette trying to kill me!"

"Now, bruh. Didn't I say don't jump to conclusions?"

"This ain't no jump, man. This is a sitting-right-in-your-face conclusion. This is a dropped-right-on-your-head conclusion. No jumping required." The two men sat in silence for several minutes.

"My wife is gonna have me 'wacked'."

"Well, you did say she was furious and she has a right to be."

"Yeah, but damn. Killed? She gonna have me killed, Cee?"

"Hell hath no fury.. "

"Yeah, but..."

"And she got that new thing goin' on with Thad. You know how that goes."

"Yeah. I do." He gulped the rest of his juice.

"If you really think so, if you really don't think she just bought a fur coat, you better start taking Ubers."

"Word?"

"These are professionals, man. Understand that."

"Yeah. I got it. Just keep following her. Damn! And I was gonna tell you to stop keeping tabs on her. Shiiit!"

"Not a problem. But you really need to watch your back. Keep tabs on *you*."

"Alright, man. I'm goin'. Got some planning to do."

"I'm here for you, my man."

"Thanks, Cee." They gave each other dap and Hiram exited Nina's.

Once on the parking lot, he walked around his truck, observing every nook and cranny. He bent down and saw nothing underneath. He popped the hood and checked the mechanisms therein. Everything seemed intact. He jumped inside and banged the steering wheel with fervent frustration.

"Gee! Isis is supposed to reactivate, not eliminate!" A new agony found him, an agony so devastating that it had no tears. He was all dried up.

Chapter Fifteen
The Official Osirian Resurrection

Two Weeks Later
Saturday, 10:00 am

"Mmmm." Thaddeus moaned as he raised himself from the vaginal feast of Georgette's cornucopia of creamy goodness. "Girl."

"Mmmm, boy." Her light green polished fingernail tips brushed across his smooth skin creating an electric shock. "Oooo!"

"Yes." He mounted her and rested his torso upon hers. "That's that force between us."

She tongued him passionately in response to the acknowledgment. "Mr. Kane."

"Yes, Mrs. Kane."

She jerked her head back onto the white cotton pillows. "What?"

"You know you Mrs. Kane. You always have been."

"Thad…"

"Georgette, you know you wanna be with me. Just admit it." She offered no reply, just a gaze of surrender. "Yeah, I know. Tired of the bullshit. I know. I gotchu, babe." He plunged into her wetness with erotic expertise, having given her an intense orgasm with his mouth magic. Her body folded into his with each stroke, promises of more pleasure wrapped her up in the ecstasy. "Yeah, that's it baby. Stay with me."

"Thad, honey. Please." Her defenses succumbed to his powerful, passionate skills and his simple, sexy words of conjugal command.

"Please? That's right. Please. Pleasing to you…for you…only you…That's right. You get it." His strokes grew stronger and Georgette grew weaker until they both climaxed, screaming, moaning in stereophonic, Dolby digital sound, a raucous Shangri-La.

Thaddeus fell back onto the bed next to her and reached for her hand. The lighted headboard cast shadows on their skin illuminating their expressions of love. She nestled her face in his shoulder while they relished the fantastical aftermath of a world they were creating.

'I do love you, Thaddeus Kane."

"I know you do." He smiled arrogantly.

She lifted her head from his shoulder. "You know I do?"

"Yes, I do."

"Aren't you gonna say it back?"

"What for? How many times have I told you what you already know?" He smacked her butt cheek and watched it jiggle. "Mrs. Kane."

She nudged him playfully. "Man..."

"Yes. Your man. I been your man."

They locked hearts, simultaneously recounting their fleeting courtship when they were both signed to Write Way Books. Thaddeus' career took off very quickly, gaining international popularity especially in Germany and Italy. He had asked her to marry him before he left to tour Europe, but she declined his inopportune proposal. Years later, Hiram recruited him to Dominion right before he captured Georgette's heart, entrepreneurial skill, and literary prestige.

They showered and ate a light breakfast, chatting about their current state of affairs.

"I am so over Hiram. I just wish he would disappear. I feel like such a fool."

"Disappear?"

"Yes. I don't want to go through everything that a divorce entails. And he is not going to be easy."

"So, you have decided that you will divorce him?"

"Yes, Thad. We talked about this."

"We did, but not from a place of certainty. You have been contemplating."

"Well, there is no more to think about now. I am done with him. I need something real. And honest. And true. And selfless. And loving." She rubbed his hands on the table.

"I understand. And I am here to be all of that."

"Yes, you are," she affirmed. "It took a whole dead girl for me to see. Now, I just want him gone. For good. Just out of my life." She picked up their plates and walked to the sink.

"But you all have children. He will never be completely gone. Take it from me, the King of co-parenting as they call it."

"Yeah. Well, we will see." She gathered their plates and continued talking. "I know he is Hendrix and Harlem's father and they think he is the sunrise and sunset, but I swear I don't even want them around him."

"He has been spending a lot of time with them since he came out of his funk, right?"

"Yes. And it's strange. I mean I know he missed them but...I don't know. I know Kendali's murder changed him. Changed all of us ."

"No doubt."

"I don't see him much. We hand off with the children and go our separate ways."

"And for now, that may be best." Thaddeus finished his coffee. "I gotta get goin'. We go on air at noon."

"Wow. The time flies."

"Yes, it does. When you're having love!" He kissed her cheek interrupting her task of loading the dishwasher. "And why are you not going again?" He hugged her from behind and she fit snugly inside his arms.

"I'm taking the children out. And Hiram has this newfound vigor about Isis and Dominion and Brad and Maceo. He is beyond excited about everything, so he wanted to do the pre-gala podcast."

"Well, I will say. I am glad the man is seemingly changing for the better."

"Seemingly." Georgette meditated on the word momentarily. "Get goin', love. I will be listening to you all."

"You know I don't even wanna go. I'd rather be with you. Right here. Doin' the wild thing all day long." He spoke into her ear and pumped his body against her derriere.

"Thad, you are nuts." She laughed and spun around to face him.

"Nuts about you." He Eskimo-kissed her. "Mustafa insisted I come. Said he talked to your ex-husband. Told us both to behave. Remember, he cried, Isis is bigger than all of us. Said he wants me on air to represent the average everyday successful male author. So, I agreed. I do anything for Big Brother Black Power Akeem." He pumped a fist.

"I know. Enjoy." They exchanged squeezes.

"And I love you, Georgette."

She blushed and he departed for the Isis Pre Launch Gala Podcast on Osiris Rising Radio, praying for a peaceful parlay.

12 Noon

"And five, four, three, two, one…" The engineer pointed at Mustafa inside the studio.

"Black Love. Black Power. Black Peace, Family. I am always honored that you all spend time with me. As much as I may come off as arrogant and cocky…" Lesli Lyn chuckled and Mustafa winked at her. "The Butterfly In The Sky is laughing at me y'all." Mustafa gave up his toothy grin while Lesli kept laughing, shaking her head, and reviewing The Flow Of The Show.

They all sat at a light oak circular high table held fast to the floor with ornately designed legs. Red, black, and green down feather cushions accented high back pub style chairs accommodating the Isis Comm founders and forgers. Gleaming oak floors polished to perfection and walls secured with bright earth tone sound proofing surrounded the communications council with Black power, art deco, modern vibrations. Jazz inspired art displayed throughout the studio and a juice bar in the corner were the finishing touches on the royal roundtable. Hiram, Lesli, Mustafa, Toni, Maceo, Brad, Thad, Monique, Brother Nati, and Nikki listened to Mustafa, waiting patiently to start the show as they sipped a variety of fresh juices and smoothies. Hiram thought of Georgette and her abandoned green drink ritual and internally snarled at Thaddeus who naturally ended up facing him at the discussion table. The possibility of Thad's involvement in the murder plot festered at the base of his brain, burning a hole in his neck. He drank his cool, kale smoothie and maintained a calm disposition.

"So, we have gathered here to give all our people, our community some history about Isis, give everyone an idea of what is coming forth and everyone's role in the experience. And first and foremost, I ask the elder in the room for permission to speak."

Brother Nati leaned forward and spoke into the microphone hanging from the ceiling. "Right on, young brother."

"Good. Good. Ashe and gratitude to you,

Brother Nati. First and foremost, we pour libations." He stood and poured water from a glass pitcher into a young lemon tree resting at the side of his chair. "To all of the ancestors who blazed trails for us, our mamas and grandmamas, papas and grandpapas, aunties, uncles, and big cousins. All the forces that conspire on our behalf. We give thanks. Ashe."

"Ashe," the council responded.

"Call out your ancestors, family," Mustafa instructed. The gathering leadership followed his mandate and Mustafa poured libations saying *ashe* in honor of their forebears.

He closed out the ritual. "To all the spirits known and unknown, *ashe*. And to our fallen sister Kendali Grace, may her spirit be at peace, *ashe*."

"Ashe!" they answered triumphantly.

He replaced the water pitcher at the table center, sat in his chair, and adjusted the microphone dangling before him.

"I wanna remind our listeners that we are also streaming live on Zing from the Isis business page. So, if you want a look-see at Isis studios, logon for the broadcast." He swigged some water and cleared his throat. "I will start with the introductions. Brother Nati Abu Akbar is a native of Seminole City and he is our elder advisor for Isis Communications. He has diligently served our community as a professor of Black Studies, author, lecturer, newspaper owner, bookstore entrepreneur, and as quiet as it's kept, the leading distributor of African centered Black studies books in the world."

Hiram craned his neck in amazement as Mustafa enumerated the magnificence of Brother Nati. He felt some shame for neglecting opportunities to build relationships with Brother Nati who stood as a righteous pillar of progress in Seminole City. He forgave himself and promised to be more assiduous in forming a bond with the elder. Mustafa continued introducing everyone and ended with Lesli Lyn, the youngest of the bunch, who was studying The Flow Of The Show which listed all the women with speaking parts. The men were there for support and audience questions.

"So, I am gonna stop talking and let my colleagues, our sisteren, share what we have going on. For Isis is the divine supreme resurrector, restorer, of Osiris.

As it was, as it is, as it shall be. Let's start with the very extraordinary Toni G! My sista! Give it up, sis."

"Brother Mustafa, it's always a pleasure. And I am grateful to you and the rest of the brothers for entrusting me with the Isis launch." She smiled at him.

"Of course, sis. Nothing but the best. And you are that."

She flashed an appreciative grin and continued. "We had to keep our numbers for the launch at a cozy 1,000. The Isis board insisted that the event be intimate, personal, and a representation of all members of our beloved industry. Authors, readers, publishers, book sellers, conventioneers, business owners, very few politicians...very few..." Toni laughed and few others giggled with her.

Maceo commented, "Right on."

"Yeah, my brother," Toni stated. "God is still working on them." Everyone laughed. "But we will have a variety of community leaders, educators, and organizers attending. For those who are not attending, the entire event will be streamed live on Zing and Wired. The sounds of the actual ceremony will be broadcast on Osiris Rising Radio." Everybody clapped and whooped after she delivered the live broadcast information. "Yeah, yeah. This will be one for the record books. The evening's itinerary will include a historical piece, a history of Black media, which is essentially a prelude to a bigger production coming from Isis. We will have some honorees to recognize; they do not know who they are."

"Ooooooo," Monique gushed. She tasted her mango blueberry smoothie.

"Yeah, sis" Toni acknowledged. "We will pay homage to pioneers, trailblazers, and innovators. And then the actual launch. We will click the button and the platform will go live." The producer played an audience cheer sound clip. Toni and several others pumped fists and waved their hands in the air. "We look forward to seeing everyone tomorrow and we are thankful for your support. This is the first of many Isis celebrations. We all the way back to Black!"

"Alright, alright. That was our favorite event executive extraordinaire, Antoinette 'Toni' Griffin, founder and CEO of The Platinum Quill. Thank you, sis. We glad to have you." He turned his body in Nikki Pearl's direction. "I am Mustafa Akeem humble servant here at Isis Comm and your host with the ghost, on Osiris Rising Radio. We are honored that you have tuned in with us for this Saturday's pre-launch gala show. Isis is resurrecting and Osiris is rising! We have our Isis initiates talking to you today. Our women of this royal roundtable are presenting you with the basics of our past, present, and future for Isis Comm. We see our call-in board is lit up like never before and we are going to take calls in a few minutes, so just hold tight on the line. Don't hang up because we want to hear from you." He hydrated his throat with a drink of water. "So, without further ado, the beautiful, incomparable co-conspirator of Black Butter Books, and marketing magician, Nikki Pearl Pennington Grant is here to share the Isis structure and marketing, sales, advertising, and promotions news. Sista Grant, say hey to the people."

"Hey, Black family and thank you Brother Akeem for this opportunity to build and grow and rise to the ultimate occasion which is Isis Communications. Brother Mustafa is way too humble, for he is the architect of this vision, this mission, which is now manifest. He brought all of us together and demanded we show up. No matter our differences, our biases, our egos, he demanded we come together in the spirit of something greater than ourselves. And here we are. All praises to God, The Creator, The Ultimate Overseer of All for this magic moment in time where we are forging a new way of being. I love you, Brother Akeem and each and every one of us sitting at this table and each and every one of our supporters, readers, publishers, authors, agents, journalists, distributors, promoters, marketers, everyone that works tirelessly to ensure that we all have the power of the written word at our fingertips."

"Yes, sista. And we love you." Brad gave Nikki a salute.

Mustafa concurred, "Yes, sista. I thank you for the good word. You inspire us."

Nikki smiled and continued. "Isis is a platform for publishing. I want to make it clear because I have been asked, 'Can I submit a manuscript?'. Isis is not a book publisher. Not at this time. Right now Isis is a distribution platform for all forms of media. Currently our focus is books. Film, TV, and music will be added in rounds. Isis is the all-seeing, all knowing, all Black, all strong, multimedia universe for books-book selling, book marketing, book promoting, and book advertising. We are concurrently streaming educational films and lecture series courtesy of Brother Nati's All Africa World Books catalogue and

Brother Mustafa's BlackOut Media catalogue. Approximately 200 Black films and TV shows will be available upon our launch..." Nikki explained Isis' initial setup to the listening audience, talked about Black Butta's lead role in advertising and sales, and encouraged everyone to get their discounted subscriptions at the pre-launch price. She then turned the mic over to Monique.

"Thanks, Nikki Pearl. That was a lotta good information simplified for us, especially me. Y'all know I'm slow." Monique chuckled and others acknowledged her humor.

Hiram humorously disagreed, "Hardly slow, Mo." He gripped his heart and lowered his gaze in reverence to her majesty. She grinned at him, simultaneously despising herself for feeling emotional at his comment. She loved Hiram in spite of his character flaws.

"That's *thee* Hiram Rivers, y'all. Always flattering. Getting everywhere with us. Dominion in full effect!" She clicked her teeth at him while the others beamed at the exchange; hearts gladdened by buried hatchets and love rising from the dirt.

Monique described more about Isis content, the customer service department, and the inner workings of the administration team. After she finished, Lesli took over and told the story of Isis Communications history, chronicling the relationships of the board members and everyone chimed in adding details, anecdotes, and color commentary to complete an awesome pre-launch podcast. Callers, chatters in the chat room, and Zingers watching on Zing Live asked questions and posted their comments for almost two hours. Brother Nati closed the broadcast with prayer. The trailblazers took turns hugging each other goodbye except Thaddeus and Hiram. They gave each other the silent street thug nod-head pop backward followed by a neck snap, each of them hoping to avoid laying the other down...permanently. Even so, love reigned supreme.

5:00 p.m.

"But mama, where are you going?" Hendrix asked. Georgette was dropping off the children after spending the day at the carnival hosted by Hamer Hill

Park. Dominion sponsored the event every year so she had to show face. Two birds with one stone was the order of the day, represent her firm and spend time with the babies. An evening with Thaddeus Kane, the cherry on top of a beautiful day.

"Just going out with friends. That's all."

"But why haven't all of us played together since we left grandma's?" Harlem inquired. She gathered her carnival winnings, a few stuffed toys and an assortment of glow sticks.

"Yeah. Why, mama?" Hendrix added, reinforcing his sister's plea.

"No reason," she answered indifferently as she texted Hiram announcing their arrival. "We will get together soon. Mama has been so busy." She tossed her phone in her handbag and turned around to face the kiddie interrogation nation in the backseat. "Remember I told you that someone very important died. Very important to our business. You met her a few times. Remember?"

"Oh yeah." Harlem sunk into the cushion of the seat, saddened by the reminder.

"I remember! Ms. Kendali!" Hendrix was proud that he recalled their mother telling them about Kendali's murder.

"Right, Hendrix!" She released a weighted sigh. "So, remember I said that mommy and daddy had to make lots of changes and help lots of people because she died?"

"Yes," they said in unison.

"So that's all that's happening. Everything will be better soon, okay?"

"Okay," Harlem agreed.

Hiram appeared in the doorway. "Hey, troops!"

"Daddy!" Hendrix screeched. He fumbled with the door latch and attempted to exit the truck, not realizing he was still buckled up.

"Hendrix, you have to unbuckle, duh?" Harlem gave her flatly stated instruction while disembarking on the other side behind the driver's seat.

Georgette stepped out and hugged her daughter. "I had so much fun with you two."

"Me too, mama."

"I love you, sweet-sweet."

"I love you too, ma." Georgette let her go and she ran into her father's arms. "Daddy!" Hendrix had finished greeting his father and started to enter the house.

Georgette called to him. "You not gonna hug me goodbye, Hendrix?"

He hesitated, turned around, and scoped his mother head to toe. She waited, internally grieved by her son's reluctance. Hiram nudged him and he walked to his mother. They embraced, Hendrix's affection half-hearted. "I love you, baby boy "

"Love you too." He hurriedly unlocked himself from his mother and raced happily into their castle while the king and queen exchanged cold glances. The king followed the prince and princess into the house and the queen hopped her chariot wondering how this was going to turn out. This was her first glimpse of the effects their separation was having on the royal court. She felt nauseous, but she knew Thaddeus would cure her ailing mind and put her heart at ease. Her phone dinged.

☐Text Message☐

Hiram: You see what happens when a child senses his mama is being slutted out like a two bit street hooker
Gee: I wonder what said child senses about his daddy fucking dead fat bitches who were essentially the hired help☐
Hiram: you are disgusting! speaking ill of the dead. you goin' to hell, Gee!
Gee: I already been. It ain't that bad.
Hiram:☐☐

"Yeah, Thaddeus. I need some of that good-good wood-wood," she crooned as she peeled out of the driveway.

8:00 p.m.

After watching movies, playing games, reading books, and doing puzzles, Hiram directed their bath and bed routine. He turned on Joe Sample and The Crusaders, lit a few incense sticks, and let the children soak in their respective bath tubs while he straightened up the bedroom that he and his wife used to share. His heart strummed an irregular guilty rhythm as sorted the laundry on their bed; he reminisced about all the love they made. The visualization of her eyes ladling a sincere love over his soul while he cradled her, and stroked her brought a sharp pain to his side. The beauty of building an empire founded in their love now morphing into a murder plot buckled his knees. He sat on the bed, pushing his tears back, whimpering. A strategy to foil the plot had been his agenda since he uncovered the truth, but now, feeling such despair, he thought he should just let it happen. "Maybe I am better off dead," he mumbled. "Maybe Kendali will be waiting for me with open arms."

"Daddy, I am all done," Harlem announced standing in front of her father in a lavender monogrammed terry cloth robe.

"What? You didn't need any help? Did you scrub your important parts?"

Harlem giggled. "Of course, Daddy. Mama taught me."

"Yes. She is a good teacher." His heart rippled with melancholy, but he forced a smile.

"You sad, Daddy? About the lady writer?"

"Yeah. But I'm okay."

"Okay." Harlem hugged his neck and Hiram conjured all of his strength to maintain his composure. He shifted the sentimental mood.

"Ooooo, you smell so good, baby girl!" He lifted her off the floor and carried her down the hall to her bedroom. She laughed and squealed as Hiram landed her onto the bed like an airplane. He kissed her cheek. "Put on your PJ's and I am going to check on your brother."

"Okay, Daddy."

Hiram found Hendrix in the midst of a crucial submarine battle with his toys.

"Boy! C'mon outta there."

"Already, Dad? A little longer?"

"You been in there long enough." Hiram splashed water on his son. "Your water's cool."

"Okay," the boy child agreed with defeated hesitation.

"Did you wash up good?"

"Yeah. Mama showed me. She said to make sure my butt is clean."

Hiram chuckled at the matter of fact tone of Hendrix's comment. "That's right, young one."

"But mama always sprays me off. But she not here to spray me." Hendrix gazed at his father, sad eyes piercing Hiram's soul.

"I will spray you."

"Great!"

Hiram hosed Hendrix while he danced under the stream. "I miss mama."

Hiram turned off the water. "What do you mean? Your mama is here."

"Not all the time. Not like she used to."

"Well, everything will be okay. Okay, son?"

"Okay."

"We just going through some changes. Everything will be alright. I promise. I love you."

"I love you too."

"C'mon. Let's go read a bedtime story with Harlem."

"Yay!"

After he read to his children and tucked them in bed, he lay on their California king for the first time in what seemed like years. The Crusaders were still giving up a symphonic soundtrack for the evening wind down. As sadness ensued he returned to his laundry chore, folding and putting away clothes, elevating his mind from the anguish of their current state of affairs. He stacked Georgette's stuff on her side of the bed and carried his stack to his closet. Shirts, pants, and underwear arranged by style and color displayed the order he required for his demanding lifestyle. He went back to the bed and studied Georgette's piles and decided to start the first phase of his foil the murder plot strategy- rekindle their romance. Putting her clothes away would soften her, moisten her concrete anger. Her closet was twice the size of his own with a vanity at the center, two free standing mirrors on opposite ends, and a seamstress station. All of her wardrobe was also organized by color and style. He placed bras and panties in the proper drawers; printed lingerie had an area of cabinets across from storage cases designated for solid ensembles. He opened a drawer and placed a printed two piece inside, smoothing out the edges realizing he had bought it for her as a 'Happy Friday' gift a while ago. He fondled the silk material admiring the handiwork of its maker. His fingers brushed the wood of the drawer and felt the bottom move. He pressed the bottom again and his hand plunged downward, his fingertips touching papers, the corners of boxes, and leather. He stepped back nervously, pondering his next move. *What lies beneath*, he thought. *Seek and ye shall find. Do I want to find?* He threw everything from the drawer onto the floor and gawked at the false bottom in disbelief. With the wood slat tilted inward, the corners of file folders, papers, and a passport were visible. He raised the board carefully and placed it next to his feet. There were two folders, a passport, and three pretty little boxes. The boxes were memento treasure chests holding her grandmother's high school ring, her mother's old college ID, and her grandfather's cufflinks. He opened a folder and thumbed through the contents which included insurance policies, birth certificates, land deeds, all things for which Hiram possessed copies. Ah, but the second folder. He flipped through its myriad of what-nots and it was way too much. Way too much information. Way too much degradation. Way too much confirmation. He tumbled to the floor, a kaleidoscope of confused emotions gnarled his spirit. The new blueprint for regaining his power came to him immediately, no need for Operation Foil The Murder Plot. Reestablishing his throne would be easier than he previously planned. *Ironically Isis, you have unwittingly resurrected your Osiris, much to my chagrin.*

Chapter Sixteen
A GALActic Affair

"Toni, my love. You really outdid yourself, sis." Lesli Lyn toasted her friend as she eyed the opulence of the Maggie Lena Walker Conservatory.

"Nothing but the best for my people."

The Walker Conservatory sat on the opposite side of Hamer Hill Park, 180 degrees from the G.W. Carter Arboretum, where the tragedy of Kendali's murder changed them forever. Tonight purposed a fresh start into a higher love of each other and the media arts. The banquet hall, decorated in gold, bright blues, oranges, greens, and silver, hosted 1,000 attendees. The theme was, of course, The Osirian Resurrection so there were various artistic interpretations of the cosmic love story hanging throughout on floor-to-ceiling banners. Gold pyramid centerpieces, blue metallic table cloths, and matching blue and orange cushioned chairs were clearly inspired by an intergalactic, ritualistic, celebration of the ancients. Palm trees placed strategically around the room swayed to the music while buoyant party goers, dressed in their African best, enjoyed the merriment of the occasion. Big screen monitors were on display on each side of the stage. A black star-spangled backdrop draped the walls of the stage and a display of wax figures depicting the miracle of Isis resurrecting Osiris while their kingdom of star gypsies watched, awed the celebrants. More monitors hung above the stage and all around the room so that no one would miss a second of the festivities. Depictions of the royal ancients on silk posters were suspended from the rafters and still others were pitched on pedestals twelve-feet tall throughout the ballroom to complete the re-creation of a sacred African palace.

"Girl! I can feel the spirit of our ancestors in the room." Lesli stomped her feet. "Just look at us. We are some beautiful people!" She chugged her champagne.

"That we are. That we are, sis." Toni scanned the room. "I am so glad Mustafa encouraged people to wear African-inspired garb."

"Me too!" Lesli swirled around in a green and white Kente printed strapless mermaid gown with her signature silver butterfly pumps, earrings, bracelet and necklace.

"Yes, Fly. You are FLY! Always."

"As are you, dearest sister." Lesli bowed her wild afro toward Toni and she spun around in her all white tux with African Kente vest, bow tie, and shoes. After her spin she stopped to behold the vision of Geronimo Blackfoot making an entrance in a simple black tux, dramatically adorned with an indigenous American feather headdress atop his head. "Now, you know I like the girls, but what is that?"

"Oh, you about to go straight?"

"He could probably change me. My God!"

"You don't recognize him? The detective?"

"From the PQ?"

"Yes."

"Girl, you know that night is all a blur. I don't like to think about it."

"Well, he was the detective on the scene."

"I am overjoyed they locked that savage Samaan up."

"Definitely. And throw away the gotdamn key."

"I met him a few times over the years."

"Ewww," Lesli grimaced.

"Yeah. I didn't know about all that evil, but I knew he was crazy."

"He's a rotten one for sure."

"But back to more pleasant things. Phew, chile. Dat thang is fine." Toni gawked at Geronimo in awe of his beauty topped with ancestral reverence.

"You see who he's with?"

"I do. She not with her husband no more?"

"Toni? You ain't know? They've been separated for a while now. No hopes for reconciliation. At least that's what I hear."

"Word?"

"Word."

"Whoo-hoo! With her fine ass. Toya know she-"

"Toni G," Lesli chided. "Down, girl. Behave. You doin' too much now. Stay in your lane."

Toni chortled and drank more of her cocktail. "I know, L-Double. I'm cool. I'm just sayin'. They would make millions on the sex tape."

"Gurrrl…"

"I feel like everybody is watching us." Toya let her orange feather wrap drop from her shoulders and dangle at her waist.

"They are," Geronimo informed.

"I wonder why."

"It's a lot to look at, love." Her eyes twinkled inside his and they mirrored smiles. The bar seemed to be the longest walk of their lives as people ogled the stunning pair, both tall, statuesque, comely, and feathered.

"What would you like, good people?" the bartender asked.

"Champagne, Tea?"

"Yes. That's good."

"Two champagnes, brother."

"I gotcha."

While the bartenders buzzed behind the bar, Toya and Geronimo pretended to ignore the paparazzi.

"Wow. Why don't they just take pictures? I mean for real."

"They probably will. Don't trip, sweetness."

"You know I am a behind-the-camera kinda girl I don't even like taking pictures."

"I know. It's amazing that you have gotten away with that all these years."

"What? Taking pictures?"

"*Not* taking pictures."

"Well, I was busy snapping up everyone else."

"Do you think you will ever go back to it? The creative director thing?"

"I don't think so. I am making other plans.

The bartender returned with their champagne glasses and a bottle.

"Your spirits, my man," he said lining up the flutes and the open bottle on the bar.

"We get a bottle too?" Geronimo asked.

"Yeah. For my people." The young dude pointed at Geronimo's headdress. "I love your attitude. Representin' the hootie hoo."

"My man," Geronimo concurred giving the brother extended pound. He gave him a generous tip and they floated to their table. After greeting the other seated guests, they sat. "So, what are your plans, Tea?"

"I have been thinking. I am going to finish what Kendali started." Toya drank the fizzy liquor. "I am going to eradicate this child sex trafficking scourge. It's our duty. Our responsibility."

"It is."

"I feel you have been brought into my life for many reasons, but one reason for sure. With you, I have a ready-made security team because it is a dangerous business. Eradicating this evil. Her dedication to the annihilation of these savages got her killed." Geronimo offered a half nod. "I know you don't agree."

"I don't necessarily disagree either."

"Right. So what do you think?"

"I think I am here to help you do whatever you want to do."

"The Stacy Capricorn Foundation. That's the name. You like?"

"I absolutely love it. An awesome way to pay homage to her. Her life. Her courage. Her books. Yes, love."

"I am glad to know this. I feel such relief."

"Relief?"

"Yes. I wasn't sure how you would receive my new mission."

"Ahhh. So, you don't know that I love you?"

Toya's mouth dropped open, her bottom lip heavy with surprise and her heart beating at the speed of sound. Geronimo leaned over and sucked the astonishment away as she caressed his shoulder while the paparazzi cooed at the love birds.

Bree was ravishing in a blue, gold, yellow peacock feather African print gown. Metallic gold makeup sparkle on her deep cocoa skin complemented by antique gold arm bracelets, gold feather pumps, and an evening pouch the same print as her dress. A pile of gold spangled goddess braids was her crown. She managed to enter undetected by Maceo and the others who had no idea that she had returned from The Motherland. The rest of the attendees noticed her, a few fans stopping her for a welcome-home hug and quick chat. She worked her way to the opposite end of the ballroom and slinked up behind Maceo where he stood in a circle with Isis' heavy hitters and guests, including Brad, Mustafa, Thaddeus, Titus, and Vaughn, Monique's husband.

"Guess who."

Maceo stopped laughing at Brad's joke, recognizing his sister-from-another-mister's voice immediately. He spun around. "Aubrey Nicole McDaniels!" He swept her up in his embrace and dunked his head into her neck. She submerged herself in his love and the brethren cheered them on with whoops and howls. The sisters of Isis were nearby in a huddle and heard the clamor. Nikki rushed over, the train of her all yellow batik pattern ensemble trailing behind her.

"Bree Whee!"

Maceo gently lowered his sister on her gold heeled feet and she jumped all over his wife. "Nikki Nikki Nuuu!!!" she harmonized. They hugged each other dancing and bouncing around the floor. Bree stepped back to look at Nikki. "You are gorgeous! Stunning as usual."

"Reflection, baby girl." Nikki squeezed her hand.

Bree turned to Maceo. "I have something for you Big Bro." She retrieved a flash drive from her purse. "This, my good brother, is my magnum opus."

"Whaaat? Magnum opus?" He accepted her offering.

"Yes. Better than the Just Enough series."

"Better?" Nikki chirped.

"Better, sis."

"You know I will start reading tonight." He pocketed the drive inside his tuxedo jacket. He hugged her again while Nikki held onto her fingers. "This is one of the best surprises. I love you, Bree."

"And I love you, Maceo." She kissed his cheek.

Nikki shook her hand. "Come on over with us," she ordered cocking her wild afro in the direction of the other women who were smiling at the reunion.

"Absolutely," she agreed following an excited Nikki to the sisters circle.

After Monique, Shante, Lesli, Toni, Aminah, Charlene (Brad's wife), gave her a warm greeting, taking turns with hugs and kisses, a waiter approached with a tray of champagne flutes. The women emptied the tray quickly except for Nikki. She asked the server, "Where is the guy who had the sparkling cider?"

The waiter responded, "There are several, ma'am. I will send one over."

"Thanks so much."

"Wayment. Cider?" Bree tilted her head sideways.

"Yeah."

"Oh Em Geeee!!!!" Bree squealed.

"What is it?" Monique asked.

Bree started jumping up and down in a circle and stomping her spiked heels onto the floor.

"Ayyye!"

"What? What?" Shante was interested in Bree's hysteria. The others paid attention.

"Ayyye!" Bree stopped her shimmy and started rubbing Nikki's belly. "Ahhh!"

"For real, Nikki?" Monique beamed.

Nikki smirked at Bree. "You would be the one to pick up on it. And so fast."

"That would be me!" She pointed at herself. "Cuz I know ain't no way you passin' up no champagne. Uh-huh! No way!"

Nikki, Monique, and Shante laughed the loudest at Bree's antics. Aminah touched her belly. "When are you due, sista?"

"I am four months along."

"Awww, congrats, love." Aminah wrapped her arm around her waist and gave her cheek to cheek affection.

Mustafa overheard the baby news. "Whoa! Wait! My man! Did I just hear that right?" He slapped Maceo on the back.

"What?"

"You expanding the tribe?"

"What?" Maceo swallowed his bourbon and moved the glass from his lips.

"I just heard Aminah give Nikki congratulations. And they all doin' the baby dance."

"Now how could you hear that in this great big ballroom?"

"My superhero powers."

Maceo laughed at Mustafa. "Bree, must have guessed because we haven't told anyone. And Bree has her own super powers."

"My brother!" He gave Maceo a bear hug. "Well, now we gotta tell everyone." He turned to the circle of brothers.

"Aw, bruh." Maceo grimaced.

"Oh yes!" Mustafa clinked his glass with a fork. "Oh wait! Let's make the toast a complete circle of life." He bopped over to Geronimo and ushered him back to the brethren swiping a champagne flute for the detective.

"Gather 'round brothers." He glanced at Aminah as she stood in the celebratory ring of women. She caught his eye. He puffed his cheeks, pointed at her, and did a baby waddle back and forth two paces. Aminah shook her head vigorously. Mustafa did the dance again. She threw her head back laughing uncontrollably. "You next!" he shouted. Aminah laughed harder.

He turned back to Maceo. "Aminah think I'm playin' with her. We havin' a girl."

"Yeah, I think I put that girl in My Pearl."

Mustafa shifted his position in the circle closer to the brothers and they moved to tighten the ring. "Brothers! A toast." They all raised their glasses. "To our fallen sister, Kendali Grace. May she be at peace. To our brother Geronimo for helping to catch the killers!" Geronimo raised his glass dispassionately.

"Word! Black Power!" They toasted in baritone harmony.

"And to Maceo's daughter!"

"A daughter? Word?" Brad wondered.

"Word," Maceo confirmed. Brad grabbed his friend, hugging him zealously.

"May she bring us more keys to unlocking the mysteries to The Universe. More Love. More Peace. More Joy."

"Right On! Black Power! Black Love!" They drank merrily knowing the night, the days, the months, and the years promised greatness beyond their imaginations. *Salud!*

Ushers, waiters, hostesses, and security escorted folks to their tables as Teavolve prepared to serve a sit-down dinner. Toni decided to give them the opportunity to shine with Khai's blessing. He sat at a table with his latest five foot ten, mildly curvaceous, high fashion conquest 180 degrees from Hiram and Georgette. As the meal was being presented, he and Hiram stared each other down a few times. Toward the end of the first course Hiram sent his long-lost friend a text.

⎕Text Message⎕
Hiram: Bro! I see you
KD: What's up I see you 2
Hiram: She all fiyah
KD: I guess she's okay
Hiram: I am glad to see you here
KD: Where else would I be. Big night for my brother.
Hiram: Yes my brother. I love you, bro
KD: I love you back.
Hiram: Brothers Forever
KD: Ditto

Throughout the banquet hall, forty banners unfurled from the ceiling, revealing the Isis logo and motto, the divinely winged goddess depicted in sunburnt orange, auburn, white, cream, gold, and cobalt blue hues. One Vision. One Vision. One Purpose. The sound of the material flapping in the air created an awesome musicality matched by the melody of Indigenous Soul playing their version of Earth Wind & Fire's Fantasy. The crowd ooed, ahhed, and gasped at the presentation. Many rose to their feet for an ovation lasting several minutes, dancing and singing along with the band. As the music faded, Mustafa floated to the stage and stepped to the podium.

"Brothers...and sisters..." He delivered the introduction with a dramatic bass tone. The attendees roared in response. "I said, Brothers and Sistas!" Many of the partakers jumped to their feet, the men whooping and the women cooing. "Osiris...is RISEN!" Mustafa removed the microphone from its stand and dropped to one need, kneeling sideways to the crowd as they applauded his profile. He raised his face to the ceiling, an aura of pride and humility swirling around his face. He stood on his feet. "Give supreme thanks to ISIS!" He opened his arms and a video monitor descended from the rafters. Old black and white photos flashed on the screen, a prelude to the Black Media documentary, *Words As Weapons*. The segment played for eight minutes and the rest of the ceremony flowed without a hitch nor hiccup. Various Isis employees spoke describing their duties and championing the Isis mission. Community service awards were bestowed upon Monique and Toni, much to their surprise. On behalf of his father, the late great Alistair Meade, Bradford accepted a lifetime achievement award posthumously. And lastly Lesli Lyn presented Maya Walker Bambara with a trailblazer award.

Mustafa returned to the podium and two stagehands wheeled out computer terminal. Big screens descended upon the crowd all over the ballroom.

"Black family. Turn your attention to a big screen near you. For our people with us on Zing and Wired, you can see the display in its entirety. And once again we love you for joining us in the live stream. We appreciate how you show up. The Isis logo shimmered against a starry black background. Mustafa motioned for his son Biko to join him on the stage. "This is my older son Biko." He handed him the mic. "Greet the people, ibn."

"Power to our people. I am glad to be here. And we thank everyone for coming out tonight." The audience applauded his youthful eloquence. He gave his father the mic.

"Alright, alright." Mustafa faced the crowd and issued his instructions. "Everybody take out your phones and open your Isis app because I know everybody in the room has subscribed." The people murmured replies as they scrolled through their phones. "Absolutely!" "Right on!" "You know it!" Mustafa switched to his mic headset as he had been doing throughout the festivities and placed the microphone back on its stand. He logged onto the computer. He keyed in his username and password, clicked on a few items and icons, and navigated the server platform. "Biko, do the honors." He gestured for his son to press the enter key. "Everyone else, start logging in!" Biko pushed the button and a dashboard appeared displaying a variety of analytical statistics. The monitors throughout the hall had different displays, some showed the server dashboard and others displayed an Isis technician navigating the app. The attendees gasped, howled, and cheered as Isis went live all over the room. The dashboard showed the number of logins ticking up at a rapid speed. The app displayed digital banners of Kendali and her *Vixen Notebook 10* and Lesli Lyn with her first installment of *By Any Wings Necessary*. "It's official, Black fam! Isis has resurrected Osiris. We are LOVE!!!" Gold, blue, orange confetti poured from above. People blew the blow horns that were given to them in their Isis gift boxes. Pretty little cobalt blue boxes contained an array of Isis paraphernalia.

"This is it, beautiful people if mine. All for you. All for me. All for us. One vision. One mission. One purpose. We all the way-" The people joined him, yelling, "BACK TO BLACK!" The roar was like no other ever experienced in the city, for it was the roar of love.

"Now! Let's party!"

Indigenous Soul retired to a suite to eat and a DJ team took over. Love reigned supreme as everyone danced with everyone. Everybody held everybody. Even Bree and Hiram embraced at one point during the night and he Monique danced a lot of dances. Georgette hoofed it up with Maceo while Brad swung with Lesli and AJ, who played humble assistant to Toni for the occasion. Thad took a break at the bar, watching Georgette swooning inside the sway of her hips. When he saw her return to her table he texted.

⬜Text Message⬜
Thad: Ooooo
Georgette:
Thad: Meet me in the south end
Georgette: Where?
Thad: Behind the conservatory. Farthest end of the grounds. Beyond the open field. There is a garden deeper in the woods. Mother's Garden
Georgette: Oh yeah. Got it. I know where. Give me about 15 minutes
Thad: That's too long. I want you now.
Georgette: 15 Thad⬜
Thad: Okay. *kickin rocks
Georgette: stop⬜
Thad: ⬜

Georgette placed her evening bag on the table and found her husband on the dance floor, rocking with Lesli Lyn.

"May I?" She bowed to Lesli.

"Absolutely, Mrs. Rivers." Lesli curtsied and leaned against Georgette playfully.

"Thanks, Les." Lesli rejoined Titus and Toni at their table.

"Oh you really trying to gas me up, huh?" Hiram grabbed his wife with seductive force, pressing his body against hers and jouncing back and forth, his hands just above her butt.

"Just doing what we came to do," she whispered in his ear.

"Yeah. Uh-huh."

They performed for the crowd as the devoted power couple who was mastering the aftershock of a murdered author, a tawdry affair, lawsuit threats, the loss of their best employee, and all the intricacies of corporate upheaval. Playing their parts to a tee, the crowd toasted them as they moved to the center of the dance floor, a natural circle of fans formed around them. People clapped and cheered, loving their semi erotic urban tango to Koffee Brown's *After The Party*. Hiram moving her around like a rag doll and she swaying, bending, and folding to his rhythmic mandates. A five minute disco samba solidified them with the attendees and Georgette was satisfied that she had fulfilled her Dominion duty. They bowed to the crowd and Georgette left the dance floor while Hiram indulged three new dance partners, hot sexy sisters who were excited by his masterful hustle. Now, she could go get her dose of Thaddy Daddy Ding A Ling.

She scooped her glittery bag from the table and tiptoed out of the venue. The dimly lit, meticulously manicured pasture and the shadows of the moonlight drenched trees hid her well as she sauntered to Mother's Garden, barefoot, heels in hand. The flowery sanctum bloomed luxuriously a quarter mile beyond The Walker Conservatory. Its aromas saturated her olfactory senses as she neared, heightening her desire for her beloved.

He stood when he saw her walking toward him. She fell into his arms and he caressed her body with desirous intensity. Their lips discovered delicious peppermint kisses as she dropped her shoes to the ground. "Ooo, Mrs. Kane," he hummed.

"Yes, Mr. Kane," she hissed stretching her neck for him to bite. His teeth chewed on her flesh, tasting the essence of her excitement for him...for them. He backed her onto the concrete picnic table atop his tuxedo jacket that he spread out for her comfort. The overskirt of her gown provided more cushion as he leaned her back and hiked up her dress.

"No panties, babe?" His erection flapped around inside his trousers anticipating the tender sweetness of her prepared vulva.

"No, Mr. Kane." Her eyes rolled around and she yanked him closer to her. The sound of him unzipping his pants stirred her ocean, a stream of cream trickled onto her skirt.

"Yes, baby." Thaddeus pawed her hips and lifted her onto his blazing hot steel. "Ooo, yes. Georgette. Baby." He mumbled into her neck, slow stroking her heavenly hollow. He huffed and stuffed her walls with diligent dexterity.

"Please forgive me, Thad. Please, baby."

"For what?"

"For not believing in us."

"It's okay. You know now. And it's not the believing that matters, it's the knowing."

Chapter Seventeen
Stalemate

Georgette appeared from a dense thicket of trees about 100 hundred yards from the Walker Conservatory. Hiram watched from a distance resting on a bench in one of the gazebos close to the parking lot. About forty five seconds later Thaddeus emerged, walking in the opposite direction, brushing his tuxedo jacket and straightening his bow tie.

"Are you fucking for real?" He rose from his spot as Georgette neared his position. She didn't see him in the darkness. Though angry, the beauty and grace of her gait moved him, his heart pitter pattering as she sashayed in the moonlight. His sentiment fleeted; fury returned. "Georgette." She stopped and swiveled her body, following the voice...

"Who is that?"

"You don't recognize your husband's voice now?"

"Hiram, what are you doing out here? Why aren't you inside with the party?"

"Because I am out here sending my wife home after she has just had the lining fucked outta her cot."

"What are you talking about?"

"I am talking about this thing is outta control...It's gotten outta hand. Go home."

"You are not and will not tell me what to do Hiram Rivers. *You* go home."

"Oh, but I am telling you. And I am going home too. I will meet you at *OUR* castle."

"I am not leaving."

He snatched her by her forearm and she stumbled from the force. "Hiram, let go of me. What is the matter with you?" She was shaken by his hostility; he had never touched her in anger in ten years together. The shock enveloped her and fear wrapped around her body as she trembled inside his grip, which grew tighter as her fear grew stronger.

"Nothing is the matter with me. You are my muthafuckin' wife. And we gonna settle this once and for all." He pulled her close to him, strangling her arm, forcing her eyes to bulge beyond the lids. He saw tears forming at their corners and relaxed his hold ever so slightly. "You tryna have me go back to prison on a murder rap? Cuz I will kill both of y'all. I ain't playin' with you, Georgette. Take ya' ass home."

Terror arrested her face, as the caramel color melted away from her skin leaving a lifeless shadow of complexion. "Hiram, okay. Okay. Just let me go."

"Getcha ass in that fuckin truck and go. NOW!" Upon releasing her from his grasp, she floundered toward the parking lot. By now, Thaddeus noticed the commotion from the far end of the grounds. He started sprinting in Hiram's direction.

"Yeah, come get it niggaaa!" Hiram readied himself in a fighting stance. When Thaddeus was about halfway from pouncing his opponent, Mustafa waltzed onto the terrace of the main ballroom, one story up, overlooking the gardens where the fighters were preparing to brawl. He whistled to his comrades, Brad and Maceo, who were nearby and they all rushed to their brothers in battle. Thaddeus kept up his pace and just when he arrived a few feet away from Hiram, Mustafa bear hugged him from behind.

"Slow ya' roll, akh. Slow your roll."

"Nah, man. This nigga need to be laid down. Grimy son of a bit-"

"Then lay me down, muthafucka! I'm right here." Hiram opened his arms wide inviting the worthy opponent to a death match.

Brad interrupted, "Both of y'all gon' stop this right now." He balled his fists with rage. "And I mean now! Enough is enough! Hiram go home and work this out with your wife." He turned to Thaddeus. "You gotta stay away from her, man. You got to, bruh. You gotta let them see their way through this."

Mustafa loosened his bear clamp of his friend and Thaddeus defended himself. "Look, if she tells me to stay away, I will. But fuck him."

While Maceo quietly agreed with Thaddeus, he still maintained his voice of reason with the other brethren. "Thad, I get it. I have known this man longer than any of us. And I know that he has a knack for inciting rage, but let him make his transformation. Let him and his wife work out their stuff. They have had a hard way to go since Kendali's murder. Just understand that. Let us all be quiet. Sit still. Let love lead us to the right way."

"That's right on, bro," Mustafa acknowledged.

"Yes. The love." Brad rubbed Thad's shoulder and Mustafa liberated him from the bear constraint. Mustafa motioned for Maceo and Hiram to come to their side for a huddle. The men stood in a circle for a group hug with Thad and Hiram at opposite ends.

Mustafa prayed. "Oh Creator, Sustainer of all the worlds. Amongst this circle of men, my brothers whom I love with all my heart, let there be peace, light and love. Let old feelings die and new love bloom. Amen. Ashe."

"Ashe!" "Amen!" They concurred.

Maceo walked Hiram to his car while the others strolled back to the celebration.

"Maaan," Hiram bemoaned.

"It's all gonna work out, bruh. Been there, done that."

"What? You and Nikki? Pshhh! Seminole City's Black Love Royalty? Go, 'head, Mace."

"Look, man. We have been through our changes. We gettin' close to twenty years. We started young. Life happens. We didn't always show our love in the best way, but we have always known that we loved each other more than anything or anyone else. And that's why you gotta get back to the love."

"Yeah. The love." Hiram started his car and leaned on it listening to Maceo's love lesson.

"You gotta get back to where it started. And it started in love. Right?"

"Yeah. I do love her. She doesn't even know how much."

"And why doesn't she know?"

"I guess I haven't always shown her in the best way."

"Riiight. So. Correct that. Get back to the love."

"I am on it. Thanks, Mace. I love you."

"I love you, Hiram." They hugged. Hiram slid into his car and Maceo watched him drive away. Back to love.

"Gee!" Hiram called out to his wife. He closed the door behind him and slipped out of his shoes leaving them in the foyer. "Gee!" He went to his office and draped the desk chair with his tuxedo jacket. A long deep breath and a thoughtful scan of his new and improved man cave filled him with new vigor, new hope, new dreams, and new wishes. He meandered to the kitchen through the dark hallway. Clicking on the light, revealed Georgette seated at the island, her head in her hands.

"I want a divorce. I want out of this fuckin' facade." She raised her head. "This merry go round." She twisted her hands in a frenzied circular motion, her mouth agape with revulsion.

"Divorce? Fuck that. You stuck here. With me. And our children."

"Hiram, I'm serious."

"So am I. We are gonna finish what we started. And that does not include your li'l boyfriend." He grabbed a cranberry juice from the fridge and opened it. "Oh and by the way. Pardon my manners. I failed to ask. Did you have a good time with him tonight?"

"Hiram, stop. We are definitely not going to do this."

"Do what? Talk about how you let Thad run clean through you like a hot knife through butter. In the fuckin' bushes." He swigged his juice. "In the fuckin' bushes, Gee!" he screamed. "Like a two dollar hookah!"

"We will not bring up two dollar hookers, Hiram. Though you paid her much more, a hooker is a hooker."

"Georgette Rivers. We are not talking about me now."

"Why not? Since when isn't everything always about you?"

"You always said my ego is my downfall." She scoffed. "I actually started believing that bullet could have been for me. But then they caught Tasir." He placed the bottle on the counter. "Then, I uncover a plot, thinking that you are trying to kill me, but you already done your killing."

"What are you talking about? You been drinkin' tonight?"

"Not one drop. Cranberry juice and water all night." He moved closer to her, picked up the bottle, and shook it in her face. "The teetotaling tipper is what they called me at the bar this evening."

"Yeah okay."

He turned his back to her and relaxed on the edge of the cooking island.

"It was you, Gee."

"What was me?"

"All this time...and here I am right here...sleeping with the murderer." Georgette removed her overskirt, folded it, and laid it on the back of her chair.

"I think you *have* been drinking and you don't remember." She walked to the sink opposite of him and washed her hands.

"You evil, cold hearted bitch." He tapped the countertop, drumming a beat of devastation. "And she looked up to you. She liked you. She revered you."

She dried her hands with a kitchen towel. "Babe, you soundin' crazy."

"Gotdammit, Gee! Stop! You killed her! How could you?!" He spun around with the momentum of his passionate antipathy.

"What?" She feigned confusion. While she mustered a performance, Hiram stormed into his office. She nervously retrieved a bottle of water from the refrigerator and gulped down half the liquid before he reappeared in the kitchen.

"You still don't know!" he roared, slamming down the envelope he found in her closet and the furrier receipts.

Her eyes darted around the documents strewn across the kitchen counter. Max honored her with her very own envelope filled with text messages, emails, and a few photos that chronicled Hiram's debauchery and thievery. Photos of the threesome chumming it up time stamped in concordance with the time and date of encrypted text messages about their gourmet play. Charts and graphs that proved his theft of authors' royalties.

"You been rifling through my stuff?"

"Gee! That's all you have to say?"

"Why do you have my papers? You been searching through my closet?"

"No, I have not. Isn't that always the way. I wasn't even looking for it." She leaned forward on the other side of the island, her palms pressed on the edge. "How could you, Gee? She admired you so much."

"Right, admired me by fucking my husband? Admiration, Hiram?"

"Was this the only way?"

"The only way?"

"Awww, Gee. Just stop. You understand what I'm saying! You killed her!"

"I don't know what you mean."

"You know exactly what the fuck I mean. Fuuuck! You murderous bitch!" Georgette stared at the paper trail. "I cannot believe you."

"No. I can't believe you, Hiram Rivers." She stood straight up. "You have to have EVERYTHING." She waved her arms dramatically delivering her diatribe. "An insatiable pig, you are. All the money. All the power. Wife. Children. Houses. Cars. A BOYFRIEND. A mistress. And then, you had to have them *together*? I am sleeping with the devil."

"Gee. Baby." He reached for her and she moved away from him, closer to the table in the breakfast nook. "The thing with Khai was just a thing. I love you. I love us."

"Yeah, but not enough to exorcise those demons." She shook her head violently wishing it would pop from her shoulders, for it was heavy with hurt. "And then this rotten, conniving slut bitch comes along and indulges your whims...your sickness...because it *is* sick, Hiram."

"Gee, I am not gay."

"Then what the hell are you? Because I don't know anymore."

"Gee, I am your husband, your lover, your friend."

"My friend? My friend. Hmph." She massaged her neck as her head pounded with too many emotions for her spirit to decipher. The feelings swelled in her stomach like a sour soup. Hiram sighed deeply and plopped onto the breakfast nook bench, giving her his undivided attention as the heat of disgraceful culpability surged through his veins. "I mean honestly I knew."

"You knew?" He talked to her back as she stood motionless next to the table.

"Yeah. I suspected. Frat brothers. I know about the frat thing. A lot of women do, we just act like we don't. I went to college too. I recognize the movement. The interactions." She exhaled.

"Why did you still marry me? If you knew."

"Because I love you. I love us. I love everything about who we are. So what if you have a boyfriend. We are bigger than your desires. Bigger than your need for brotherly affections. I thought that one day you and Khai would cease your sexual dalliances. Probably after he found a woman crazy enough to marry him. I thought you would get over your faggot feelings. I never saw you looking at other men. I thought it was just Khai."

"Exactly, Gee."

"Yeah, but here comes this bitch. Rotten...wicked...debaucherous...man stealing...wanton...ravenous...slut...monkey...fish..."

"Gee, please." He bowed his head shamefully.

She continued, "...bitch...ass... whore. Argh!" Her hands clenched the air and pulled down the curtains of her imaginary world, landing at her sides. "I let go of the Khai thing. Thinking you would grow out of it.

"Grow out of it?"

"Yes."

"Well, Khai and I are no more. And I am not sure if you grow out of it."

"So you have to have a boyfriend. You like men now?"

"No. I really don't. I just love Khai."

"Right. That's my point. We all have phases. But here comes this bitch. And she, with all her vixen ways, indulges you in this...this...this...nastiness. The fuckin' faggotry!"

"But you didn't have to kill her, Gee."

"I didn't have to kill her and you didn't have to corrupt her, Hiram." She whirled around to face him. "You did this thing to her too...like you did to me. Make us want to do any and everything for you. Even endure a marriage with your homosexual side piece. Even engage in bisexual sex. Even build an empire. Even kill for you." Her tear ducts activated, saturating her eyes, but not falling.

"Gee, listen baby..."

"No you listen. You listen for once. You certainly have no idea how much I love us. How much I love our children. How much I absolutely love you. How much I have invested in this. Did you think I would just let you...let her... let anybody just ruin it all?" Her arms mimed her emotions. "You thought I was gonna stand by and let you run amok with this twisted bitch?" Hiram offered no conversation for his wife. "But the thing I did not see. The thing that I missed, was that you actually loved her. And you missed it too. You didn't know until that last breath left her body." One tear coursed down to her chin. "I just don't wanna love you anymore. I just don't...Gosh! I wish I could do this again. Go back to that book signing when we met. I would never..."

"Don't say it, Gee. Don't say that!"

"I wouldn't, Hiram." She sighed. "No matter. I'm divorcing you."

He pounded the table with his fists and his teeth shown in a snarl. "The hell you are!"

"I am, Hiram."

"You gonna sit right here and raise our children. With me!"

"No. I am leaving."

"Georgette Rivers. The statute of limitations never runs out on murder. Don't make me…"

"And the statute of limitations never runs out on humiliation, Mr. Pancake Switch Hitta. Fuckin' faggot." She backed into the kitchen, closer to the kitchen island, away from him, watching his fury frothing. "I don't even care anymore," she screamed. "Fuck it. I will turn all of the intel over to Myesha. She will have a field day slingin' your faggot ass around on her gossip segment."

"Oh okay. You do that. Meanwhile me and Detective Blackfoot are real friendly these days. And he would love to really solve the murder case."

Georgette sunk. Her face drained of enthusiasm. "You wouldn't dare?"

"Georgette you know me. Answer that for yourself. And you got one more time to call me a faggot!" He jumped to his feet and slinked toward her, halting halfway.

"What about our children? You would have their mother locked up?"

"What about them? They will be fine. Here with me. Their faggot father. Showing up to school befriending all the kids with two dads."

"You wouldn't?"

"Go on and try me, girl."

"Hiram, this isn't fair!"

He angled his body parallel to the floor in a charging stance, his face formed the grimace of an angry lion. She looked away. "Who gives a fuck about fair? You think I will let you just walk away from me while you run off with Thaddeus Kane? A nigga who hates me at that?!" He straightened his posture. "But just to show you I'm not completely callous. I will give you a divorce." Her countenance brightened and her body softened as he granted her wish. "After Hendrix turns 18." He shoved his hands into his pockets giving her his profile to kiss, smiling a wicked grin and rocking back and forth on his heels.

"What? Hendrix is 4, Hiram!"

"I know how old my son is."

"You are horrible. You will hold me hostage here for 14 years? *14 years?*"

He turned his head toward her. "Hostage? How can you say that? You will be here mothering and wifing. Building our empire. You have work to do. We started this thing and we gon' finish it. It's that simple."

"That simple?"

"Yeah. If he loves you so much, he will wait." He looked away so satisfied with her reaction to his mandates.

"I will not stop seeing him, Hiram."

"I know. I don't expect you to. I do demand you respect us. So, you can continue keeping up the appearance of friendship with him. Mentorship. Whatever y'all decide. But you are *my wife*. And I am *your husband*. Period."

She collapsed to her knees. Her embankment of sorrow drenched her caramel cheeks. She made no sound as her face contorted a thousand feelings of grief. Digging a pathway into her misery, her stiletto nails cursed the flesh of her thighs. Hiram walked over to his wife and held her against his torso, pudgy with tequila and sadness. Surprisingly, she surrendered to his caress, weak with anguish. Guilt, regret, relief, and a sense of peace came upon him. With all their secrets out in the open, he saw transformation as the next step for them. Their trials and tribulations would be great for Karma is the ultimate overseer, but ultimately he hoped a new foundation and a new friendship would form. He prayed she was his Isis resurrecting him and he was her Osiris redeeming her. "We are gonna be alright, Gee. It's just a stalemate. That's all."

THE END

Brooks & Kane

Visit Our website for instant gift books, giveaways, book celebrations, & The Kaleidoscope Shop!

www.PlatinumQuill.com

Made in the USA
Middletown, DE
04 June 2022

66670711R00142